Being Sixteen

"*Being Sixteen* explores all the heartache and frustration that come when a girl's perfect dreams unravel. This tender and emotional story dives past the surface, questioning everything from family traditions and friendships to faith, while remaining optimistic and lyrical. It is a touching and fresh look at life at its most hopeful—and most devastating—time."

—Becca Wilhite, author of *Bright Blue Miracle*

"I love Ally's writing! Her characters are real and interesting, her dialogue is authentic, and her descriptions are vivid and memorable. She has a deft and delicate touch when it comes to storytelling."

—Lisa Mangum, author of *The Hourglass Door*

"Allyson Braithwaite Condie's newest novel is her best yet. With clear dialogue and insightful, reflective commentary, *Being Sixteen* honestly and optimistically portrays how an eating disorder can traumatize the relationship of two sisters and their friends. This novel is a compelling and thought-provoking read for teens."

—Chris Crowe, professor of English, Brigham Young University, author of *Two Roads*

Yearbook

"An engaging, unique portrayal of high school life by a talented new author."

—Kay Lynn Mangum, bestselling author of *The Secret Journal of Brett Colton* and *A Love Like Lilly*

"I appreciated the important moral lessons learned. I highly recommend it for today's teenagers!"

—John Bytheway, bestselling author of *What I Wish I'd Known in High School*

First Day

"Condie raised the creative bar for LDS fiction in her debut novel, *Yearbook*. Now in her follow up, *First Day*, she's cleared it by a mile! Condie's characters jump off the page and will linger at your side long after you close the book."

—Jason F. Wright, author of the national bestseller *Christmas Jars*

"Ms. Condie has the unique ability to easily steer readers through each main character's viewpoint, making this book a brilliant, insightful and very enjoyable read!"

—Holly E. Newton, M.A., *Meridian Magazine*

Reunion

"*Reunion* is the story of young adults leaving high school, beginning college, and embarking on missions. It's a tangle of discovering who and what is important, falling in love, and making decisions. It's written in a warm contemporary style that explores many of the child-to-adult turning point issues."

—Jennie Hansen, *Meridian Magazine*

Freshman for President

"Condie's restrained narrative keeps the plot linear, subtly nuanced by the mysterious depression of Milo's older sister, Maura. However, even she is drawn into the campaign. Will Milo be elected President of the United States of America?"

—*ForeWord Magazine*

"The teen remains a regular guy throughout the experience—thoughtful, earnest, and likable—so most readers will empathize with his triumphs and struggles. . . . The mobilization of young voters by having a spokesperson their own age is appealing . . . and Milo's actions to capitalize on that potential seem credible."

—*School Library Journal*

BEING SIXTEEN

Other Books by

ALLYSON BRAITHWAITE CONDIE

Yearbook

First Day

Reunion

Freshman for President

BEING SIXTEEN

A NOVEL BY

Allyson Braithwaite Condie

DESERET
BOOK

SALT LAKE CITY, UTAH

For my sister, Elaine Braithwaite Vickers,

who is the kind of girl that others want to follow

Quotations on pages 182 and 195 are from Jeffrey R. Holland, "To Young Women," *Ensign*, November 2005, 28, 29.

Visit us at DeseretBook.com

Library of Congress Cataloging-in-Publication Data

Condie, Allyson Braithwaite.
    Being sixteen / Allyson Braithwaite Condie.
        p. cm.
    Summary: The year Juliet turns sixteen includes everything from her first date to quitting the basketball team, but when her younger sister, Carly, develops an eating disorder, Juliet must rely on her family and her faith for strength.
    ISBN 978-1-60641-233-6 (paperbound)
    1. American fiction—21st century. [1. Sisters—Fiction. 2. Dating (Social customs)—Fiction. 3. High schools—Fiction. 4. Schools—Fiction. 5. Eating disorders—Fiction. 6. Mormons—Fiction. 7. Family life—Fiction.] I. Title.
    PZ7.C7586Be 2010
    [Fic]—dc22   2009031910

Printed in the United States of America
Malloy Lithographing Incorporated, Ann Arbor, MI

10   9   8   7   6   5   4   3   2   1

PROLOGUE

The night of my sixteenth birthday, I didn't even bother to make a wish when I blew out the candles on the cake. It was my sixteenth birthday, after all. My wishes had already come true.

When you are Mormon, there are things you can pretty much count on happening when you reach a certain age. There are rites of passage in every culture, but in ours the big ones for girls are these:

When you are born, you receive a name and a blessing.

When you turn eight, you are baptized and confirmed.

When you turn twelve, you get to go to Young Women.

And, of course, there's the most magical age of all: sixteen. When you turn sixteen, you can start dating. And driving. And living.

I counted the candles on my cake as the flames flickered in the summer breeze. I heard the cheers of my friends and family, and as I tasted cake and summer and the promise of good times to come, I thought, *This is going to be a good year. Maybe the best year of my life.*

I had no idea.

CHAPTER 1

August

When I was little, having a birthday in early August meant wading-pool parties and popsicles. It meant sitting with my friends at the picnic table on our back patio, laughing and talking and trying to eat my ice cream before it melted all over my paper plate. It meant staying up as late as I wanted to, playing tag or hide-and-go-seek or other night games with the neighborhood kids. It meant never having to go to school on my birthday. I loved it.

But the year I turned sixteen, having an August birthday became the worst kind of torture. All school year long, I had to wait and watch while everyone else celebrated their birthdays. One by one, my friends started going to dances and out on dates, and soon I was the only one who couldn't take a turn driving anywhere and who had to sit at home watching movies on prom night. The year I turned sixteen was the year I cursed my August birthday.

There were lots of reasons I couldn't wait to turn sixteen, but, of course, most of them had something to do with driving—and dating.

One of the reasons was Old Blue, the hideous old sedan that both of my two older sisters had driven before they left home. Large and blue—obviously—Old Blue sat in our driveway like a beached whale. But it meant

I'd have access to my own means of transportation; I wasn't about to be picky.

Another reason I couldn't wait for my birthday was that I'd finally be connected to the modern world. My parents refused to buy any of us girls cell phones until we turned sixteen. They stuck to their guns even when my older sister Maddie turned fifteen and bought a toy cell phone. She walked around in public, talking into it, trying to shame them into buying her a real one. It didn't work.

Turning sixteen also meant that I could go to dances—including prom. I didn't have to stay at home anymore wondering about every-thing—who was dancing with whom, what everyone looked like, and how it might feel to walk onto a dance floor wearing a beautiful dress and holding the hand of a guy in a tux.

And there was one more reason that I looked forward to being six-teen: Nate Carmine. Nate was the kind of clean-cut, good-looking guy that girls want to go out with and that parents want their daughters to date. He had tangly dark hair and celery-green eyes, and that combina-tion of confidence and kindness that is irresistible in a very good way.

And you know what? Nate liked *me*.

"What was your favorite birthday ever?" my best friend Megan asked me as we drove home from the evening session of our summer basketball camp. Correction. *I* was driving. *I was driving!* Old Blue sailed along the roads, large and in charge, with me behind the wheel.

I glanced over at Megan, who'd been my best friend since we were in the same fifth-grade class. Looking at her reminded me of looking at my-self in a mirror—even though we don't have similar faces, we're about the same height and we both have long brown hair. Once in a while, people used to ask us if we were sisters.

"I don't know. Twelve? That was a good one. I got to start going to Young Women, and I had an awesome birthday party," I said.

"Oh, yeah. I remember that party."

"Remember how we had that cake in the shape of a hoop and all those little cupcakes decorated like basketballs?"

"And your parents had one of the members of the college team come and sign autographs and shoot hoops with us."

"Like I said—that was a good one."

Time to turn onto Megan's street. I flicked the turn signal on with an exaggerated gesture. "Please notice that I am signaling at least two seconds in advance of my turn—"

Megan reached over and flicked the lever back. "Wait. Go to your house instead. Your mom invited me over for cake."

"Did she?" I asked. "Did she invite anyone else?"

"Maybe," Megan said, grinning. "I don't know."

"She's throwing me a surprise party, isn't she?"

"Juliet!" Megan rolled her eyes. "Way to ruin the surprise."

"I'll act surprised," I promised. "So is she?"

"I'm not telling you!"

"She totally is," I said with satisfaction. "I knew it." Both my older sisters had had surprise parties for their sixteenth birthdays, but usually the parties happened earlier in the day. Emma and Maddie had school on their sixteenth birthdays, so my mom had to get creative. For Em's birthday, Mom invited Em's friends over for breakfast, and for Maddie's, she asked for special permission to take Maddie and her friends off-campus for lunch.

Nothing special had happened at breakfast for me. During the lunch break from basketball camp, Dad and I made a mad dash to get my license at the Department of Motor Vehicles, but that wasn't a surprise. We'd planned on doing that for weeks. Even though getting my license was very, very exciting, and even though I got to play ball all day long at basketball camp, I have to admit that I hoped for something extra, too. Something with surprises, and people I loved, and cake. Definitely cake.

I pulled into the driveway and bounded up the steps, Megan hurrying to keep up with me. My house was dark and quiet. "Helloooo—" I called out, opening the front door. Nothing. They were probably hiding behind the couches. I flipped on the light. "Hey—"

Still nothing. Nothing and no one. I turned to Megan, who smirked a little. "What's going on?" I demanded.

"Maybe we should try the backyard," she suggested, and I practically ran through the living room into the kitchen. I threw open the back door.

"Surprise!" everyone shouted.

"Happy birthday!" my sister Maddie called. "How does it feel to be sixteen?"

I just stood there, smiling, soaking it all in.

It wasn't dark yet, only dusky, and the golden, glowing light of the sunset turned everyone and everything beautiful. My parents and my sisters were there. My friends were there, and, yes, Nate Carmine was there, too, standing next to my dad. Dad must have said something funny because Nate started to laugh, and at that moment he glanced over and saw me. His smile widened a little as his eyes met mine.

The evening wind threatened to blow out the candles on the cake that my mom carried toward me—my favorite kind of cake, chocolate. I knew the frosting was homemade and deliciously rich. As Mom got closer, I leaned over and swiped my finger along the edge of the cake and popped the frosting into my mouth.

"*Juliet!*" my mom said, laughing. She held the cake closer to me. "At least blow out the candles first."

I took a deep breath and closed my eyes, ready to wish. But nothing came to mind. My life was full of good things. So I opened my eyes and leaned in to blow out all of the candles. I did it all in one breath, and everyone cheered. The smoke drifted up as the first stars started coming out, little bright lights in a darkening blue sky.

CHAPTER 2

I almost slept through my alarm the next morning. Nate and I had stayed up talking and holding hands until the end of the party. Then I spent the next hour or so remembering all the talking and holding hands. I was tired. For a second or two I wished that I could sleep in instead of going to basketball camp.

But then I remembered that I had a driver's license and that I didn't need to have Mom or Dad take me anymore. That got me out of bed and into the driver's seat of Old Blue pretty quickly. I was backing out of the driveway when the front door opened and my younger sister appeared. "Wait for me!" she yelled.

All freedom comes with a price. I was so excited about driving on my own again that I'd forgotten something. *Someone,* actually—my fourteen-year-old sister, Carly, who needed a ride to her first day of cheerleading practice.

"Sorry," I called back.

Carly climbed in and slammed the door shut. "You were going to leave without me, weren't you?" she accused.

"Sorry," I said again. "I guess I was a little excited."

Carly snapped her seat belt on and rolled her eyes at me. "*I guess.*"

I rolled down my window. Old Blue's air conditioning was

unpredictable at best, and it was already getting warm. "So where are you practicing?"

"At the high school."

"I know *that*, Carly. I'm driving you there right now. *Where* at the high school?"

"I don't know. The main gym, maybe?"

"You can't be practicing in the main gym. That's where we're practicing. It's been reserved for basketball camp all week. We're using the auxiliary gyms too."

"I swear they said we were practicing at the high school."

"That can't be right."

"Maybe there's going to be a fight," Carly theorized.

"I think we would win. No offense, but you guys are cheerleaders."

"But if it was a dance-off, *we* would win," Carly said, and we both started laughing at the idea.

Driving with Carly reminded me of the times that my older sister Maddie gave *me* rides to summer camp, back when she was a senior and I hoped to make the freshman team. I had felt pretty proud of the fact that my sister was the best player on the team. I had looked up to her, and I hoped that Carly looked up to me, in spite of the fact that I had almost left her behind that morning.

There are four of us Kendall girls. Emma is the oldest. Usually, she goes by Em, but right now she's officially Sister Kendall and serving a mission in Spain. Maddie is a sophomore in college. I'm next—Juliet— and then Carly, who's starting her freshman year at South High. Out of the four of us, she's the only one who doesn't care about playing on the basketball team.

"You could make the freshman team easy, you know," I told Carly for the fiftieth time. "I've seen most of the girls your age playing at camp. You're better than all of them."

"I thought we were done having this conversation." Carly didn't bother to hide the exasperation in her voice. "I decided to try out for cheerleading instead. I made the freshman cheer squad *months* ago. Remember? What makes you think I'm going to change my mind now?"

"Nothing." We pulled into South High's parking lot. "It's just that I can't imagine cheering for a sport when you could be *playing* one."

"And I can't imagine running around chasing a ball when you could be dancing and yelling and pumping up a huge crowd of people."

"Ooh, touché." I parked the car and we both climbed out. "I know. All I'm saying is that it would be fun if you were on the team. We could play together."

"We can still play together, stupid. We have a hoop in our backyard."

"I know, but we could go on all the trips together too."

"Like you and Maddie."

"Well, yeah. And like Maddie and Em."

"Someone had to break the mold. And besides, won't you be glad when you have your own personal cheerleader? I'll dress up in my cheer uniform and come to every single home game. I'll stand in the bleachers and spell out your name." She cupped her hands around her mouth and yelled, "Gimme a J!"

She drew a few stares from the other basketball players and cheerleaders heading for the gym. "Thanks, Carly."

"Don't mention it."

"So how can I return the favor?"

"All you have to do is stop talking about how I could have played basketball. And you could come see me cheer at some of the freshman games. That's all."

"Okay."

"I mean it." She suddenly became serious. "I'm cheerleading now. I don't want to spend any more time talking about what I'm *not* doing."

Carly and I both turned out to be right. Both the cheerleaders and the basketball team thought they had reserved the main gym. The head basketball coach, Coach Giles, and the cheerleading adviser started talking and gesturing at each other. Carly caught my eye and mouthed the words "dance-off" at me, and I laughed. This wasn't so bad. We were still hanging out a lot. It was all right if the last Kendall girl didn't carry on the basketball tradition.

No one wanted to back down, so while Coach Giles placed a phone call to the administration to settle the problem, we shared the main gym.

"This is kind of ridiculous," Megan told me during a passing drill.

"I know," I called back. "What do you bet we're the ones who end up out in the cold?" We could use only half the court, and I had to keep checking behind me to make sure I didn't inadvertently become part of a cheerleading routine.

Megan shook her head. "Not with five state championships behind us. I bet Coach Giles talks the cheer adviser into changing her time or something."

Someone threw a wild pass and it sailed toward the cheerleaders. Carly stepped forward and caught the ball. Then she dribbled forward to the three-point line and shot it. The ball sailed through the net. She left her hand up for a second, admiring her shot. Then she grinned at me and ran back to the rest of her group.

"It's too bad she isn't trying out," Megan observed.

"Tell me about it."

Our practice ended first so I went into the locker room to shower, and then I waited on the bleachers for Carly to finish. It got kind of boring watching them choreograph dances and go over and over the same thirty-second cheer, but you could tell Carly was loving it. And that she was good at it, too.

"So, what did you think?" she asked me afterward.

"I liked how you hit that three," I said. "Not bad for a cheerleader."

"I caught you dancing along when we were practicing the routine for halftime," she shot back. "Not bad for a basketball player."

Together we walked through the front doors of the school. Carly grabbed my arm. "I hope you aren't tired of surprises, Juliet."

"What do you mean?" Then I realized what she meant. Right in front of us, parked next to the sidewalk, was Nate's car—with Nate standing next to it. I hurried toward him, unable to keep from grinning. "Hey, what are you doing here?"

"I wanted to take you on your first date."

"Right now?"

"Yeah, right now. Are you busy?"

"I guess not." I looked over at Carly. She looked at me with an expression that I knew had been on my face two years ago, when I was the freshman watching Maddie and Em go out with guys. The look that said *I can't wait until it's my turn.*

"We'll have to take Carly home first," I began, but she interrupted me.

"I'll get a ride home with Savannah. You go ahead."

"Thanks, Carly."

Nate opened the door for me and I climbed into the car. A skinny glass vase full of pink lilies sat in the cup holder next to my seat. Their fragrance filled the car.

"Hey, what are these?"

"A birthday present."

"But you already gave me a birthday present at my party last night. You guys all went in on the Sports Fanatic gift certificate."

"I know. But some things, you know, are meant to be given when you're not in a crowd. Like flowers . . . and this."

"This" was a kiss. It was broad daylight, and in the middle of the parking lot, and he kissed me on the cheek. But it was still a kiss, and it still made my heart race. "Thanks," I said to Nate, hoping he wouldn't notice me blushing a little.

"I thought maybe I'd take you to breakfast. Are you hungry?"

"You have no idea. I slept through my alarm this morning and I didn't have time to eat."

"What about thirsty?"

"That too."

"Look in the glove compartment," he told me, and I opened it up to find a bottle of lemon-lime Powerade. My favorite.

"Nate, you're the best. You even remembered what flavor I like."

"Of course I did. What kind of loser do you take me for? I'd never bring you fruit punch."

I was too busy chugging down the Powerade to talk. I put the lid back on the empty bottle and looked over at Nate, who laughed at me. "I guess you *were* thirsty."

"Seriously, Nate. Flowers, breakfast, even Powerade . . . you didn't forget anything."

"I've had a long time to plan it all. I've been waiting to take you out for months."

"So is it worth the wait?" I teased him.

"Of course."

Smiling at Nate, sitting in his sun-warmed car and looking at his bright green eyes, I felt like I had finally arrived at the place I wanted to be.

CHAPTER 3

As always, chaos reigned in the lunchroom on the first day of school. Confused freshman wandered into lines; people called out their orders to the workers behind the counters. Someone struggled through one of the swinging cafeteria doors with a tower of paper cups in plastic sleeves.

I didn't see my sister with all of the other freshmen, but I knew we had the same lunch period so I kept an eye out for her. I remembered all too well how stressful that first day was for me two years earlier, when I'd stuck to my fellow freshman Megan like glue. I got caught up in the wrong lunch line and ended up with a desiccated hamburger patty on a sad little bun instead of the sandwich I'd meant to get. I had walked out into a cafeteria that was crowded with people who knew their place, and I had no idea where mine would be. I had looked around for Maddie wistfully, even though I knew she was in a different lunch period.

Megan and I had ended up sitting on the floor against the wall with some other discouraged-looking freshmen and eating our lunches on the fringes of the crowd. We were both fairly confident and assertive, but we'd lost a little of our nerve, faced with all of those upperclassmen, with all of that noise, and with those horrible hamburgers sitting on our scratched plastic trays.

Things were different now. I knew where I was going. I skipped the food line, dodging neatly around the clusters of waiting people. I brought my lunch from home and only needed to buy a drink. (I'm a sucker for the school's little cartons of chocolate milk.) I grabbed one out of the icy tub at the end of the line, dropped my exact change into the cashier's plastic cup, and sailed into the cafeteria.

Nate waited for me at our usual table from the year before, the one at the end of the long line of windows. When he saw me, his face lit up and he waved at me. I waved back.

"There's your boyfriend," said a voice behind me, and I turned in surprise to find Carly standing right there.

"He's not my boyfriend," I said automatically, and she laughed.

Mormon teens are encouraged not to have steady boyfriends or girl-friends. So Nate and I weren't officially dating. His parents had a no con-secutive dates rule, meaning we could go out with each other as long as we went out with different people in between. My mom and dad were pretty happy about the rule, since it saved my parents from worrying about me having a boyfriend *and* from having to be the bad guys.

"How's your day been?" I asked Carly. She looked remarkably con-fident, standing there in the cafeteria in her cheerleading uniform. Since the football teams had games that night, the entire cheer squad wore their uniforms to school; it automatically marked Carly as someone who belonged to a group. Savannah and a few of Carly's other friends were already sitting at a table and waving at her.

"Pretty great," she said, and only then did I see a little flicker of some-thing that might have been uncertainty cross her face. She shrugged. "You know. It's way better than middle school, but it's still school."

I noticed that her hands were empty. "Where's your lunch?"

But she had already called, "See you, Jule," over her shoulder and headed off toward her friends.

Nate pulled the chair next to him out for me. I sat down and scooted a few inches closer. "At last," he said, grinning at me. "I've been waiting to see you all day."

"You saw me after second period," I reminded him.

"Yeah, but it's not the same as having a class together." He put his arm around me briefly. It was one of the gestures of his that I loved, one that said, *I like you and I don't care who knows it.*

Our friend Max arrived with his lunch and rolled his eyes at us. "Am I interrupting anything here?"

"You're always interrupting," Nate shot back, and Max laughed. "Where's everyone else?"

As if on cue, Megan, Chelsea, Hanna, and a few more of our friends arrived at our table en masse. As they sat down, I glanced over at Carly's table. She and her friends had been joined by some guys from the football team. I noticed with surprise that some of them were juniors and seniors.

"I still can't believe Carly is a cheerleader," Megan said, following my gaze.

"Why? What's wrong with cheerleaders?" Nate asked.

"There is *nothing* wrong with cheerleaders," Max said, watching the girls in their flippy short skirts.

"That's my little sister you're checking out," I reminded him, and he turned back to our table.

"There isn't anything wrong with cheerleaders," I agreed, "but the rest of my sisters and me, we all—"

"Play basketball," Megan finished. "Hey, speaking of basketball, we're still meeting at your house tonight, right?" Megan and I planned to practice every evening until basketball tryouts in October. Nothing would stop us from making varsity.

"Oh, I meant to tell you. I can't tonight. I have a meeting with a member of the bishopric."

"Uh-oh. What did you do?" Max teased.

"Nothing. It's my birthday interview, that's all."

Chelsea, who wasn't LDS, looked surprised. "You get interviewed every year on your birthday?"

"Yeah. Everyone does." I shrugged. "They want to know how you're doing."

Chelsea nodded. A lot of Mormons go to our school—Max, Nate,

Megan, and myself among them—so Chelsea and Hanna and our other friends are used to us talking about Church stuff.

We were finishing lunch when Megan leaned over and spoke to me in a low voice. "Isn't that Jaydon Fullmer throwing Carly over his shoulder?"

"*What?*" I turned to look.

A circle of senior football players stood near Carly's table. One of them did have a cheerleader thrown over his shoulder. When he turned, I could see the girl's face and her long brown ponytail tied with blue-and-gold ribbons to match her uniform. It *was* Carly. She laughed and screamed, the other football players cheered, and almost everyone in the cafeteria turned to watch the show.

"Yeah, it is." Something about the whole scene made me uncomfortable. I knew a lot of those guys. Some of them were good guys—and some weren't. In my opinion, the one who threw Carly over his shoulder fell into the second category. Even though I suspected Carly didn't mind the attention, even though she laughed and pretended to be mad at him when he set her down a few seconds later, something about the whole thing made me worry.

She was a freshman. She should be hanging out with the other scrawny little people in the ninth-grade hall after she finished eating, not flirting with the senior football players. And guys should not feel free to throw her around.

"I didn't know she knew so many seniors," Megan said.

"Me either." I made a mental note to talk to Carly about Jaydon as soon as I could.

Bishop Mercer shook my hand at the end of my interview later that night. "Thank you for coming in this evening, Juliet. We're so glad to have you in our ward. You're the kind of girl that others want to follow."

"Thanks, bishop."

"I'll see you on Sunday."

"See you then."

Before I left the building, I stopped to look at Emma's missionary plaque for a second. Most of the other photos showed the missionaries in a studio, but Em stood outside our house in front of the pink magnolia tree in our yard. The photographer, a friend of ours, made Em laugh at the moment she took the picture. I liked looking at it and remembering the sound of Em's laughter. I missed her.

I left Em behind and started walking home. Even with my newly minted driver's license, I wasn't tempted to drive Old Blue to church. I loved the walk between my house and the church, especially in summer, especially with an August sunset glowing pink and gold over the mountains and the warm air touching my skin.

I loved my church building. I could tell you every little thing about it. There was a pattern in the rocks on the wall behind the pulpit that resembled a face if you knew where to look. The carpet used to be teal before they remodeled the building, but you could still see pieces of the old carpet if you looked in the wooden hymnal holders on the back of each pew, where they'd forgotten to replace the teal lining with the newer beige. The nursery smelled like glue and fruit snacks, and the piano in the Young Women's room had a sticky key down low in the bass register. The trees outside the church were green and pretty, but they weren't anything special until the fall. Then the leaves turned a burning, bright shade of yellow, as if the sunlight they had absorbed all summer shone back out of them.

And, of course, I loved more than just the building. I loved the Church itself, the Church with a capital C—The Church of Jesus Christ of Latter-day Saints. I loved being Mormon. I loved bearing my testimony. I loved singing the hymns, even though I didn't have the best voice. I loved Heavenly Father and Jesus Christ. I loved reading my scriptures for my seminary assignments. I liked saying the words out loud as I read to make sure I took it all in.

As I turned the corner onto my street, the oldest Koch boy zipped past me on his bike. "Wait for us!" his little sister and brother called from behind, and soon they passed me. The little girl pedaled furiously on her bicycle, and the smallest brother ran as hard as he could. They wanted to be wherever their brother was going.

Seeing them made me smile. I remembered being the little kid on the bike, calling after Emma and Maddie on summer evenings. I remembered standing up on the pedals to go faster, not wanting to be left behind, checking back over my shoulder to make sure that Carly still followed.

I thought about what Bishop Mercer had said: *You're the kind of girl that others want to follow.* Then I thought about Carly. Things seemed to be changing a little between us. It wasn't so much that she decided not to play basketball, although I had to admit that I still felt a little sad about that. It was more that she hadn't wanted to listen to me earlier that afternoon when I tried to warn her about Jaydon Fullmer. She didn't trust me the way I trusted my older sisters; she laughed at me and brushed me off.

If I really am the kind of girl that others want to follow, then why doesn't my own sister want to follow me? I tried not to let the question weigh on me for too long. It was still summer, and I was almost home.

CHAPTER 4

September

A few weeks later I stood in the kitchen, wearing my sweats and a T-shirt and eating a warmed-up dinner of leftovers made up of two parts macaroni and cheese, one part old lasagna, and one part ramen noodles. And yes, it tasted as disgusting as it sounds, but my mom hadn't cooked anything new that night. She and my dad had a date planned: dinner and a movie.

"We'll be home around ten," my mom said, hunting around in the closet for her dress coat. "Will you be home by then?" She took another look at me. "Are you going anywhere?"

"I'm insulted," I said, striking a pose with my bowl and spoon. "Don't I look like I'm going out?"

"No Nate tonight?"

"He's on a date. You know the rule his parents have. We went out last Friday, so he's taking someone else out this weekend."

"Oh, right. What about Megan?"

"She's in the same group. They all went to the new miniature golf place."

"Isn't there a football game tonight?" my dad asked, walking into the room with Carly right behind him. "You could go to that."

"I could," I agreed. "Or I could stay here and eat leftovers and go to bed at nine. Do you think it's kind of scary that that sounds really appealing to me right now?"

"I do," Carly interrupted. "You can drive! You can go *anywhere*!"

My mom pulled on her coat. "Well, if you do leave the house, be sure to lock up. And Carly, your curfew is 11:30. Please don't break it again."

"Have fun on your date!" I called out to my parents, who held hands as they walked down the driveway. They waved and I watched them from the window. After they climbed into the car, my dad revved the engine and honked the horn. I dropped the curtain, rolling my eyes. Parents these days. I'd probably catch them kissing on the front porch later that night.

I sighed. I felt trashed from playing basketball with Megan every day after school and from a lot of late nights studying. Going to bed early didn't seem like a bad idea. Still, Carly had a point. There *was* something so wrong about being sixteen and home on a Friday night.

Carly came back into the kitchen while I rinsed out my bowl and debated the merits of chocolate milk versus strawberry milk. "So if you're not doing anything anyway, can you give me a ride to the game? And Savannah?"

"Can't you get Savannah's mom or dad to take you?"

"We could, but it's so much less embarrassing if you drive. Besides, where's your school spirit?" She couldn't quite keep a straight face. Even Carly doesn't use terms like "school spirit" seriously.

"I'm using up all my school spirit to make the varsity team. I am not going to sit on the bench this year."

"That's the good thing about being a cheerleader," Carly told me. "We all get to cheer. No one has to sit out."

"Yeah, yeah," I said. Then I realized I hadn't even asked her about the freshman football game she'd cheered at that afternoon. "How did everything go today, anyway? I swear I'm going to come and watch you before the season is over. But our practices always seem to be at the same time as your games."

"It was fun. Our team totally killed them. Then we went and watched the junior varsity game. I hope I'm on that squad next year."

"See? You *are* like the rest of us. You want to be the best too."

"You're right. You're so right. You're *always* right." She paused for a second. "Will you *please* give us a ride?"

"Okay, okay." I stood up. "But you'll have to wait for me to get ready. If I'm going to drive you guys all the way over there, I might as well stay and watch the game."

"Thank you, thank you, thank you, Juliet!" She reached for the phone to call Savannah.

"But if you want to go to the dance after the game, you'll have to get a ride home with Savannah's parents. I'm not going to stay for that."

She already held the phone to her ear. "No problem."

The gym was dark and loud and hot, the way it always is at a post-game dance. People were clustered and crowded everywhere, changing like chameleons under the flashing colored lights.

"I think we're some of the only upperclassmen here," Chelsea observed dryly.

"No, there are some seniors over there." Max pointed to a bunch of freshly showered football players. "And over there," he added, pointing again.

"Still, we're definitely in the minority," I said. All of the freshmen and sophomores were out in full force for the first dance of the year, dressed up and standing around in nervous little groups. "The amount of perfume in here could kill a person. Remind me again how I ended up here."

"We don't have anything better to do and the DJ is supposed to be good tonight," Hanna reminded me. Next to Megan, Hanna was my best friend. She was a senior and played on the basketball team too. She took no prisoners on the court and was fiercely competitive—characteristics I could respect.

She was also the kind of girl who could turn anything into a party. "Get out here on the dance floor, people!" she called out, already dancing.

We all joined her. It took some doing—Chelsea and Aaron and I had to push a protesting Max out into the middle of the room. At first, everyone but Hanna still felt a little self-conscious. Eventually, though, we realized that the music *was* good and remembered that we were free and young and happy. So we danced. And, not to brag or anything, but I'm a pretty good dancer. Having two older sisters who always want you to help them choreograph dance routines to their favorite pop songs will do that to you.

It wasn't until a while later, during the first slow song, that I spotted Carly dancing with Jaydon. Dancing way too close with Jaydon.

I grabbed Max by the hand. "Dance with me, okay?"

"Sure." Max looked surprised, but he followed me out to the floor. "What's the occasion?"

"What do you mean?"

"I don't think we've danced since you and Nate started going out."

"Oh." I didn't know what to say to that. "Sorry."

"So what *is* the occasion?"

"I need to check on my sister. So we need to dance over in that direction."

"All right." Max grinned. "Should we waltz our way over there?"

"Do you know *how* to waltz?"

"Not really. But we could act like we do."

"I kind of hoped we could try *not* to draw attention to ourselves for a minute. I want to sneak up on them so I can see what's going on."

Max narrowed his eyes and stuck his arm out dramatically, pulling mine with him. He sort of tangoed me for a few steps until we were closer to Carly. People gave us strange looks as we passed them, and I started laughing. "Max! This isn't sneaking."

"It isn't? I thought a secret agent would dance like this."

"Maybe in your world. You're acting like a freshman. Actually, I take that back. Freshmen aren't this weird." We were right next to Carly and Jaydon. I couldn't believe that my sister hadn't noticed us. She was all wrapped up in Jaydon, who danced so close to her that he looked like a parasite. It was bad enough when a guy wanted to dance like that with me; it was worse watching some guy dance like that with my sister.

"Yuck," I whispered to Max. "Look at him."

"He's all over her," Max agreed. "Are you going to say anything to him?"

"Yeah. Turn me so I'm facing them." Max obliged. My eyes met Jaydon's and I said in my most cheerful, I-totally-see-what-you're-doing voice, "Hey, Jaydon! Hey, Carly! Are you guys having fun?"

Jaydon gave me a look that clearly said he wished I'd mind my own business, but he did pull away from Carly a little. She glared at me and said, "Yeah, we are." Her voice sounded clipped and annoyed and she turned away from me.

The song ended a few seconds later. "I'll be right back," I told Max and followed Carly off the dance floor. She walked toward Savannah and her other friends; Jaydon went back to his friends, who were standing near the DJ table and acting as if they owned the place.

Carly glanced over her shoulder. When she saw me following her, she stopped in her tracks. "What was that all about?" she hissed.

"Whoa," I said, surprised. I knew she was annoyed with me, but I didn't expect her to freak out. "Nothing. I only wanted to remind you that Jaydon is kind of a jerk, in case you couldn't tell from the way he didn't give you any space."

"*Juliet.* I don't need you breathing down my neck. It's humiliating!"

"I wanted to—"

She interrupted me and grabbed my arm. "You are *embarrassing* me. Please leave me alone." I heard a note of desperation in her voice and I suddenly felt stupid. It was her life, after all. I shouldn't follow her around and treat her like a little kid. How could she handle the situation with Jaydon herself if I kept popping up at every turn?

"Okay," I said. "I'll meet you at Old Blue at 11:15 so we can get home on time, all right?"

Carly relaxed and let go of my arm. "All right."

"How did it go?" Max asked after I'd made my way back to my friends.

"Not as well as I hoped. She says I'm embarrassing her."

"She thinks you're embarrassing her?" Hanna said. "She hasn't seen anything yet." She gestured for us to move aside. "I'm going to do the worm. Make some space."

"Oh, no," Chelsea and Max said in unison.

The dance was still going strong at 11:15, but I had to make sure Carly was home by curfew. Things had gotten incredibly crowded during the last hour or so and I couldn't find her anywhere in the crush of people. Maybe she'd gone out to the car to wait for me.

"I'd better leave," I told my friends. "I have to get Carly home on time."

"See you later," Chelsea said. "We'll probably go pretty soon too. There isn't enough room to breathe anymore."

"See you." I waved to them and made my way through the crowd and out the doors. As they closed, all the laughing and music and shouting vanished. For a few seconds, as I stood there in the sudden quiet of the cool autumn night, it seemed like I was the only soul in the world.

The doors opened and shut again, and then Carly said, "Juliet?"

I turned around. She didn't seem angry anymore, thank goodness. "Are you ready to go home?"

"No. I hate having such an early curfew." We walked to the parking lot together, both of us taking deep breaths of the crisp, autumn air.

"That's not *my* fault, remember?"

"I know. Thanks for taking me home. You could have stayed longer."

"I wanted to go anyway. I had fun, but it isn't the same without Nate there." Then I stopped. "Wait. What about Savannah?"

"She decided to get a ride home with Jaydon and his friends. They offered me a ride, too, but I thought you'd probably freak out, so I said no."

"You've got that right," I said. "Plus there's the little matter of the curfew issue."

"I know, but what will Mom and Dad really do? They'll get mad and tell me not to do it again, but that's it."

"They are getting *so* lazy in their old age," I agreed. "But here you are anyway, coming home on time."

"Yeah, well, it's not worth fighting you *and* them. Anyway, that dance was getting lame. If I'm going to get in trouble, I want it to be for something good."

We climbed inside of Old Blue. I started the car and the radio began blasting away, still turned up loud from when we sang along to the music on the way to the game. Carly reached over to turn the volume down. "What don't you like about Jaydon, anyway?"

Well, I thought, *to start with, he's the kind of guy that refers to fresh-man girls as "fresh meat." And besides that, he was all over you on the dance floor, and I've seen him act that way with about seventy-five other girls over the years. And I had biology with him last year and every other thing he said involved some kind of gross innuendo.*

But I didn't want to hurt her feelings, and I knew she would think I was being a protective older sister. So instead I said, "He's a lot older than you. And when I had a class with him last year, he always bragged to his friends about what a big player he is."

"Three years isn't *that* much older."

"Yeah, but in high school the age difference matters. In high school it's like dog years or something. Each year in high school counts for about seven years."

"Right. So that means you're ancient?"

"Ouch, Carly."

"Seriously, though, when doesn't the age thing matter so much?" she asked me, sounding wistful.

"Maybe in college. Or maybe when you're a junior it's okay to date a senior. I don't know. It depends."

"I think it's when you're sixteen," Carly said. "That's the age when everything changes."

"You think so?"

"I know so."

We drove the rest of the way home in silence. I meant to talk to Carly more about Jaydon and dating and everything, but I started thinking about Nate and wondering about his date that night.

Our street looked dark except for a small, welcoming constellation of porch lights and streetlights. I could tell that someone at our house had waited up for us because the kitchen light was still on. My cell phone rang as we pulled into the driveway.

"We're not late, are we?" Carly asked. "Is it Mom and Dad?"

"Nope, it's Nate." I parked the car and picked up the phone. "Hey,

Nate. Can you hang on for a second?" I turned to Carly. "Will you tell Mom or Dad I'll be right in? I'm going to talk to Nate out here for a minute."

"Maybe I'll stay here. *You* didn't give *me* any privacy earlier tonight."

"Carly."

"All right, all right." She got out of the car with a huff. As I watched her go up the front steps, I felt a little pang of empathy. It was easy to remember how I felt just two years ago.

CHAPTER 5

October

On Monday after school, the sight of Old Blue in the parking lot stopped me dead in my tracks. Even from a distance I could tell that something had happened to my ancient blue behemoth. There was writing all over the car windows and a white foamy substance that appeared to be whipped cream sprayed across the sides and hood.

My car was perfectly fine when we'd come to school a few hours earlier but something had obviously happened in the interim. Carly saw the mess at the same time I did. "Oh, no! Did someone trash Old Blue?"

I started walking as fast as I could. "That better not be paint on the windows. Why would someone go after Old Blue? There are so many other cars out here—"

Carly caught on quicker than I did. "Juliet! I bet it's Nate!"

"Why would Nate ruin my car?"

"He didn't *ruin* it! I bet he's asking you to the homecoming dance!"

"Really?" The two of us hurried to the car, and sure enough, she was right. The words on the windows spelled out: JULIET, WILL YOU GO TO HOMECOMING WITH ME? in white soapy letters (not paint, thank goodness). White soap stripes covered the car and blue-and-gold balloons filled the backseat.

I started to smile, feeling both excitement and relief. Of course.

I should have known. "It must have taken him forever to do this. I wonder if he skipped a class or something?"

"You're going to homecoming!" Carly jumped up and down. "Aren't you excited?"

"Of course I am." In fact, I felt practically giddy and couldn't quit grinning like an idiot in the middle of the parking lot. A group of juniors stared as they walked by the car and I waved at them, relishing the attention.

"Help me get some of this off, will you? I'm never going to be able to drive unless we scrape a little of the soap off the windows."

Carly didn't move. She stood completely still, a look of horror on her face.

"What? What's wrong?"

"What if it isn't Nate?"

"Who else would it be?" I asked, confused.

"Jule, Stewey Simpson asked me last week if you had a date to the dance yet and I told him that you didn't."

"You did *what*?" Stewey Simpson was my age. He'd never been kissed, but he really *wanted* to be kissed. Everyone in our high school knew that, because Stewey talked about it all the time, and he always asked really popular girls to dances, and then he tried to kiss them at the end of the night. Sometimes he even said that he *had* kissed them, but the girls always dispelled the rumor. Getting asked to a dance by Stewey Simpson was a no-win situation. You could be a jerk and tell him no, or you could go with him and try not to be kissed by him all night.

"I'm sorry! I didn't think he asked with a purpose . . ."

"It's Stewey Simpson! Of course he had a purpose! We have to figure out who this is," I told her. *"Now."*

The windows were forgotten in the urgency of the situation. Who cared about soap when something so important—the identity of the boy asking me to homecoming—was on the line? Carly and I popped balloons furiously. There were pieces of paper with letters written on them in some of the balloons. We threw the emptied balloons on the floor, not even caring about the mess.

"I found a T!" Carly said, excited. "Nate's name has a T . . ." She started to trail off.

"So does Stewey's," I finished. I covered my face with my hands. "What if it's him?"

"Well, even if it is, that's kind of a good sign," Carly attempted to console me. "He only asks really popular girls to dances."

"That doesn't make me feel any better. I do not want my first formal dance to be with Stewey Simpson. I do not want my first *kiss* to be with Stewey Simpson. Do you understand me?"

Carly stopped popping balloons. "You haven't ever kissed anyone?"

"Have *you*?" I asked, surprised.

"Maybe," she said with a little smile. Before I could ask her what she meant, she started bugging me again. "Not even Nate?"

"No, I haven't. Not even Nate. Not yet. Okay?"

"Okay. Sorry. I thought—" She broke off, and then a second later, she squealed. "There's an A in this one!"

"Oh, thank goodness. It has to be Nate, then."

"Unless—" Carly hesitated.

"Unless what?"

"Unless Stewey used his full name."

It took me a second to spell it out in my mind. *"Stewart."* I groaned. "Do you think he did?"

"There's only one way to find out."

I started popping balloons faster. "Hurry. We have to pop these balloons like my life depends on it."

Carly nodded. "Because it kind of does."

I pulled the car into the car wash, shifted into park, and sat back. Lined up along the dashboard were letters spelling out N-A-T-E C-A-R-M-I-N-E. I kept glancing at them, and they made me smile every time.

"I knew it was Nate before we found all the letters," I told Carly, as the spray hit Old Blue. "I knew it when we found the coupon to the car wash in that balloon. Who else would be so thoughtful?" I wished that everyone in the world could feel as happy as I did at that moment. I was going to my first formal dance with someone wonderful, someone I liked, someone who also liked me. In my good mood, I even hoped that Stewey would find someone wonderful to go with. A beautiful senior girl, maybe; perhaps her kiss would turn him into a prince. Anything could happen.

The pink-and-blue suds started dappling over the car, turning purple as they slid into each other. "I love this," I said happily.

"You love what? Going to the car wash?"

"Yeah. Don't you? It's so relaxing. All you have to do is sit here and watch the soap and the water. Remember how we used to come here with Dad when we were little?"

"I never liked it," Carly informed me. "It's freaky. What if one of these machines malfunctions? We'd be trapped in here with no way out."

"We would find a way out." The water sheeted down, washing the purple suds away. "Come on. Don't ruin Old Blue's fun. It's been ages since she's had a real car wash."

We pulled out of the bay and climbed out of the car to take a look. There were still some streaks in a few places on the windows where the soap had been, but for the most part, everything looked clean.

"He even used the kind of soap that washes off easily," Carly said. "Good old Nate."

There was something in her tone I didn't like. "Is something wrong with that?"

"No, of course not." But her tone hadn't changed, and I started to get mad.

"Don't you like Nate?"

"Of course I do. But—sometimes he seems too good to be true." She shrugged.

I opened the car door and climbed back inside, literally biting my tongue so that I wouldn't make a snide comment about Jaydon.

Carly got in too. "Are you mad at me?"

"No."

"Yes, you are. If I apologize a lot and tell you that Nate is the best guy ever, will you take me to the drugstore?"

"No."

"I'm just jealous, Jule, you know that. You know I like Nate." She was back to her teasing, laughing self. "Please, please, please—"

"Fine. But only because it's on the way home. What do you need to get there anyway?"

"Hair dye. I'm thinking about going red."

No surprise there. Carly loved experimenting with her hair. She'd always been more daring than I was that way. I never dyed or highlighted my hair. But there was a first time for everything. When we got to the drugstore, I got out too.

"I won't be long," Carly said, sounding surprised. "Are you coming in?"

"Sure. I want to look at the colors. I could use a change."

Once we were inside, I didn't know where to look. "Where do they keep the hair dye here?"

"I don't know. We'll find it." We made our way through the displays of bags of candy and cheap Halloween decorations. Carly and I both jumped as a motion-activated witch started cackling at us as we passed a display.

"Halloween is out of control," Carly muttered, and I had to agree. We edged around another display of tacky costumes and face paint.

"Here we go." I'd found the right aisle. Carly started browsing the reds while I looked through the browns. Maybe something a little darker would make me look more dramatic. Maddie had the darkest hair out of all of us and I'd always loved how she looked.

"What do you think of this color?" I asked Carly, holding up a box, but she was gone. I looked at the box for a little longer and then at the do-it-yourself highlights. When Carly didn't come back, I wandered up to the front of the store. To my surprise, she'd finished up with the cashier and had started for the doors.

"Thanks a lot for waiting for me," I said, falling into step beside her as we walked toward Old Blue.

"Sorry. I thought you were coming."

"What color did you get?"

"Red." Carly opened the car door and stuffed the plastic bags she carried underneath the seat. "I decided to get some makeup and some cough drops, too. What about you?"

"I didn't end up buying anything. I thought you were coming back."

"You did? Sorry. Do you want to go back inside? I can help you find a color."

I thought about it for a second. "No. I probably shouldn't experiment right before homecoming anyway."

"That was fun—the way Nate asked you."

"It *was* fun. Kind of nerve-wracking, but fun."

"You don't think Mom would let me go to homecoming, do you?" Carly asked wistfully.

I turned and stared at her. "Are you serious? You're fourteen. *I'm* barely going to homecoming for the first time."

"I'm just kidding." Carly turned to look out the window, where a few faint soapy letters were still visible. She traced their outlines along the glass.

"Um, I have a little problem." Megan's voice came from the dressing room next to mine.

"What is it?" That was Carly, in the room on my other side. Megan and I had abandoned our regularly scheduled after-school basketball practice to go shopping for our homecoming dresses, and Carly had begged to come along. Of course, she couldn't resist trying on something too.

"I can't reach to zip up my dress."

"Me either," I said.

"Same here," Carly agreed.

"That's a relief," said Megan. "I was starting to wonder if I had abnormally short arms."

We all came out and converged on the three-way mirror at the end of the hall. I zipped Carly up, Megan zipped me up, and Carly zipped up Megan's dress. Then we all turned to look in the mirrors.

We looked completely different from the three girls in jeans and T-shirts who had entered the dressing rooms a few moments earlier.

Carly said something first. "Ugh. This one makes me look fat."

"Please shut up *now*," Megan said jokingly. "What are you anyway—a size four? You're so skinny."

"Actually, I'm a two." Carly made a face as she tried to adjust the neckline of the dress. "I'm going to try something else on. Maybe something black. Everyone looks thinner in black." She left the dressing room, heading for the racks in the store.

Megan and I looked at our reflections in the mirror again. "I like the one you're wearing," I told Megan. "You look beautiful." Megan had worked all summer as a lifeguard and the cream-colored dress looked great against her tan skin.

"I like it too. But maybe I should try on some other things to make sure."

"What about me?" I looked at myself in the mirror. The burgundy dress I wore looked pretty, but I didn't look earth-shatteringly beautiful in it. And I was going for earth-shatteringly beautiful.

"Try on a red one like Carly's," Megan suggested.

"I don't think so. Maybe I should go for black too."

I didn't bother to change out of the burgundy dress before I went back out into the store. I saw Carly standing near the dresses, still wearing the red dress and looking in another mirror.

"Can you believe how fat I look?" she asked when she saw me.

"You need to give it a rest," I told her. "You know you're skinny."

"Yeah, but try wearing a cheerleading uniform. You can't have any extra fat! There's nowhere to hide it!" She looked at me. "I think we need to find you another dress. That one's okay, but you could do better."

"I know. Megan thinks I should try one like yours, but I don't know if I want to go for red."

"You don't want to stand out?"

"I do, but—" I shrugged. "I guess I want to be more subtle."

Together we searched the racks. It didn't take long before Carly found something for me: a sapphire-colored dress, beautiful and long. "Oh, I like it," I said, taking the dress from her. "But it has spaghetti straps."

"Try it on anyway. Mom can fix anything. Look, it comes with this little matching wrap. She could use the fabric from that."

I took the dress with me back into the dressing room and pulled it on. Then I looked in the mirror, hoping that the dress looked as good on me as had on the hanger. It looked even better, and it fit perfectly. I met my own gaze in the mirror and smiled. The sapphire color made my blue eyes more noticeable.

"Do you need me to zip you up?" Carly asked.

"I've got it." I opened the door. "What do you think?"

"Oh, you look gorgeous." Megan raised her eyebrows. "But do you think your parents are going to go for the spaghetti straps?"

"My mom can fix it. She ended up making sleeves for most of my sisters' dresses."

"You should definitely get that one, then. You look amazing."

Carly looked at me wistfully. "Do you think I could borrow it sometime? I love it."

"Of course. Mom might have to hem it for you, though." I'm a couple of inches taller than Carly, who is the shortest of us sisters.

"It's *never* going to be my turn," Carly complained.

"Less than two years, Carly. Not that much longer."

"It feels like forever."

"Believe me, I know. At least your birthday is in June, not August."

"June's not *that* much better than August," Carly argued.

"Well, at least you won't have to go straight to homecoming right after basketball tryouts," Megan added. "I still can't believe that our last day of tryouts is the same day as the dance."

"It is?" Carly looked at me. "Did you know that, Juliet?"

"Yeah. Kind of lame, huh? We're barely going to have time to go to dinner and the dance."

Megan and I went back into the dressing rooms to change into our clothes. I carefully hung the dress back up on its padded hanger and smoothed out the skirt. "Carly?" I called. "Do you need me to unzip you?"

When she didn't answer, I opened the door and went back out into the store. There she stood, wearing a frosting-pink dress that fit her perfectly and turning around slowly in front of the three-way mirror. She didn't see me. She looked gorgeous.

I smiled and stepped back, wanting to let her live in the moment. I wished I hadn't left my cell phone at home so that I could take a picture of her. A beautiful girl in a beautiful dress, right on the verge of everything wonderful.

Only later did I realize that she hadn't been smiling.

CHAPTER 6

The gym echoed with sounds—shoes squeaking, balls thunking, and every now and then the sound of a perfectly shot ball flying through the net. *Swish.* That one was mine.

I went to grab another ball and saw a girl standing on the periphery and looking nervous. I knew her; she was Abby Ellington, one of the few ninth graders invited to try out for the junior varsity and varsity teams. Two years ago, that had been me. I'd been uncertain but hopeful as I walked into the gym that first day. "Juliet!" Maddie had called to me, and she'd passed me the ball. I'd caught it and walked onto the floor feeling like a million bucks. Even though I'd ended up on the freshman team, I'd still felt like I'd been singled out and welcomed that day at tryouts.

I caught Abby's eye and passed her the ball. She smiled and dribbled it onto the court, and then took a three-point shot. She missed, but barely, and I thought it was gutsy and cool that she had gone for the three like that.

It made me miss Carly. That was something she would do.

A few minutes later, I was starting a layup when a whistle shrilled across the court. I made the shot and turned around, surprised. It wasn't time to start yet. We usually had a full half hour to warm up before try-outs officially began.

Coach Slater, the brand-new junior varsity coach, stood in the middle of the floor and blew her whistle again.

"We heard you the first time," muttered Hanna next to me, and I tried not to laugh. Where was Coach Giles?

"Okay, ladies, I need your attention." Coach Slater put her hands on her hips. It was her first year at South, and none of us really knew anything about her except her name and that she seemed pretty young. I guessed she was about my sister Emma's age.

It took a few moments for all the basketballs to be still and for people to realize that we had a stranger in charge of tryouts. Coach Slater was impatient. She blew her whistle again. Megan passed her ball over to me at the last second, and I caught it and held it. Coach Slater glared at me as she began speaking. "*Please* put the balls away and gather in the bleachers so we can have a brief meeting to start the tryouts. Thank you."

"A meeting?" Megan said to me. "What's going on?"

I shrugged, not wanting Coach Slater to glare at me again.

When we all sat in the bleachers, subdued and confused by the change of events, Coach Slater gave us the scoop. "Coach Giles received a phone call last night from a college in California. They offered her a job as the head coach of their women's basketball team. She left today to determine whether or not she's interested in accepting the offer."

Those of us who had played on the team before looked at each other. The news wasn't a complete surprise, but the timing was. Because of the school's many state championships, Coach Giles had fielded offers from colleges and universities before. She'd always turned them down. But last year, her youngest son had graduated and gone off to college, and she admitted that she was more open to the idea of leaving than before. Still, she'd assured us that she planned to stay at our high school for at least one more year.

"Anyway, let's get started." Coach Slater paused, looking down at her clipboard as if she needed it for reference.

Hanna raised her hand. "Um, Coach Slater? Why is she interviewing *now*? I thought she would stay here this year for sure. Isn't hiring over for the year?"

"Apparently the coach was fired for some ethics violations," Coach Slater said. "They are looking to replace him as soon as possible."

"*Ethics* violations?" Hanna said to me. "That sounds scandalous."

Coach Slater looked pointedly in our direction. "Ms. Kendall, I know your sisters were basketball stars, but that doesn't mean you get to talk while I'm giving you instructions."

What? I hadn't said anything. Hanna was the one who'd whispered, and Megan had thrown the ball at the last second. And how did Coach Slater know that I was a Kendall?

I didn't want to seem like a whiner, so I only said, "Okay."

Megan asked the question on all of our minds. "Coach Slater? Who's going to be the one making the cuts during tryouts?"

I expected Coach Slater to bite Megan's head off but she didn't. "Coach Giles plans to be back tomorrow and will take over the tryouts from there. Even if she accepts the job in California, she plans to be here long enough to select this year's team and coach one or two of the games to help with the transition while the administration chooses a new head coach to replace her."

Megan asked another question. "Are *you* going to be the new head coach?"

Coach Slater permitted herself a small smile. "That *may* be the case. The administration hasn't decided yet. They're waiting to hear if Coach Giles will stay or not."

A new head coach. I couldn't even imagine it. I'd sat in the South High bleachers for years as a spectator and as a JV player, watching Coach Giles lead the South High School Lady Panthers varsity team. This was supposed to be the year I was finally out on the floor, the last Kendall girl playing for the legendary coach.

I called Maddie the minute I got out of the gym. "Maddie. Guess what? Coach Giles might move to California to work at a college there."

"*What?* When?"

"She's looking at the school right now. If she takes the job, she'll leave almost immediately."

"That *stinks*. I mean, that's great for her, but that stinks if she's leaving."

"Tell me about it. I've waited all my life to play varsity for her, and right when I have a chance to finally make it—"

"Shoot, Jule, I have to go. I'm sorry. I have a late class starting right now and the professor just saw me standing outside the door. I'll call you later, okay?"

"Oh, okay."

I looked at the cell phone in my hand, feeling stupid. What was the point of having one of these things if you didn't even have anyone to talk to? Megan and Hanna had already gone home. Nate had a student government meeting. And I couldn't talk to Carly, either. She was still cheering for a freshman football game over on the football field. I was supposed to give her a ride home.

I wandered over to the chain-link fence that separated the track and the football field from the rest of the campus. As I went through the gate and walked toward the bleachers my spirits lifted a little, and I smiled to myself. The track was the place where I'd truly gotten to know Nate.

A couple of weeks into track season, Megan had talked me into coming to practice and giving the high jump a try. The team didn't have any high jumpers and the girls' track coach, Coach Walker, was ecstatic to see me.

However, she knew nothing about the high jump. She did her best—she asked a couple of athletes from the university track team to come give me pointers for a few days. After that, I was on my own. I'd spent my life being coached, so it felt weird to coach myself. I liked it fine, but I didn't feel the same passion for high jumping that I did for basketball. I didn't know if I would keep jumping.

And then one day Nate Carmine came over to the high-jump pit. "Hey."

"What's up?" I wasn't sure why he'd come over to talk to me. We didn't know each other very well—although I admitted to myself that I wouldn't mind knowing him better. He seemed nice, and when girls in my grade talked about cute guys, they always mentioned Nate. *With good reason,* I thought, looking at him.

"I was watching you jump and I wondered if you'd teach me how," Nate said.

He'd been watching me jump? How embarrassing. High jumping wasn't the most graceful event in the track world. Well, maybe if you did it right, but I was still learning.

"I don't know what I'm doing. I don't even have a coach."

"I know. That's why I think it's so cool that you're doing it. Come on. Teach me."

I glanced around. Hardly anyone else was left on the track—the distance runners were out running around town and the sprinters had finished up with their workout. So pretty much the only person who would see me humiliating myself in front of a cute guy was the cute guy himself. Why not?

"Okay, but it's kind of hard to explain."

"Just tell me how you do it."

"I pick up as much speed as I can, and then I take off hard from my left foot, rotate my shoulders, arch my back—" I shrugged. "Maybe it'd be easier if I showed you."

"All right."

I went over and set the bar as low as I could, praying that I wouldn't knock it off while I showed Nate what to do. Luckily I cleared it easily. I started to slide off the mats, but before I could move, Nate crashed through the bar headfirst and belly flopped next to me.

"Are you okay?" I asked, trying not to laugh. "What on earth was *that?*"

"I chickened out at the last minute and thought I'd take it head on," he gasped. "I don't think I can breathe."

Then I *did* start to laugh. One of the cutest guys at our high school had tried to impress *me* and had belly flopped instead. Suddenly, I knew that was what had happened. I knew it because of the way he looked at me while I laughed. That was the beginning, the very beginning, of Nate and me.

I climbed up into the metal bleachers and looked for my sister in the lineup of blue-and-gold uniforms and bouncing ponytails. Carly and the other cheerleaders jumped and danced, trying to keep warm and pump up the crowd. The rows weren't very full—only a few dozen people were scattered in the bleachers, probably friends or girlfriends or parents of the players. I pulled my jacket tighter. The sun was about to go down.

My cell phone rang. Nate. My day suddenly got a little bit brighter.

"Hey," I said. "What's up?"

"Our meeting's over. Are you still at the school?"

"Yeah, I'm over here in the bleachers waiting for Carly."

"I'll come find you."

Soon I saw him walking onto the track. I loved the way that boy walked, confident and smooth but without strutting. Some of the girls turned to watch Nate instead of the game. He spotted me right away and climbed up into the stands to sit right next to me. "Hey, Jule. How did tryouts go?"

Finally, someone who wanted to listen. "Crazy. Get this—Coach Giles wasn't there. She's checking out a job in California and she's probably going to leave South."

"You're kidding me."

"I'm not. I wish I was."

"You've waited forever to play for her!"

"I know."

Nate put his arm around me, and I leaned my head against his shoulder.

"I'm sorry, Juliet. That's no good. But you'll still have a great season."

There are so many things to like about Nate. He doesn't care if I'm wearing my T-shirt and sweats from tryouts; he still thinks I'm cute. He listens. He cares. He's funny and good-looking and doesn't mind showing the world that he likes me.

We sat together like that until the game ended.

For once, Carly didn't say anything about how cute Nate looked or about how much fun she had cheering for the football team. She waited quietly while Nate and I said good-bye and she didn't have much to say on the drive home.

"Everything okay?" I asked.

"Not really."

"What's wrong?"

Carly took a moment to answer. "I'm just really tired."

I kept driving, thinking about Nate and Coach Giles and tryouts and homecoming and the report cards our teachers had handed out earlier that day. I had a lot on my mind.

"I got a C in history," Carly said suddenly.

"You did?" My voice betrayed the surprise I felt. Carly always excelled in school, just like Em and Maddie. Another Kendall trait, though one I didn't share. I worked hard, and I'd never failed a class, but I wasn't crazy smart like my sisters. My grades were always good enough that I wasn't in danger of being kicked off a team or anything, but they weren't anything special. Sometimes it made me feel stupid when teachers expected me to be brilliant. I felt like I disappointed them when I turned out to be average.

But I knew this was a big deal to Carly. Unlike me, she'd never had a C before. "What happened?"

"I tried. I swear I did. But there's so much to do. Do you think Mom and Dad are going to freak out? Do you think they're going to make me quit cheer?"

"I'm sure they'll understand. It's a C, not an F. Mom and Dad aren't ogres."

"I know, but I've never gotten a grade this low before!" Her voice sounded panicked and worried, not the way it usually did: spunky, sassy, full of confidence. "I got As and Bs in all my other classes. That has to count for something, doesn't it?"

"I'm sure it will."

"I hope so. If they make me quit cheer—" She couldn't even finish the sentence.

"Why is cheer so important to you?" I knew the minute I asked that it was a stupid question. "Never mind. I know. Because you feel about it the way I feel about basketball."

"Exactly."

I turned into our driveway and Carly gathered her bag into her arms and sat up straight. "I'll get back on top of things next semester." She sounded in control again. "I'm sure everything will be fine."

I was sure of it too. That was part of being a Kendall. We worked hard, we did our best, and we assumed that everything would be fine.

Even now, I don't see what's so bad about that. Is assuming that everything will go wrong a better way to live?

So even though I felt supremely unlucky because Coach Giles might leave right when I would (hopefully) finally make the varsity team, I knew that Coach Giles truly deserved to have her shot at the big time, and that I would have a great season and do well anyway. And even though I felt worried about my sister, I also knew things would be okay. I knew that Carly would get back on top of her grades and that she would eventually figure out that Jaydon was a loser. I knew I had Nate and Megan and Hanna, and all my other friends, and my sisters. I knew that my parents loved me. I knew that I believed in the gospel. I knew that everything happened for a reason. I knew that I was a lucky person, a person who had it all together. And I knew I was strong.

But here's what I didn't know:

You can suffer a little loss and be okay. You can say good-bye to a person if you know that they are off to something great. It's when the losses are too big and when the destination is too permanent, or uncertain, that I run into trouble and doubt my own strength. I know that now. But I didn't know it then.

CHAPTER 7

"Oatmeal or cereal?" Mom asked me.

"Um, cereal." I grabbed the box of Wheaties and sat down at the table, shaking the brown flakes into the bowl. I followed the routine set by my older sisters for the week of basketball tryouts: eat healthy, drink water like crazy all day long to stay hydrated, and get eight hours of sleep every single night. And while I slept, I dreamed about basketball. I wondered if my sisters had too.

Mom poured me a glass of orange juice.

"Thanks," I told her.

Dad came into the room looking foggy and tired, the way he always does until he eats breakfast. He'd spent twenty years getting up early for work and hadn't yet gotten used to it.

"Ugh," I said, swallowing my first bite of Wheaties. Breakfast of Champions indeed. "I should have gone with the oatmeal, Mom."

"Oatmeal?" Dad said, sounding slightly more alert. "You made oatmeal?"

"Jule, you're in charge of the lesson for family home evening tonight," Mom reminded me as she dished up a bowl of oatmeal for my dad.

"I know. I'm the only one who bothers to change the board these days," I griped, gesturing pointedly at the family home evening pegboard

44

hanging in its honored place on the wall. The board had a spot for all the components of family home evening—prayer, scripture, lesson, treat—and a little wooden disc for each family member. My "Juliet" disc hung on the hook under Lesson.

According to the family home evening board, Em and Maddie were lazy. Their names hadn't moved from the extra hook on the end in a very long time. Of course, since they weren't home, they had a good reason to skip family home evening. Carly always said we were the only family in the world who used their board even when the kids were out of Primary, but I liked the routine of it all. I liked knowing what to expect.

Carly came into the kitchen, looking perfect as usual. She always got up earlier than the rest of us and it showed—hair bouncy and shiny and curled; makeup impeccable; and necklace and earrings complementing her outfit.

"Honey, what do you want for breakfast?" Mom asked.

"I already ate." Carly pulled my keys out of the bowl on the counter where I kept them and tossed them to me. "Come on, Jule. We're going to be late."

"Hold on." I gulped the last of my orange juice and put my glass in the dishwasher. "Let me run upstairs and brush my teeth."

"Wait. What time should we have family home evening tonight?" Mom asked.

"I'm not going to be home until six-thirty or seven," I told her. "Remember? It's the second night of tryouts."

"Of course I remember, sweetie. Good luck."

"That means I won't be home until late either," Carly reminded Mom.

"If you don't want to wait around for Juliet to finish, I could come pick you up after work," Dad offered.

"That's okay. I don't mind waiting," Carly said. I shot her a look. I knew exactly why she didn't mind waiting. When I finished practice, I often found her hanging around in the halls or sitting on the bleachers with Jaydon Fullmer and his friends.

"All right," Mom said. "I'll save you each a plate of dinner in the fridge if you're not home in time."

"Sounds good," I called over my shoulder as I pounded up the stairs.

"Ugh," I said, checking my teeth in the rearview mirror. "I think I still have Wheaties stuck in my molars."

"*Gross,* Jule." Carly was the pickiest person I knew about brushing her teeth. She brushed them after every meal and sometimes at random times during the day. She even carried a toothbrush and a little tube of toothpaste in her backpack. "Why are you eating Wheaties anyway? You hate them."

"For good luck. It's what Em and Maddie always ate during the week of tryouts. I ate them last year, too, and I made the JV team. I'm not going to tempt fate by messing with tradition."

"You're so superstitious." Carly rolled her eyes. "Do you have to do everything exactly the way Em and Maddie did it?"

"Hey, it worked for them. I figure it has to work for me."

Carly muttered something under her breath that sounded like, "It doesn't always happen that way."

"What?"

"Nothing."

Two things changed that second day of tryouts. First, Coach Giles was back. Second, I realized that I'd forgotten one of the most important Kendall traditions of all—prayer.

Back when I was a freshman, I'd been in the locker room changing after one of our games when I noticed Maddie alone on a bench. The rest of the varsity team laughed and talked as they dressed for their game and I wondered why she wasn't with them. Maddie leaned over, elbows propped on her thighs and her hands clasped in front of her. Her forehead rested on her hands. "Hey, Madd—" I began, and then I realized she was praying. She looked up at me.

"Sorry I interrupted you."

She smiled at me. "No problem."

"I didn't know you prayed before the games."

"Every time. I learned it from Em."

From that day on, I did the same thing. Even though I wanted to ask for us to win, I didn't. Instead, I prayed that I would play my best and that the team would be able to work together so that we could be proud of the outcome. My testimony was strong before that day, but it felt like it deepened and grew even more as I followed Maddie's example. Heavenly Father always answered my prayers in some way. If I felt nervous and jumpy, I found calm and peace; if I felt tired and worried, I found strength and energy.

Right before tryouts, I found a bench in an empty corner of the cavernous locker room, away from the rest of the girls. It wasn't *exactly* the same place where I first found Maddie praying, but I could still imagine that my feet were in same spot on the tile floor where her feet had been—and Em's feet before hers. I took a deep breath and closed my eyes.

"Do you want me to warm yours up?" I pulled my plastic-wrapped dinner plate out of the fridge.

"No, I'll eat mine after family home evening." Carly reached past me and grabbed the pitcher of Crystal Light. "I'm more thirsty than anything."

"How are you not starving?" I started the microwave.

"One of the other cheerleaders brought some treats to practice."

"Girls, is that you?" Mom called from the living room.

"It's us," Carly called back.

My parents came into the kitchen. "How did tryouts go?" Dad asked.

"Great," I said. The microwave beeped, and I pulled my plate out. "Much better than yesterday." After my prayer in the locker room I'd felt strong and ready to show what I could do after all my months of practice and preparation.

My dad grinned at me. "Good for you."

"So what do you have planned for the lesson tonight?" Carly asked, sitting down next to me at the kitchen table. "I have a lot of homework."

"Too bad for you," I said, taking a bite of my dinner. "Ouch." The food was still hot, so I set my fork back down. "I planned on reading and discussing the book of Isaiah."

"Very funny."

"Actually, I thought we could put together a package or something for Em. We haven't done that in a while."

"That's a good idea," Dad said. "She e-mailed a couple of weeks ago asking for one of those little hymnbooks in Spanish. I picked one up at the distribution center but I haven't sent it to her yet."

"She also wanted peanut butter," Mom added.

"What else do you think she needs?" Dad wondered.

"Let's print off her latest e-mail and look for clues." I grinned and headed for the computer in the family room.

Family home evening that night turned into a scavenger hunt. We had to rummage through the pantry to find an unopened jar of peanut butter, go through Emma's jewelry to find a necklace to replace one she'd broken, and locate the right kind of box for mailing everything to Spain. Then Mom decided that we might as well make a care package for Maddie, so she and Dad made a quick trip to the store for some extra treats.

While they were gone, Carly and I wrote letters to Emma and put her package together. "Do you think this is enough?" I asked Carly, arranging the items in the box. "It seems like we need something else. I don't know what, though."

"*I* know." Carly suddenly got a mischievous glint in her eye. "I'll be right back."

"Okay, but hurry. I'm almost ready to tape this up."

Carly ran upstairs and then came back down with something hidden behind her back.

"What do you have?"

Carly held out her offering, and I burst out laughing. "Oh, *yes*. I can't believe I didn't think of that."

Carly held a small Strawberry Shortcake doll that had once been mine before I handed it down to her. One of the doll's eyes was halfway scraped off and she had a weird little smile on her face and not much of her red curly hair left on her pink plastic head. Emma claimed that Strawberry freaked her out, so we used to tuck the doll under her pillow or hide it in her backpack to hear her scream.

"Let's make it so Strawberry's head barely peeks out of the tissue paper. Then it will be the first thing Em sees." Carly giggled.

"That's perfect." We nestled the paper around Strawberry's head and checked the effect. The doll's disembodied little head with its painted-on smile and dead eyes stared directly at us from the tissue paper nest.

"Wow, that's good. That's even creeping me out." Carly shuddered, and I started laughing again.

"What's so funny, girls?" Mom walked into the kitchen with her arms full of shopping bags.

"Nothing," I said innocently, closing the box. "Nothing at all. We just finished."

Since Dad was in charge of refreshments, we all went out for ice cream. Carly kept making me laugh. Whenever Mom or Dad weren't looking, she'd stop eating her shake and stare at me with a creepy frozen smile and one of her eyes half shut like Strawberry's. Every time she did it I laughed so hard that I almost choked on my smoothie.

When I went up to bed that night, I paused at the kitchen table to look at the two brown cardboard boxes: one for Maddie and one for Emma. One of the corners of Emma's box had popped up a little, so I rummaged around in the kitchen drawer to find the packing tape.

"Want me to help you with that?"

Carly's voice made me jump a mile. "You almost made me wet my pants," I complained as she moved out of the darkened area near the fridge.

"I know. You should have seen yourself jump." Carly came over and held the corner while I taped it down, the tape shiny and smooth along the edge of the box. When I finished, we both stood there looking at the packages for a second.

"Maddie only lives a few hours away." Carly scooted Emma's package over so that it sat next to Maddie's. "Why are we sending her stuff she can buy at the store?"

"Well, wouldn't you want to know that everyone at home cared about you? I would. You'd better send me something good when I go away to college."

"Right." Carly looked a little sad. "Who's going to send stuff to me? You'll all be gone already."

"Mom and Dad will. I will too. No one will forget about you."

Carly grinned again. "What do you think Emma will do when she opens that box and finds out that Strawberry followed her all the way to Spain?"

"She actually *will* wet her pants."

That night, I dreamed that the box, captained by Strawberry Shortcake, sailed all the way to Spain on a bright blue sea. In my dream we'd packed the box so well and so tightly that the salt water of the ocean didn't even dampen the cardboard, didn't even seep through the edges. When it drifted onto the shore at Emma's feet, and she picked it up, everything inside was safe and sound.

CHAPTER 8

"Help," I said.

Carly looked at me and took it all in: my tangled ponytail, my basketball gear, my sweaty face without a trace of makeup, and my completely panicked expression.

Basketball tryouts went late. Very late. In exactly one hour Nate was due to pick me up for dinner and the homecoming dance. I could only hope that Carly and Savannah would be able to transform me in time. I'd promised them they'd have two or three hours; now they had only one.

"No problem," Carly said confidently. "Hurry and take a shower, and Savannah and I will be ready the second you're finished."

"Wait!" Savannah exclaimed. "Let's take a 'before' picture."

"Oh, right, I almost forgot." Carly ran to get her camera.

I did my best to stifle my impatience. I'd never be ready in time without their help and if they needed a "before" picture, they could have one. Whatever it took to keep them happy.

"Don't smile," Carly added as she held up the camera. "Frown. It makes the 'before' and 'after' pictures so much more dramatic."

I frowned for them and then bolted for the shower.

"You have five minutes!" Carly called after me.

"I've been waiting for months to go to a dance with Nate," I told Carly as she finished blow-drying my hair straight. "I want to look beautiful. Do you think there's still time?"

"Of course," Carly said soothingly, turning off the hair dryer. "You *are* beautiful."

"You know what I mean. I want to be first-dance beautiful." We had a long way to go and only about thirty minutes left. I'd showered and my hair was dry, but it wasn't styled yet and I wasn't wearing any makeup.

"You will be. Your hair is going to look amazing and your dress is perfect." She lifted a section of hair and spritzed it with something. "Can you believe it? You're finally going to your first dance! Aren't you excited?"

"Yeah, but I can't stop thinking about basketball. Coach Giles isn't going to post the list of who made varsity until Monday morning. How am I supposed to wait until then?"

"You did fine at tryouts, right?"

"Yeah." I'd been unbelievably relieved when Coach Giles arrived back in time to conduct the tryouts after the first day. Something about Coach Slater put me on edge and I didn't play as well for her. I thought I'd passed the stage where someone could get in my mind and mess up my game, but apparently that wasn't the case.

"Then you need to stop worrying about it. Necklace."

Savannah handed Carly my necklace.

"You need to take a break from thinking about whether or not you'll make varsity. Just concentrate on having fun with Nate."

"You're right."

"Of course I am. Now stop talking. I have to do your makeup and you're going to mess me up."

Carly's face appeared in front of me, serious and focused. "No mascara," I reminded her, ignoring her instructions to be quiet. "I always forget I'm wearing it and smear it everywhere."

"That's why they have *waterproof* mascara, Jule. Now, seriously. Stop talking."

Carly spent the next few minutes working on my face, her eyebrows furrowed in concentration. I took a deep breath and tried to relax.

"Oh, you look beautiful," Savannah told me.

"Doesn't she?" Carly sounded proud. "You owe me for this, Juliet."

"When you go to your first dance, I'll return the favor."

"Please. The only makeup you know how to apply is lip gloss. Close your eyes. I need to do your eyeliner."

"Well, then, maybe I'll help you with your hair."

"You *are* good at that when you want to be," Carly conceded. "Okay. I'm almost done. Don't look yet, though."

I opened one eye and peeked in the mirror.

"Juliet!" Carly was indignant. "You cheated!"

I opened both eyes and looked at myself. "Wow. You did a good job. My eyes look so different." Carly had gone to town with the eyeliner, the eye shadow, and the mascara, but somehow I still liked the effect. I looked dramatic.

"I know."

"Are you sure it's not too much? I mean, I like the way it looks, but do I look like I'm in an '80s girl band?"

Savannah laughed. "*No,* Juliet."

Mom came into the room as Carly fixed one last stray piece of hair. I turned around so Mom could see how I looked. She'd seen me in the dress before, of course, but never with my makeup on and my hair done.

"What do you think, Mom?"

You would think my mom would be used to her daughters getting dressed up for dances. I'm the third girl in the family, after all. But here's what I love about my mom: she gets just as excited for Carly and me when we do things as she did for Em, who was the first.

She covered her mouth with her hand and she shook her head, speechless for a moment. Then she gave me a hug. "You are so lovely."

Of course, it's great to get a good reaction from your mom, but the one you're really hoping to dazzle is your date. So it made me *very* happy to see Nate's jaw actually drop when I opened the door.

"Juliet. Wow. I don't even know what to say!"

"Tell her she's beautiful!" Carly called from the other room.

"Carly!" I exclaimed, laughing.

"You are, of course," Nate said, smiling at me.

"Don't leave until we get the 'after' picture!" Carly called out.

"We're going to have to take a few pictures before we leave," I warned Nate. "My mom wants some, and Carly wants to document the miracle she performed. I got home from tryouts only an hour ago."

"How did it go?"

"Pretty well, I think."

My mom, my dad, Carly, and Savannah all came into the room. Dad told me I looked beautiful, gave me a kiss, and said hello to Nate. Then he bailed out, not wanting to wait around for all of the picture-taking. My mom restrained herself and took only a couple of pictures. Then it was Carly's turn.

"Smile like this is the happiest moment of your life," Carly directed.

That wasn't hard to do.

"So where are you taking me?" I asked Nate once we were in his car. It was already almost nine o'clock. Thanks to tryouts, we barely had time for dinner before we went to the dance.

"You'll see." He glanced over at me, the car swerved a tiny bit, and he laughed. "This is kind of embarrassing. I'm having a hard time keeping my eyes on the road."

"Are we meeting up with anyone else?"

"No. The rest of the group went to dinner earlier. You know Max. He thought he'd die if he had to wait until nine to eat. We'll meet up with them at the dance, but for now it's just you and me. Is that all right?"

"Of course."

We arrived at Nate's house a few minutes later. "Welcome to

Restaurant Carmine. My family has something planned for us. I hope you don't mind."

"Not at all. That sounds great." I always liked being around Nate's family.

To my surprise, Nate guided me away from the front door and along the path that led to his backyard. "We're eating back here?" I asked, shivering a little. It was still warm for October, but I could definitely feel a chill in the air.

"Actually, we're eating in the garden shed."

I laughed, but as we rounded the corner, I realized he was serious. Luminarias lined the path that led to the stone shed, and the shed door stood open. The white paper bags glowed brightly against the darkness of the backyard.

"This is beautiful! I can't believe you thought of this."

"Um, actually, I didn't." Nate looked sheepish. "My mom did. We tried to think of something different to do instead of eating at a restaurant or in our dining room."

A table set for two stood inside the shed door. Candles and flowers decorated the table and white paper lanterns hung from the ceiling. "Wow. Does it always look like this in here?"

Nate laughed. "Are you kidding? It never looks like this. My dad had to haul out the lawn mower and a bunch of other junk before we could set everything up."

The shed still smelled faintly of potting soil and the gasoline from the lawn mower, but mostly it smelled like vanilla-scented candles and the warm bread that Nate's thirteen-year-old sister, Jessica, brought in for us. I noticed that she'd dressed up in a dark church dress and an apron. She grinned at me. "I'll be your waitress tonight," she informed me, and I grinned back.

Nate pulled out a chair for me, and Jessica handed me a pen and a card made of thick cream-colored paper. "Please indicate which meal you would like this evening," she said, adopting a formal tone.

"Hmmm." I looked at the card, which had a menu printed on it in a fancy font. There were two options: *Marinated Shrimp with Garden*

Vegetables and Sparkling Cider or *House Specialty Pizza with Non-Alcoholic Beer of Root.* I started to laugh. "Jess, did you write this menu?"

"Perhaps." Somehow she maintained a straight face.

Would it be terribly uncouth if I picked the pizza? I was starving from practice, and as good as the shrimp sounded, I didn't know if it would fill me up.

Nate leaned to whisper in my ear, "Pick whatever you want. We have plenty of both."

While I hesitated, Nate made a mark on his card and handed it to Jessica. As if to influence my decision, my stomach growled faintly. I hoped Nate couldn't hear it. I made a check mark in the box next to the pizza and handed my card to Jessica. "Thank you."

"You're welcome," she said politely, and then she ran back to the house with the cards in her hand. A few seconds later, we heard a cheer go up from the house.

"What was that all about?" I asked Nate.

"You must have chosen the pizza."

I nodded.

"That's what they were hoping you'd pick."

"Why?"

"The younger kids and my dad helped make it."

"Uh-oh. Who made the shrimp?" I didn't want to offend anyone.

Nate laughed. "It's actually takeout. They spent so much time making the pizza dough that they forgot to marinate the shrimp. Dad just got back with a substitute from a restaurant right before we got here."

I started to laugh. "I love your family."

"Wait until you see the pizza. I think the girls ended up deciding to make it into the shape of a heart."

"How romantic."

"No kidding. Hey, since we're talking about romantic stuff—what do you think of the flowers?"

"The flowers? They're beautiful." I looked at them closely for the first time. Pink lilies. Exactly like the flowers he'd given me for my birthday.

"Nate, you're the best." I couldn't believe everything he'd done for me. There were traces of magic in the air: a basketball player transformed into a princess, a garden shed into a romantic restaurant. I wondered what other transformations might take place that night.

At the homecoming dance later, Nate and I didn't even make it through our first dance before someone interrupted us. We had put our arms around each other and as we started to dance beneath the dim, romantic lights, I thought to myself, *I could do this forever.* Then someone called my name and I turned.

"I've been looking everywhere for you!"

"We just got here." I tried not to let Megan know that I was the tiniest bit annoyed that she hadn't waited until the song ended.

"Me too, but I stopped by Coach Giles's office on my way in. I wanted to see if she'd posted the final team list on her door before she went home for the weekend."

Megan's date shrugged. "There was no stopping her."

All my annoyance was gone. "And?"

"It's there."

My heart started to pound. "You're kidding me. Did you see my name?"

"Maybe I did, maybe I didn't." Megan winked at me. "You should definitely go check it out, though."

I looked at Nate. He didn't even hesitate. "Let's go," he said, grabbing my hand.

We left the darkened cafeteria and went out into the hall. The school is usually dim at night, but Megan or someone must have found the hall lights and turned them on, because there was a lighted path right to Coach Giles's classroom. Sure enough, a piece of white paper was taped to the door.

I stopped before we were close enough to read the list. "Maybe I don't want to know."

Nate stopped with me. He still held my hand. "I think you want to know, Jule. Megan wouldn't find you and tell you about it if it wasn't good news. Besides, if anyone deserves to make the varsity team, it's you."

"Okay." I took a deep breath and looked for my name.

It was right where I wanted it to be. There under Varsity Team, the last name on the list—Juliet Kendall.

Nate read it at the same time I did. "All right!" he yelled, and he grabbed me in a bear hug. We held on tight for a moment, and then Nate pulled back and looked at me. It was one of those looks where the person is really looking at you, really seeing you.

At first, I noticed everything about that moment. The fluorescent light buzzing and popping overhead, threatening to give out at any moment. The dinginess of our school hallway at night, without throngs of students to give it life. The sounds of other students somewhere in the building, making me wonder if someone was about to come around the corner and catch the two of us standing there, almost kissing, in front of Coach Giles's classroom door.

Then Nate leaned closer, and we were no longer almost kissing. There was nothing "almost" about it. I closed my eyes, and all of the things I'd noticed earlier simply disappeared.

"Sorry," Nate said a few moments later. "I didn't plan on doing that. But I couldn't wait."

"I don't mind at all." I glanced around me. "Although I have to admit I never thought my first kiss would be in the halls of South High."

"I didn't think mine would be, either," Nate admitted. "How about this. Let's say it never happened."

I must have looked stunned, because he hurried to explain. "Then I'll have an excuse to get it right next time."

Next time. I grinned at him, and we walked back to the dance together, our hands touching. My feet, however, didn't touch the floor.

I made the varsity basketball team.

Nate Carmine kissed me.

Nate Carmine kissed *me*.

So here's the problem with walking on air. Obviously, you have to come back to earth sometime. That's a given. The problem comes when you realize how much you liked flying.

CHAPTER 9

November

At our team practice the next Monday, Coach Giles announced that she had accepted the job in California. She promised to stay long enough to coach our first game at the end of November, but then she'd be gone for good.

The news spread like wildfire through our little town and through the Kendall family in particular. Maddie decided to stay home a few extra days during Thanksgiving vacation so she could be in the stands to watch Coach Giles's final game at South High. Em sent an e-mail from Spain for us to give to Coach after the game.

Emma also wrote to me: "Congratulations on making the varsity team, Jule! Way to keep the Kendall tradition alive. Play hard. Give it your all. I know you don't need me to tell you that."

I didn't, but I also didn't mind hearing it again. *Play hard. Give it your all.* Those were the things the Kendall girls did best.

Maddie came home the Tuesday before Thanksgiving. "I couldn't wait to get here," she said, breathless, as she hauled a giant bag of laundry in from her car. "So I thought I'd come home right after class today. Mom, what's for dinner?"

"You're a walking stereotype, you know that?" I said as I helped her carry the huge bundle down the hall to the laundry room.

"I know," she admitted. Once we'd gotten rid of the bag, she threw her arms around me. "Oh, it's so good to be home. I can't wait for Thanksgiving dinner. What should we do Saturday night? We should totally have a girls' night, right?"

"Yeah. Oh, wait."

"Don't tell me you have a date."

"I do. With Nate. But I can change it. I can see if he wants to go to lunch or something instead. What do you want to do?"

"We should watch *X-Men* in honor of Em." Em has a giant crush on Hugh Jackman, even with his Wolverine hair.

"And we can decorate the Christmas tree." I loved opening the boxes of decorations from years past and hanging them on the tree with my sisters.

"And play Clue."

"Oh, yeah, that's a given. We *have* to play Clue." The four of us girls had developed our own rules and way to play the game, which had evolved over years of rainy Saturday afternoons, long summer days, and sick days home from school. Yes, there are other board games, and, yes, sometimes we play them, but no other game can really compete with Clue.

"I can't wait!" Maddie squealed, making me laugh. I had missed her laugh; she is the loudest and most enthusiastic of all my sisters.

We were still without Em, but at least we were at three-quarters strength instead of half.

"You love it when everyone's home, don't you?" Carly asked a few days later. "Like when Emma and Maddie are both around."

"Yeah, of course. Don't you?"

"It's all right. But it's really . . . loud. And no one lets me forget I'm the baby of the family. It's like Emma and Maddie don't realize I've grown up."

I had to admit she had a point. Maddie and Em always called her Baby Sister. They meant it as a term of endearment, but I could see how it might get old.

"And Maddie always takes charge." Carly shrugged. "I know you have fun with them. I know you've worked really hard to bridge the gap between you guys. But it's different for me. It's like—I mean, I love them, and I've always looked up to them, but for me there *is* no bridge. I'm not their friend like you are. I'm just their little sister."

"That's not true—" I started to say, but right then Maddie came into the family room.

She carried a tray full of food and grinned from ear to ear. "Here we go! Kendall Sisters' Night!"

I laughed. "It is going to get *so* wild. I can already tell."

"It really is," Maddie said. "The three of us haven't been together since when? Your birthday? That was months ago! We have movies to watch! Games of Clue to play! Gossip to catch up on! Like, for example, why a certain senior boy called Carly last night."

A car honked outside. "Juliet can fill you in," Carly said, reaching for her hoodie. "That's my ride. I'm going over to Savannah's."

"You're not staying?" Maddie sounded surprised. "Come on, Carly. You can miss it! Juliet canceled a *date* for this!"

"That's *her* problem," Carly muttered, so quietly that only I could hear her. I gave her an exasperated look, and she shrugged.

"I made brownies!" Maddie said. "You love brownies!"

Carly caught my eye, and I bit my lip. I could see why she felt like the older sisters treated her like a baby. It was as though Maddie thought that all she had to do was tell Carly that we'd made a treat and she'd immediately want to stay. "I'll have some later." The horn honked again in the driveway. "See you guys!"

The front door closed behind her, and Maddie turned to look at me. "What's up with Carly, anyway?"

"What do you mean?"

"She's been grumpy all weekend."

"She's a freshman," I said. "Remember being a freshman? You can't go anywhere without a ride, you can't date, all your friends are changing. It's not the easiest year. We all went through it."

"And she's really skinny."

"She's *always* been really skinny." It was true. Carly had always been the smallest sister.

"And she's acting kind of weird about food." Maddie must have been able to tell from the look on my face that I didn't know what she meant because she went on. "Carly hardly ever eats with the rest of us, except at dinnertime when she can't get around it. And when she does, she cuts her food up really small and puts tons of salt and pepper on everything."

"So what?"

"It reminds me of a roommate I had last year. She had bulimia."

"Carly doesn't have an eating disorder," I said. "Mom and Dad and I would know if she did."

"Are you sure?" Maddie must have sensed my frustration and she held up her hands. "Okay, okay. I'm done. We can talk about something else. I only wanted to tell you to keep an eye on her."

"Fine." As if I needed Maddie to tell me that, anyway. What kind of a Kendall sister did she take me for?

"So can you tell me what's up with this whole Jaydon Fullmer thing?"

Now *that* was a concern I could get behind. "Yeah, that *is* weird. She seems to really like him. He always flirts with her in the halls and at dances."

Maddie shuddered. "Gross. Jaydon Fullmer! He was a jerk even back when I went to school with him. Do Mom and Dad know that she's hanging out with him?"

"I don't know." I had the same worries about Jaydon that Maddie did, but her continued interrogation made me feel defensive. If she wanted to know all about Carly's life, why didn't she ask Carly?

Maddie sighed. "Well, let's get started. I didn't mean to ruin everything. I just wanted to point it out."

She turned on the movie and we divided up the brownies. Later, when the movie was over, the thick, sticky-sweet taste of the brownies lingered in my mouth, and our conversation about Carly lingered in my mind.

Was everything okay with her? Were the changes in her due to something as simple as working out too hard for cheer or flirting too much with the wrong guy? Or was something really wrong?

Girls' night ended a little prematurely when my parents came home from their movie and Maddie got a phone call from a guy in her college ward. We never did get to play Clue, but it wouldn't have been the same without Emma and Carly anyway.

Left alone in the living room, I couldn't stop the questions about Carly from cycling through my mind. And I started remembering things that hadn't worried me much when they happened but now that I thought about them, they seemed strange. Like the night after Thanksgiving, when I saw Carly standing in the kitchen in the dark and eating the rest of the banana cream pie straight out of the pie dish. Or the fact that I'd never actually seen her eating anything for lunch at school. And the way she avoided eating dinner with me after practice and always said she'd eat later instead.

There could be explanations for those things, I thought to myself. *Maybe she was really hungry the night after Thanksgiving. Maybe she doesn't like to eat in front of Jaydon and all his friends at their table, so she eats before or after she comes to the cafeteria. Maybe people do bring a lot of snacks to share at cheer practice.*

But I still couldn't stop thinking about what Maddie had said.

I went into the family room and turned on the computer. As soon as it was up and running, I Googled "eating disorders." After a few seconds I ended up at the National Eating Disorders Association's Web site.

I found a link listing the warning signs and symptoms of bulimia. As I read through the list, it didn't make me feel any better. I had to admit that some of it sounded like Carly. *Extreme concern with body weight and shape.* Carly always talked about how fat she looked and how much she worried about looking perfect in her cheer uniform. *Excessive, rigid exercise regimen despite weather, fatigue, illness, or injury.* She never, ever missed practice, even if she was sick. *Evidence of binge-eating. Evidence of purging behaviors including laxatives or diuretics.* Yikes. They were all scary, but one in particular freaked me out: *Calluses on the back of hands and knuckles from self-induced vomiting.* I had noticed some scratches on Carly's index finger one day and asked her what had happened. She said she got them from doing lifts and things at cheer practice. *That could be true,* I told myself. *Don't freak out yet.*

My cell phone rang right as I was in the middle of reading a list of possible health consequences. I glanced at my watch. Ten minutes to midnight. Who would call so late? I looked at the display and recognized Savannah's cell phone number. It must be Carly.

"Hey."

"Hey, Jule. Can you come pick me up?"

"Sure. Are you still at Savannah's?"

"Yeah. Can you hurry? Mom and Dad said I could stay out until midnight tonight. I didn't realize it was so late. Do you think they'll count it if you pick me up by midnight? Or do you think I have to actually be *home* by midnight?"

I laughed. "I don't know. I'll be right there."

"Thanks, Jule. You're the best."

Before I shut down the computer, I cleared out the history. I didn't want Carly to know what I'd been researching. I couldn't clear out my mind, though. It was full of horrible words that would not go away: *vomiting, laxative abuse, discoloration of the teeth, purging, depression, electrolyte imbalance, organ failure, death.*

When I got to Savannah's house, Carly stood outside in the freezing air waiting for me. She'd zipped up her yellow hoodie tight and pulled the hood over her head to keep herself warm. I hadn't even stopped Old Blue before Carly ran down the driveway and started to open the door. "Go, go, go!" she said as she climbed inside. "I don't want anyone to see that I'm leaving!"

"I've never driven a getaway car before." I killed the headlights and backed out of the driveway as stealthily as I could. Carly laughed. "Why don't you want anyone to see you leave?" I asked.

"Because it will be more mysterious that way, if I sort of disappear. They'll be like 'Where's Carly?' and then they'll miss me and think about me more than if I'd made this big deal about saying good-bye. You've got to be a little hard to get, right?"

"I guess so. Who's 'they,' anyway?"

"Oh, no one," she said airily.

Stupid Jaydon. "Did Savannah's parents let her invite seniors over?"

"No, of course not. She invited kids our age and a couple of sopho-mores." She looked over at me. "I know what you're thinking, Juliet. But I'm not *only* interested in Jaydon Fullmer. There are some pretty cute sophomore guys, too."

"That's good to hear."

"Did you guys have fun at home? Are there any brownies left?"

"Yeah, we saved you some."

"Oh, good. I probably shouldn't eat any, though. The holidays are going to make me *so* fat!"

I didn't know what else to say, so all I said was, "You're not fat, Carly."

Maddie hadn't needed to tell me to keep an eye on Carly. I would look out for her because looking out for each other is one of the most important parts of being a Kendall girl.

CHAPTER 10

Don't look up. Don't look up.

Of course I looked up. We'd never had such a big crowd for a non-play-off game. The stands were full of people wearing South High blue and gold, people who had come to witness the end of an era. Everyone was squished right up next to each other on our old, creaky wooden bleachers. I knew those bleachers. I'd been sitting in them for years, watching my sisters play.

Now I was the one being watched. I felt some of the pressure and I felt nervous—a glittery, bright kind of nervousness that felt exciting, too. And underneath all of that I felt something else. I felt ready.

When I made a practice layup and a few people cheered, I decided that warming up in front of a crowd wasn't half bad. It made even layups and shooting around seem full of significance. I couldn't wait to play. *Let's go.*

The buzzer sounded. As we headed for the bench, I looked up into the stands one final time before the game started. I found my family: Mom, Dad, Maddie, and Carly. I'd spotted Nate and Max and our other friends earlier. Megan and Hanna, of course, were right with me. We were part of the same team.

So almost everyone I cared about was in the gym. The coach I had spent my whole life idolizing and my whole high school career learning from was coaching her last game. I was playing varsity for the first time, and I was starting. My sisters were (almost) all there. My friends were there.

There was no question. We had to win.

When I'm playing basketball and I really get in the zone, I hear everything that matters and I tune out everything that doesn't. The sounds of the game are sharp and clear: Whistles. The squeak of basketball shoes. The voices of my teammates, and the sound of the ball bouncing, the rim rattling, the net swishing, the fans cheering when a shot is good.

On the very first play of the game I saw a chance and I took it. Megan cut up to the top of the key and set a perfect screen on my defender. Two dribbles later, I took my dad's signature fade-away jumper and got nothing but net. The crowd went wild, and I saw Coach Giles clapping on the sidelines. "That's it, Juliet!" she yelled.

I couldn't wipe the smile off my face as I ran back down the court. Electricity seemed to be running through the crowd, through our team, through my own veins. I'm great at assists but I'm not the star, and I hardly ever score the first points in a game. What a way to start the night. And I had a feeling it would only get better and better from there.

The final score was 65–48. Almost before the buzzer finished sounding, our whole team turned and ran for Coach Giles. She laughed and put her hands up as though trying to fend us off, but then she opened her arms and we all swarmed her, hugging her and shouting. I had the ball when the buzzer sounded; I hung onto it and gave it to Coach. She held it over her head and we all cheered wildly.

"We did it!" Megan yelled, throwing her arms around me. I hugged her back. We had come such a long way together, from our city recreation games to our first high school varsity game. All the summer camps and after-school practices paid off.

People came out of the stands to congratulate Coach and wish her well. Maddie and my parents made their way down to the court.

"Good game!" Maddie called to me, and I grinned.

Molly and Hanna, our team captains, hooked up a microphone. A few minutes later, Molly's voice broke through the crowd's excited chatter and cheers. "We want to take a minute and talk about Coach Giles."

It took the crowd a little while to settle down, but soon everyone in the bleachers and out on the floor had quieted down and turned to look at Molly.

"As most of you know, tonight is Coach's last game." Molly paused, and I could tell she was fighting tears. "She's spent a lot of years helping the girls at South High achieve their dreams, and so we want to wish her the best as she goes on to reach for her own."

Coach Giles smiled and wiped her eyes. So did other parents and players in the crowd.

"So we want Coach Giles to know that we aren't going to forget her." Molly held up a blue-and-gold basketball jersey. "We're retiring this jersey in honor of you, Coach. For the rest of the season, and for as long as games are played at South High, we'll remember you."

Hanna handed the jersey and the mike to Coach Giles amid a cacophony of cheers and yells from the stands. Coach smiled and the crowd hushed for her. "This is a great way to end my time at South High," she began. "Not only with a win, but with everyone playing hard. I am honored to be a part of this basketball program and to work with the young women here. South High will always be a part of me, so it means a lot to me to know that I will also be a part of the school." She looked down at the jersey for a moment. "I don't know what else to say, except to thank you and to tell you that I won't ever forget this. It has been my privilege."

The crowd was quiet as the captains hoisted the jersey up to the rafters. When it reached the top, everyone burst into cheers. The number they'd given Coach Giles was 5—the number of state championships she'd won while at South High.

It took a while, but eventually Maddie made her way to where I stood. At last the two of us were face-to-face with Coach Giles.

"Oh, my Kendall girls," Coach said, hugging us.

"We need a picture with you, Coach," Maddie said. "We don't have one of you with all the Kendall sisters." I saw her dart a quick glance at Carly, who was talking to a group of girls not too far away. "All the basketball-playing girls, anyway."

Coach Giles laughed. "But Emma is in Spain! We'll still be missing one."

"I already thought of that." Maddie reached into her bag and pulled out an 8x10 shot of Em's head. "I'll put it in between us. I'm going to make her a little shorter than me, though. It's only fair."

Coach Giles laughed again. Maddie, fake Em, and I arranged ourselves around Coach Giles. "Now we have all the girls," Maddie said.

"Almost." I looked over at Carly.

As my mom took the picture, Carly turned. I saw her look at us as we grinned for the camera, and I felt a little ache. She had chosen to do something different; we hadn't meant to exclude her. I hoped she understood. I couldn't read the expression on her face. Maybe there wasn't anything to read.

Mom looked at the digital camera. "It's a good one."

"I want you to send me that picture," Coach Giles said.

"Of course we will." Maddie gave her one last hug. "You'll always be our coach."

That was true for Maddie, but not for me. I would start under a new regime on Monday. I looked over to where Coach Slater stood talking to one of the parents. Her voice carried across to me—"They played well, but there are a few things I plan on changing for next time."

"Geez, can't that Slater girl wait until Coach Giles is out of the building?" Maddie muttered to me.

"You know her? She's new this year."

"I remember her from when Em played with her. She had a chip on her shoulder then, too."

"She doesn't like me very much."

"That's not surprising. She and Emma really got into it a few times

69

when they were both on the team. You know Em. She never holds anything in."

"That's true." It was one of the reasons we all thought Emma would be a great missionary. She wasn't afraid of saying what she thought and she was passionate about things that mattered to her.

We were some of the last people to leave the gym. My parents and Maddie kept running into old friends and former teammates. Finally, my family walked out to the parking lot to say good-bye to Maddie. She had to get back to school and work, which she'd already missed to see the game.

"Drive safely," my mom said, giving her a kiss.

"I will." Maddie sighed. "I feel all blue and nostalgic. I can't believe it's all over."

"Hey, what are you saying?" I pretended to be mad. "It's not over yet. I'm still playing."

"You're right. Sorry, Jule."

The four of us waved until she pulled out of the parking lot.

"Remember when we could barely fit everyone in one car?" Mom asked Dad. "Now it's just the two of us. Unless you want to ride with us, Carly?"

"I think I'll go with Jule."

Dad laughed. "Now it really *is* just the two of us." He opened the car door for Mom. "See you girls at home in a few minutes. Great game, Juliet."

"Thanks, Dad."

Carly and I walked toward Old Blue. I hadn't been able to talk to Nate after the game, so I reached into the pocket of my sweatshirt to see if he'd called on my cell. I couldn't find it.

"Shoot. I think I left my cell phone in my gym locker."

"Do you want to go get it?" Carly asked. "I bet they haven't locked up yet."

"Yeah, let's give it a try."

We ran back to the gym. We passed a few people on the way, but when we got to the gym itself it was almost empty. Almost. Coach Giles stood in the middle of the floor with her head tipped back, looking up at the retired jersey in the rafters. Her husband stood next to her.

I stopped and Carly almost ran into me. "Juliet, what are you—"

"Shh," I said. Carly fell silent.

Coach Giles and her husband stood there for a few more moments and then Coach Giles's husband put his arm around her. Together, they walked across the floor and out the doors at the other end of the gym. When they went outside, the lights went off. A janitor somewhere must have been waiting for Coach Giles to leave.

She had gone from everything to nothing, from being swamped with people to being almost alone, from standing in the center of the light to walking out into the dark. And now she would start over somewhere new with nothing, and leave everything behind.

How could she do it?

"How are we going to get out of here?" Carly asked, bringing me back to reality. "I can't see anything!"

"I guess I'll have to wait until later to get my phone," I said, turning around. "It's way too dark for us to try to get to the locker room. Let's go back out the way we came."

"Okay." Carly grabbed my hand. "Lead on."

I thought I knew where I was going, but I led us straight into a wall. "Oof. That wasn't right."

"This is the blind leading the blind," Carly complained.

"*You* take a turn, then."

"Okay." She led me around the wall. Then, feeling carefully, we inched along the floor to the stairs and climbed them together. When we reached the top, the darkness lifted a little because of the illuminated signs near the exit door. The light wasn't very strong, but we could see our way out. Carly let go of my hand.

CHAPTER 11

December

Kendall girls don't swear. Not even if they are really, really mad. But they do slam lockers. So I did. I slammed the door to my basketball locker as hard as I could. Then I opened it up and slammed it again.

"Do you feel better?" Megan asked me.

"No. Maybe." I sighed and sat down on the bench to unlace my shoes. I felt a little sheepish even though only Megan and Hanna had seen me slam the locker. "That practice stunk."

"It *was* really weird," Megan agreed. "We didn't spend that much time on drills and conditioning even when we were freshmen. How many minutes did we get to play at the end—five?"

"I can't believe she's having JV and varsity be completely separate teams." I shook my head. "We've never done it that way at South."

"I feel like someone died or something," Hanna said. "I can't believe Coach Giles is really gone."

"I know. Me either." And I couldn't believe Coach Slater was the new head coach, and I didn't understand why she disliked me so much. I had hoped that everything would be fine and that she would have noticed how well I'd played in the first game.

She hadn't. Or if she had, she didn't care. That became apparent right from the beginning of practice, which she had started out by saying,

"We're going to change things up a little." You could see she was absolutely thrilled to be in charge. She rarely smiled, but she smiled then as she looked down at the notes on her clipboard. "First of all, we're going to start wearing knee pads in all our games. We need to be vigilant about protecting against injury."

We all looked at each other. *Knee pads?* Basketball players don't wear knee pads. We're not skateboarding or playing baseball.

"Next, we're going to have a team cheer before each game. I want each of you to write a team cheer tonight and submit it to me tomorrow morning. I'll pick the best one and we'll use that cheer before each game to rally team spirit."

Ha, I thought to myself. *Little do you know that I have an advantage. My sister the cheerleader can help with this one.*

Still, we all exchanged glances again. This was as weird as the knee pads. We were having a cheer-writing competition? Wouldn't our time be better spent, say, practicing basketball?

"Finally, on game days, you will dress up for the entire school day. I know you've been doing that already, but I want us to take it to the next level and show people how serious South High girls are about their team spirit. So this means no more skirts and sweaters. Only actual dresses. And no sandals or flip-flops or bare legs. You need to wear dress shoes and nylons."

"Can I wear my prom dress?" Hanna asked in an innocent voice.

I ducked my head, knowing that making eye contact with Megan or Hanna would be fatal—I would start laughing and not be able to stop. I *had* to get Coach Slater to respect me as a player. Laughing in her face wouldn't help.

"If it fits the criteria, then yes, you may. And while I'm thinking about it, you need to do something about your hair."

"My hair?" Hanna said, reaching up to touch it. She always wore her bright blonde hair in two pigtails for games. It was kind of her trademark.

"I want you to start pulling it back in a single ponytail like everyone else. Any other questions?" Coach Slater asked, staring down the rest of us.

No one said anything. Hanna looked mad, but she stayed quiet too.

What was there to say? We would be a knee-pad-wearing, cheer-writing, prom-dress-wearing basketball team with identical hairstyles.

"Okay. Let's get started. Oh, and Alisha, let's have you go blue today. Juliet, you're with the white team."

That's when I knew for sure she didn't like me. As a starter, I should have been wearing my jersey with the blue side out and playing on the same team with the other starters during the scrimmage. By having me change it to the white side and having Alisha wear blue, Coach Slater basically demoted me. In front of everyone.

"I don't get it," Hanna said now, closing her locker. "Why is she changing things around? Everything went fine in our last game. You played great, too. Why try to fix what isn't broken?"

"I don't know."

"Maybe she wants to prove that she doesn't have to use Coach Giles's system to win," Megan said.

"Maybe she wants to change everything just because she can," I fumed. "I bet she's not going to let me start in Friday's game."

"And what's the deal about not telling us who's going to start until the day of the game?" Hanna continued. I could tell she worried about her position too. "Coach Giles *always* let us know the day before."

"Like I said, I think she's trying to do stuff her way," Megan said.

"Are you defending her?" Hanna asked.

Megan shook her head. "No. It's driving me crazy too. Coach Giles has been coaching us one way, and changing it up now makes things harder. But we have to try to make it work. Coach Slater is the coach now. Hopefully she knows what she's doing." She shut her locker without slamming it and slung her bag over her shoulder.

"You'll start," I told Hanna as the three of us walked out into the gym. "You're a senior. She won't mess with you."

"She sure messed with both of us today," Hanna pointed out. Coach Slater had made Hanna play center, which wasn't her usual position.

"I don't like being messed with," I said.

"But what are you going to do about it?" Megan asked.

"I have no idea." I started walking toward Old Blue. "I guess tonight

Maybe that's the way to Coach Slater's heart."

"It's either that or knee pads," Hanna agreed.

If I'd had a locker at home, I would have slammed it too. But I didn't, so I threw down my pencil instead.

I didn't think I had anger management issues, but after three hours of homework on top of the world's most frustrating basketball practice, the last thing I wanted to do was write a cheer. Carly had locked herself in her room to work on her homework, so I didn't want to bother her by asking her for help. After an hour, all I had were three stupid lines:

Pride, Honor, Panther Spirit

Come on team, let's hear it

GO, PANTHERS!

Pathetic, but the best I could do. I sighed and went to type it up on the computer even though it was so short I might as well have jotted it down on a Post-it note. Once I finished, I took the paper and went to Carly's room. Her door was finally open, which I took as a good sign. "Hey, Carly?"

"What?" She was working, her head bent down.

"Can you listen to a cheer I wrote?"

She turned around and stared at me. "You wrote a *cheer*?"

"Yeah."

"Why?"

"It's kind of a long story. Coach Slater is having a competition to see which of us can write the best cheer. Then we're going to do the cheer before every game."

"Seriously?"

"Yeah. So will you listen to mine?"

"I guess."

I wondered what was up with Carly. She usually wasn't so terse. "All right." I cleared my throat, feeling unbelievably self-conscious even though my audience had only one member. How did Carly scream out cheers in front of hundreds of people?

When I finished, I looked to her for approval. "So, what do you think?"

"Is that all there is?"

"Well, yeah." I tried to defend my sad little cheer. "It's supposed to be kind of a short rally cry, you know, that we can do before the game. It's for the team, not for the crowd."

"It's fine, then."

"Thanks." I'd hoped for a little more help, but she seemed preoccupied. Besides, did it really matter anyway?

"How's basketball going?" Carly started rearranging the papers on her desk.

"Don't ask. Coach Slater made us do drills for almost three hours this afternoon."

"You don't like her, do you?"

"Coach Slater? Not so much. I don't think she's going to have me start in the game on Friday."

"Hasn't she heard that Kendall girls are automatically supposed to play varsity and get all the playing time?"

Did Carly *want* to make me mad? "That's not it. It shouldn't matter what Maddie and Emma did. It matters what *I* do. And I had a good game on Tuesday, remember? I think she just doesn't like me. Or maybe she doesn't like Em. They played together, I guess." Time for a change of subject. "So what's up with you? Is something wrong?" I flopped onto the floor next to her bed.

"Nothing's wrong. I'm just trying to get my homework done."

"Hey, what are all these?" I pulled out a plastic bag from under her bed. It was filled with candy—miniature Snickers bars, individual Reese's Peanut Butter Cups. "Oh, yum. Can I have some?"

Carly jumped out of her chair. "*No.* Put that back."

"Okay, okay. Sorry."

Carly pulled the bag out of my hands and stuffed it into her closet instead. "They're for cheerleading. We're making candy bar signs for the freshman boys' basketball team."

I rolled my eyes. How lame. The cheerleaders treated the football and basketball players like they were gods. "So what are you working on?"

"History. I have a test coming up."

"Well, I guess I should let you study." I waited for a second, but she didn't contradict me so I got up to leave. I wanted to talk more but the set of her shoulders told me that it wasn't the right time.

I went back to my room feeling a little strange. I'd worried so much about my older sisters leaving for college and missions and marriage. I'd always counted on Carly being around. Now I realized that someone didn't have to leave physically for a relationship to change. Carly and I had always been close, and I counted on that. I needed it. I thought that she did too.

I turned in my cheer to Coach Slater's office the next morning and hoped that would be the end of it. But it wasn't. She singled me out at practice. "Juliet, I hear your sister is a cheerleader."

"Yeah, she is."

"So I imagine she was helpful when you wrote this." She held up a copy of my cheer.

Was she accusing me of cheerleading plagiarism? "No, actually, I—"

"It doesn't matter. It's still the best cheer." She handed everyone a copy, and Hanna and Megan grinned at me. "Go over the words on your own tonight. We'll start doing the cheer at our game on Friday. Now, does everyone have their knee pads?"

Friday finally came. I ironed my favorite dress, bought nylons to go with it (yuck—I hated nylons), and wore my best dress shoes, the ones with the highest heels. I packed my bag before school so that I wouldn't have to do it right before the game, and I checked six times to make sure my knee pads were inside. I checked so many times that Carly got tired of waiting for me and went to sit in Old Blue, honking the horn until I came out to drive us to school.

"We're going to be late," she told me when I finally got into the car.

"We'll make it. We still have ten minutes."

"Are you nervous about the game?"

"I'm fine." I sighed. "I think. I hope she lets me start."

I ducked into my first-period class right before the bell. Hanna, who sat a few rows in front of me, caught my eye and stuck her legs into the aisle. I started laughing silently. She wore a dress and nylons and dress shoes, like Coach Slater had decreed, but she wore something else, too. Knee pads. Hanna's dress was short so you could see them perfectly, bright white against her black nylons and the black of her dress.

"Only a few hours until our fate is decided," Hanna said cheerfully after class.

"Don't remind me."

"Think positive. It's going to be fine. We're both going to start. I can feel it."

"Has Coach Slater seen you yet?"

"No, but I'm hoping I'll run into her in the halls." Hanna waved as she headed off to her next class. "I'll see you at lunch."

"What happened to Hanna?" Nate came to stand beside me. "Did she get injured at practice?"

I laughed. "No. It's an inside joke." I started to tell him about Coach Slater's new rules, but he interrupted me.

"Sorry. I just saw Megan. I've got to catch her and tell her what happened at our student government meeting yesterday."

"Oh, okay. See you later."

Nate was already hurrying away. "See you!" he called over his shoulder.

Megan turned and smiled when Nate called out her name to get her attention. She was dressed up, too, of course, and she looked great. They disappeared into the crowded hallways together.

It was stupid, but I felt kind of alone as I walked to my next class.

CHAPTER 12

"All right. Here's the starting lineup for tonight's game." Coach Slater stood in front of us with her list in her hand. She paused, and I found myself holding my breath.

"Hanna. Molly. Megan."

Megan was starting! "Go Meg," I whispered to her under my breath.

"Alisha. Cara."

She didn't call my name.

I think one of the hardest feelings in the world is when you're ready for something, totally ready, and something or someone keeps you from doing it.

Sitting on the bench felt all wrong. For one awful moment, in the silence after Coach Slater read the names, I thought I might cry. But I didn't. I set my shoulders and told myself, *It's not over yet.*

I watched each play with my hands clenched and my legs tensed, ready to spring up and run out on the court at a moment's notice. Megan's first shot went a little wild, but she found her rhythm soon enough. Coach Slater put Hanna back in at forward and she played well too. And I had to admit that Alisha did fine. She took—and missed—a lot of shots, but she also made a few.

After a while I glanced up into the bleachers. I saw my mom and dad and Nate and Max, but I couldn't see Carly. What did they think about me sitting on the bench? Did they feel sorry for me? Angry for me?

It doesn't matter what they think, I told myself. *Get your head back in the game.*

With an effort, I brought my mind back to the play happening in front of me. I didn't want Coach Slater to accuse me of daydreaming. I stared in her direction, willing her to turn and look at me and send me into the game. "Come on, come on," I muttered under my breath.

When Coach Slater finally pulled Alisha out and sent me in at the end of the first quarter, I felt like I might explode as I ran onto the floor. The ref handed Hanna the ball, she passed it to me, and I took control. Three trips down the floor, two assists, and a three that I barely missed. Not bad.

The whistle blew. A time-out. I ran over to the sidelines.

"Good job, everyone," Coach Slater said. She looked at me. "I want us to run a play to get Juliet another open look at that three. Okay, Juliet?"

I nodded. My role on the team wasn't usually to score points—I usually made the plays happen for other people—but if Coach Slater wanted me to shoot, I would do it. I would do whatever she told me to do if it meant I could play.

We ran out onto the floor again. The play worked the way we planned it—two screens, a cut to the outside, and Juliet Kendall wide open for the three. Only I hesitated, and then I wasn't so wide open anymore. As their guard rushed out to defend me, she left Cara all alone at the top of the key. I made a quick bounce pass to her, and she hit the shot.

Time-out again. "Juliet, I thought I told you to take the shot."

"I meant to, but I waited too long and then I saw Cara—"

"Do what I tell you. Let's try that play again."

I felt rattled. *The pass worked. Cara made the shot, didn't she?* I wanted to trust my instincts, but it seemed like Coach Slater was telling me to ignore them. But she was the coach. Maybe Megan had it right. Maybe Coach Slater wanted to turn me into more of a shooting guard.

The moment I had a look at the basket, I took the next shot.

It wasn't a good opening. I didn't trust my instincts. I did what Coach Slater told me to do. The ball rattled off the rim and the other team grabbed the rebound. We ran back down the court.

I felt like I'd let the team down. Coach Slater must have agreed because she pulled me out and didn't put me in again until the end of the fourth quarter. By then, we were ahead by ten points. I played fine, but I didn't make the difference between a win and a loss; I didn't feel like I'd helped at all. I started to wonder what I had to do to convince Coach that I could play. Maybe I needed to practice dramatic last-second shots or something. Maybe I should figure out a way to dunk. *That* would get her attention.

The buzzer sounded as the clock ran down to zero. I turned and handed the ball to the ref. Megan came up next to me and we bumped shoulders.

"Great game," I said, and I meant it. "You were on fire. What did you have—fifteen points?"

"I think so."

After we shook hands with the other team, we all grabbed our warm-ups and followed Coach Slater back into the locker room for the post-game meeting. I looked back over my shoulder once but I still didn't see Carly. I couldn't help but feel like my life had been turned upside down. It seemed like I was trapped in an alternate universe, while somewhere else things were happening the way they were meant to happen. Maybe somewhere else Juliet Kendall started in a game for her real coach, Coach Giles, while Carly cheered in the stands.

When I got home I found Carly upstairs in the bathroom we shared, brushing her teeth.

"Hey."

"Hey." She spat into the sink and frowned at herself in the mirror. "How long have you been home?"

"I just got here."

"Sorry I missed your game. But Mom and Dad have that new rule about me only going out once on the weekends, and tomorrow night is Savannah's birthday."

"Oh, right." My parents worried that Carly had too much going on with cheerleading, school, Mutual, and socializing. They thought she might be spreading herself too thin.

"I figured you wouldn't be mad because I came to one of your games earlier in the week."

"I'm not mad. Sorry if it seems that way. Tonight was kind of lame. I didn't get to start." I decided I didn't want to think about it or talk about it anymore. "How did your homework go?"

"Fine. I'm finished." Carly took one last look at her face in the mirror and then turned away.

Something silvery fell to the ground when she moved away: one of those medicine packets where you can punch the pills out through the tinfoil backing. Almost all the holes had been popped open.

"Hey, you dropped this," I said, handing her the foil packet.

Carly snatched it from my hand. "My decongestant. I've been stuffed up all week."

"So what are you doing now?"

She sighed exaggeratedly. "Nothing." Then she turned and walked back toward her room. "Nothing, nothing, nothing. I never do anything."

She seemed down, but I didn't have time to talk to her. Nate was on his way over to pick me up for our date. And Carly didn't seem to be in the mood to talk anyway. "That's not true," I called after her, but I didn't get a response.

A little while later, I heard the doorbell ring. "I think that's Nate," I called out to Carly. "Can you get the door for me? I'm trying to finish my makeup."

No response. She was probably listening to her iPod. Or ignoring me. Only a few weeks ago, Carly would have hurried to answer the door for the chance to chat with Nate for a few seconds. What was going on with her?

The doorbell rang again. I decided lip gloss would have to be enough and ran down the stairs.

"Sorry, I'm a little early," Nate said when I opened the door. "Are you ready?"

"Close enough." I grabbed my jacket and called back up the stairs. "Carly! I'm leaving!" Nothing.

"What's Carly doing home on a Friday night?" Nate asked as we walked to his car.

"New rule. She can go out only once on the weekends."

"That must be killing her."

"She doesn't like it, that's for sure."

I expected Nate to take my hand as we walked to his car, but he didn't. That seemed a little strange. He opened the car door for me, though, and once we were both inside he turned to me and smiled.

"So do you feel okay about the game tonight?"

"I guess. I'm glad we won. And it's great that Megan and Hanna both got to start."

"Maybe you should wear your knee pads with your dress on the next game day. Maybe that was Hanna's good-luck charm."

"Maybe I will."

We were both quiet for a few seconds, which was also weird. Usually we had too much to say to each other. I was about to ask him if he'd heard our new pre-game basketball cheer when my cell phone rang.

"It's Maddie," I said, glancing at the display. "She must be wondering how the game went." I put the phone back into my pocket. "I'll call her back later."

"You can call her now—if you want."

Why did he say that? We had kind of an unspoken rule that we didn't take other calls while we were out together, unless it was our parents. Something seemed a little off. "Nate?"

"Yeah?"

"Is anything wrong?" The minute the words were out of my mouth, I wanted to take them back. I suddenly decided that if anything *was* wrong, I didn't want to hear about it. Not right then.

"No. Why?"

"I don't know. You seem a little tired or something."

"That's probably it. Planning this Sub-for-Santa thing for student government is killing me."

I wondered to myself when I had started analyzing his every move. So he didn't hold my hand while we walked to the car. So he seemed a little quieter than usual. So what? Why did I worry about *everything* lately? I had enough stress in my life with basketball and worrying about my sister. I didn't need to add drama where it didn't exist, like in my relationship with Nate.

"So," I said brightly, in my most teasing, enthusiastic, I'm-Juliet-Kendall-and-nothing-gets-me-down tone, "what can I do to help you? Do we need to get you a Santa suit or something?"

Nate laughed, and then, finally, reached for my hand.

After Nate dropped me off later that night and after I walked into our darkened house, I suddenly felt exhausted. It was like my body knew that I didn't have to perform anymore. I stood in the dark foyer for a minute, bone-tired from the game and the date—tired of all of it. I closed my eyes and let my shoulders slump.

My phone beeped again, and I pulled it out of my pocket to find a text message from Maddie: *How was your game?*

I texted her back: *It went okay. I didn't get to start.* I stood there for a few minutes, waiting to see if she would text or call back. Nothing happened. She was probably out doing something fun with her college friends.

I went into the kitchen and opened the freezer. Mom had bought some Rocky Road ice cream, my favorite. I wanted to stay up a little longer in case Maddie called back. Maybe a little sugar would help. I pulled out the carton, surprised at how light it felt. I opened it up. Only a little sliver of ice cream, barely enough for a single scoop, remained along the bottom.

My parents weren't home yet. I hadn't eaten any. Carly was the only one who'd been home all evening. Had she eaten almost a whole carton of ice cream by herself while we were all out?

Now that I was looking at the question directly, I could see the answer was yes. And I could see other things, too. Things I'd noticed but ignored.

The way she avoided eating with the family. Her slipping grades. The way she'd been withdrawing a little more. Brushing her teeth obsessively. Worrying about her weight. Bags of candy stashed under her bed. I'd been a fool to believe her excuse about making signs for the basketball players.

And I couldn't get the image of that foil packet out of my mind. Did Carly really have a cold? Or could they be something besides decongestants? Laxatives, maybe, like the Web site had mentioned? I didn't know what laxatives looked like. I made a mental note to myself to look the next time I went to the store.

I dug out the last little spoonful of ice cream and popped it in my mouth. It tasted sweet and cool, and it melted way too fast on my tongue, and then there was nothing left. I threw the carton in the trash and climbed up the stairs to my room. Carly's door was closed and her room was dark so I didn't stop. I wouldn't have known what to say, or how to say it, anyway.

CHAPTER 13

I should have kept a running list of Things I Never Thought I'd Do the Year I Turned Sixteen. It could include items such as:

Sit on the bench for the majority of every basketball game.

Wear knee pads, a mouth guard, and ankle braces in aforementioned basketball games.

Write a cheer.

And the latest addition to the list: Buy laxatives.

I stood in the aisle of the store and stared at the boxes. Who knew there would be so many kinds? Some were even chocolate-flavored and looked like squares of candy. I looked around, wondering if I dared to ask a store employee. *Excuse me—which kind of laxative is the most popular? No, not with old people. With teenage girls.*

I didn't have the courage, plus it was Saturday afternoon and the store teemed with holiday shoppers. I ended up choosing a small box with pink pills and burying it underneath the other items in my basket: the nylons to replace the ones I'd torn the week before, the flour and sugar my mom asked me to pick up for Christmas cookies, and the bag of Nate's favorite candy that I planned to give him as part of his Christmas present.

I must have imagined the weirdness between Nate and me, because the next time we went out everything was back to normal. Including the good-night kiss on the steps of my front porch. I must have been paranoid or something.

I hadn't imagined the weirdness at basketball, though. Coach Slater still wouldn't let me start, and she also made us wear mouth guards and ankle braces in addition to the knee pads. Hanna threatened to show up at practice one day in her brother's football uniform to illustrate how ridiculous this was all becoming, but of course she didn't. She started every game, so she didn't want to rock the boat. I, on the other hand, should probably go for it. It couldn't make things worse. The prayers I said before each game were getting harder and harder to say. What good did it do to ask for help to play my best if I never even played?

The cashier rang up my items and didn't glance twice at the laxatives. Apparently they fell into the category of things that are embarrassing to buy but don't cause cashiers a moment's thought. Like underwear or feminine products.

Maddie called as I climbed into the car. I hurried to answer the phone. It had been more than a week since I'd talked to her, which was longer than we usually went without updating each other on our lives.

"What's up?" Maddie asked. "Are you at home?"

"No, I'm out. Buying laxatives."

"What?"

"I'm kind of worried that Carly has been taking them," I explained. "She dropped something a few nights ago that I thought looked like laxative pills, but I didn't get a close enough look so I bought some at the store today." I rustled around in the plastic grocery sack and pulled out the small box. "I'm going to look at them right now, before I go home."

"So? What do you think?" Maddie sounded worried.

"Hold on. I haven't opened them yet." I opened the box and looked at the contents. Pretty basic, a bunch of little pink pills in a foil package. There were about a million other things packaged that way. Fancy cough drops, for example. And, to give Carly credit, the little red decongestant pills we usually took when we had colds or allergies *were* packaged the same way.

I didn't know what I expected: some kind of giant warning in red letters, maybe, that said, *DO NOT USE TO SUPPORT YOUR EATING DISORDER.*

"So . . ." Maddie said again.

"The results are inconclusive." I turned the pills over in my hand. "It does look a little like the decongestant package. I can't be sure. I don't know. I guess I'm a pretty lousy detective."

"Oh." Maddie was quiet. "Have you talked to Mom and Dad about her lately?"

"There hasn't been anything to talk about. I found a bunch of candy bars under the bed a while ago but she had a good excuse for them being there, and I don't think Mom and Dad will think she's lying. She's been kind of moody for the last couple of weeks, but I think that's because Mom and Dad restricted how much she goes out on the weekends. And who knows—maybe she really *was* taking a decongestant."

"Have you noticed her throwing up lately?"

I was exasperated. "Look, Maddie, I'm not following her around night and day. I'm not keeping a journal about what I see her eat. I'm keeping an eye on her—like *you* asked me to, remember? And I'm not going to turn this into a big deal when I can't prove that it is. It's easy for you to assume you know everything when you don't have to live here and spy on your own sister." I threw the pills down in disgust. "I shouldn't have even been doing this."

Maddie didn't speak for a second. "I'm sorry. You're right. I think I worry so much because it doesn't seem like there's anything I can do. And every time I come home, Carly seems different. It's easy to notice how different when I'm gone for a few weeks at a time."

"Mom and Dad and I are paying attention, too."

"I know." Neither of us said anything for a moment.

"I do have some good news, though," I said, breaking the silence. "I think she's over her crush on Jaydon Fullmer. I haven't heard her talk about him for a while, and I haven't seen them together in the halls, either."

"That *is* good news." Maddie paused. "I have some good news too, but I'm not sure you'll be crazy about it."

"Try me. What's up?"

"I'm not coming home for Christmas."

"*What?* Where else would you go?"

"My roommate and I found these super cheap tickets to Costa Rica. We thought it would be fun to go backpacking for a couple of weeks and get out of the snow, and I have enough money left from working this summer to do it. We're both minoring in Spanish, so this would be good for us."

"But why right now? Couldn't you go over spring break or during the summer or—" I'd been looking forward to Maddie's visit so much. I'd hoped we could make up for the Thanksgiving visit and spend time with Carly.

"I want to take the chance while I have it. Who knows if I'll be able to get away later? I checked with Mom and Dad, and they said it would be okay. And with Em gone, it seemed like this would be a good year to miss."

"Thanks a lot."

"You know what I mean. Look, I'll be back for New Year's. I'll even be able to see a couple of your games before I have to go back to school. I don't want to miss out on this trip, though. This is a once-in-a-lifetime opportunity, you know?"

"Sure."

"Jule, I promise I'm not abandoning you with the Carly thing. I'll be there for most of the holidays. Christmas is the only part I'll miss."

"Fine." I decided not to point out that Christmas was the most important part. Who cared about New Year's?

"What are you going to do about the laxatives?"

"I don't know. Bake them into brownies for Coach Slater?" I'd heard of pranks like that, but of course I'd never done anything so mean. I had to admit that the temptation was strong.

Maddie laughed. "Didn't you get any playing time in your last game?"

"Not much. Again."

"Is the team winning games?"

"We're doing okay. Not as well as we did last year."

"She'll figure it out."

Yeah, right, I thought, but I didn't say that to Maddie. I said what I always did when the subject came up. "I hope so."

I hung up the phone and looked at the empty box in my hand again. What now? I didn't want to take the laxatives home with me.

There was a trash can in front of the store. I got back out of the car and threw the box and the pills away, no wiser than I'd been before.

Soon I had another item to add to my list of things I never thought I'd do: Give my almost-boyfriend permission to go out with my best friend.

On Monday, Nate and I were the first people at our table at lunch. As we sat down, he said, "I have kind of a weird question for you."

"What is it?"

"There's this combined student government thing this weekend at Parker High and we're supposed to bring a date. Since you and I went out last weekend, I thought I might take Megan. You know, because she's on student government and everything."

I was silent for a moment. "That's not a question."

"I know. I mean, so I guess I wanted to ask—would you care if I took her?"

Um, yes, I wanted to say. *Of course I would care. She's my best friend! You're my almost-boyfriend!* But I didn't want to seem needy or insecure so I didn't say that.

"You would," Nate said, watching me. "You would care. Okay. That's no problem. Who do you think I should take?"

Then I felt like a jerk for not trusting him and Megan. It made sense that he might want to take her. It was safe, even. She was one of his best friends. Besides, I'd gone out with a guy from my English class a few weeks earlier and Nate had trusted me. But still, something in me didn't want him to take Megan. They already hung out a lot doing student government stuff. They were close.

"Um, I don't know. Hanna?" I knew who Hanna had a crush on, and it wasn't Nate.

"I thought about asking her. But I overheard her talking about her plans this weekend and it sounds like she's busy on Saturday night." He shrugged. "It's no problem. I'll find someone else."

I started to feel like I'd made a big deal out of nothing. And who did I want him to ask, anyway? Some super-cute girl I didn't even know? "Oh, go ahead and take Megan. She's fun. She's your friend. I'm sure she'd love to go with you."

"Are you sure?"

"I'm sure."

At that moment, Max and Megan and Hanna arrived at the table and Nate changed the subject. "Big game on Friday night, right?"

"You know it," Hanna said. We were playing our crosstown rivals, Eastview High, right before the varsity boys played them. Eastview was always our toughest competition. "You guys are coming, right?"

"I'll be there for sure. Max, are you with me?" Nate grinned.

"That depends. Will there be any cheerleaders?"

Hanna, Megan, and I all threw our straw wrappers at him.

"There might be some," I told him, "but don't even *try* to flirt with Carly."

"You're pretty protective," Max said.

"Of course I am. She's my little sister."

Everyone kept talking about the game and the rivalry and how we hoped we'd be able to repeat last year's sweep, when both the girls' and boys' varsity teams beat Eastview in overtime. I remembered that game. I'd been sitting on the bench cheering for the varsity girls.

I couldn't stand to think about sitting on the bench again this year. I'd written the cheer, run the drills, worn the stupid mouth guard and knee pads, done everything I'd been asked to do, whether it had anything to do with basketball or not, and it hadn't made any difference. There was only one thing left to try. I had to talk to Coach Slater.

CHAPTER 14

I decided to approach Coach Slater before I lost my courage. So when she dismissed us at practice that day, I tried to be as low-key and professional as possible. "Coach Slater, can I talk to you for a second?"

"Sure," she said, folding her arms across her chest. "What is it?" The other girls on the team looked at me curiously as they gathered their stuff together.

"I kind of hoped that I could talk to you in private."

"I don't have much time. Can you talk to me out here?"

"Um, I guess." Most of the girls were heading for the locker room, so maybe it would be okay. Hanna and Megan both gave me surprised looks on their way out of the gym. I hadn't told them I planned to talk to Coach Slater. "I wondered—" I stopped. This was painful and embarrassing, but I had to know, so I didn't let myself off the hook. "I was wondering why you haven't been starting me."

"Well, the reason is simple." She paused, as if she expected me to fill it in for her.

I couldn't, though, so I waited.

"Because you're not the best point guard on the team. Alisha is."

I wanted to argue with her, but I tried to stay calm. "Alisha is a great player. But I had more assists in that first game than she's had in any game since."

"And Alisha has scored more points."

I didn't want this to turn into a bash-Alisha session. "I know she scores a lot of points, but she also shoots the ball a lot. I bet our percentages are really close. Coach Giles thought—"

"I think Coach Giles valued a different kind of game than I do."

That's for sure, I thought to myself, but of course I didn't say it. Instead I said, "Oh."

"Look, Juliet, you're a good player. But Alisha is better, and Catherine has flashes of brilliance, so I like to give her some playing time too. She has a lot of promise for a sophomore. Even though we'll still have you next year, we're going to need another good point guard in the wings when Alisha graduates this spring. Try to think long-term. Try to think about the team. That's what I have to do."

I couldn't stand it. "I *do* think about the team. That's why I lead the team in assists!"

"I'm not going to argue about this with you," Coach Slater said. "I'm the coach. You're the player. You're going to have to trust me. Is there anything else you wanted to talk about?"

Not with you, I thought. "No, that's it."

I didn't want to talk to Hanna or Megan, either. I was too humiliated. So I didn't go back to the locker room to change. Instead, I grabbed my stuff and went straight out to Old Blue. I needed to talk to one of my sisters, and I wanted to talk to someone face-to-face, not over the phone. That meant Carly. I wondered if she'd had cheer practice in the auxiliary gym today. Before I could go back and check, I found a note on Old Blue: *Practice canceled today. I found a ride home. C.*

As I drove away, I tried to ignore the humiliation that still burned in me from my conversation with Coach Slater. Why had I even tried to talk to her? We didn't understand each other. She'd thought I was a trouble-maker and a mediocre player right from the start, and it didn't seem like there was anything I could do to convince her otherwise. I didn't know how much longer I could keep banging my head against that particular brick wall.

When I got home, Carly's bedroom door was closed. That seemed to be happening more and more. I knocked. "Carly?"

"What?"

"Can I come in?"

"I guess."

I opened the door and went inside her room. She and I used to share it before Emma moved out and I took over her old room. Not for the first time, I noticed how different Carly's room looked now that it was just hers. I'm kind of messy. Carly is a neat freak. She hangs her clothes up in the closet according to color and all the books on her shelves are alphabetized. She sat at her desk, which was also super-organized: one little cup of pencils and pens, one lamp, and one neat little notebook, which she closed as I walked through the door.

"This place is freaky-clean," I said, trying to joke with her. "I can still see the vacuum lines on the floor." I could, too.

"Is that what you wanted to come in and tell me?" She sounded sarcastic and snotty.

"You don't have to bite my head off." I had second thoughts about telling her what Coach Slater said after practice. You can't really open your heart to someone who's in a crummy mood. But I still didn't want to be alone. Maybe the best thing to do was to distract myself from thinking about basketball. "I'm going to run a couple of errands. I wondered if you wanted to come."

"Right now?

"Well, yeah."

To my surprise, Carly nodded. "I guess I could stand to get out of the house." She grabbed her hoodie, and together we went down the stairs and climbed into Old Blue. The heater always took its sweet time getting started, so Carly and I were both shivering as I started down the street.

"Where are we going, anyway?" Carly asked.

"To the store to pick up the photo Christmas cards for Mom, and then I thought maybe we could go to a movie or something."

"No Christmas shopping? Don't you need to get something for Nate?"

"I already did. I ordered it online."

"What did you get him?"

"A University of Arizona sweatshirt."

"What made you think of that?"

"He's always wanted to go there for college, and he's a big Wildcats fan. Plus, I asked Max for advice and that's what he suggested." (Max's exact words had been, "Get him something to do with sports. Don't try to give him anything meaningful.")

"Oh." I wondered if Carly was offended that I hadn't taken *her* advice about what to give Nate. She'd suggested I give him something meaningful—make him a playlist of our favorite songs and put together a photo album of pictures of the two of us together. I'd figured I should go with what Max said. He was a guy, after all.

"What movie are we going to see?"

"There's a showing of *When Stars Align* in an hour. Do you want to see that one?"

"Sure."

"I'm pretty sure Nate won't be heartbroken if I see it without him. Besides, I need a break. I'm sick of practicing and sick of studying." I nudged my cell phone toward her. "Will you send Mom and Dad a text telling them that we'll be home late for dinner?"

As we drove to the store, Carly's mood seemed to improve in spite of herself. I felt a little better too. It was hard not to feel okay about things with the Christmas music on the radio and the deep snow that had fallen the night before lining the streets and hiding the dead brown grass. I started to think that maybe it wasn't such a big deal that Maddie would be gone for the holidays this year. She'd be back again next Christmas and so would Emma. Next year would be great.

Wait a minute, I thought. *When did I start doing* that *again?* It had been a long time since I'd been in the habit of wishing time away. Since I'd turned sixteen, in fact.

A long line of people waited at the photo counter. Old people wearing coats, young mothers holding babies in bright woolly winter hats, husbands out on errands for their wives. Carly shifted from one foot to the other, impatient. "Do you care if I wait for you in the car?" she asked.

"I guess not." She took off and I sighed, watching her walk toward the doors near the pharmacy. So much for spending time together. I turned back to the line, willing it to go faster so that we could make it to our movie on time. On purpose, I didn't look over to see if Carly went outside or not. I didn't really want to know if she went over to the registers to buy laxatives or candy instead. Spying on her was getting really old.

Twenty minutes later I finally climbed back into the car with the Christmas cards. Carly sat in the passenger seat, waiting for me. She held out her hand. "Let's see. What picture did Mom decide to use?"

I opened up the envelope and slid out one of the cards. "The one we took right before Emma left in May." In the photo, my family sat on the steps of our house, dressed up but not too formal. The early-evening lighting was perfect. The red brick of our house made a warm, almost-glowing background. My parents looked especially radiant, surrounded by their girls.

Only seven months had passed, but things had already changed. Em was gone, of course, and Carly looked different. She'd gotten a haircut and grown up a little, but that was only part of it. Her smile seemed more subdued these days.

"You look so different," Carly said.

"*I* do?" I'd been so focused on everyone else that I hadn't really looked at myself. I sat next to Maddie at the edge of the picture. My hair looked lighter from the sun and my skin was tan since I'd been outside so much for track. "I'm a lot paler now."

"It's not that," Carly said. "You look sassy in this picture."

"Sassy?" I looked closer. My face smiled back at me. Carly was right. There was a confidence about me that showed in the picture, in my posture, even. I remembered suddenly that I had come straight from a track meet and had barely enough time to shower and get dressed. After the picture-taking, I'd gone with my friends to a movie, and then I'd studied late into the night for the ACT. I was a girl who was going places, and it showed in the picture.

"I was actually going to say the same thing about you," I told Carly.

"Really? I think I look better now." She scrutinized the picture. "That skirt—ugh. Totally unflattering. And I look like such a baby. I think my face has changed since this picture. Don't you?" She held the photo up next to her cheek and looked at me hopefully.

"I don't know," I said, taking the card back from her and tucking it into the envelope with the rest. I didn't want to look at it anymore. It made me kind of sad. I missed springtime. I missed Maddie. I missed Emma. I missed the younger, more innocent Carly. I missed feeling the way I'd felt when that picture had been taken: confident and glowing.

We went to the same movie theater we'd gone to since we were little, the one right down the hill from our house. The popcorny smell of the lobby made me nostalgic. "Remember when we used to walk down here and go to movies all the time in the summer?"

Carly nodded. "And we saved up our allowance for treats. You'd buy the popcorn, and I'd buy two drinks."

"I want root beer," I teased her, but she reached for her purse. "Okay."

She got in one of the concession lines and I got in another. It was exactly like old times when we competed to see whose line moved more quickly.

"I'm going to beat you," Carly said, smiling at me when I got stuck behind a family with little kids who took their candy selections very seriously.

"If you do, don't forget to save the seats." Another old rule of ours. Whoever made it through concessions first was in charge of finding the best spots possible.

Carly did beat me. She sailed through the line long before the kids in front of me finished deciding on their Red Vines. The theater was already dark when I went inside. It didn't take long to find my sister—she sat in our favorite area, halfway up the stadium seating and to the right, on the aisle. As I climbed up the stairs in the dark with the sounds of whispering and rustling around me, I felt like I had stepped back into my childhood for a minute. I almost expected to see a ten-year-old Carly waiting for me, thrilled to have beaten me into the theater and bouncing a little in her seat.

I sat down next to her, careful not to spill the popcorn.

"Perfect timing," she whispered to me, taking a handful of the buttery puffs. The opening credits scrolled up on the screen.

It was the cheesy kind of romantic movie that had nothing to do with the way things happened in real life, which was exactly what I needed—a giant dose of escapism. I did miss holding hands with Nate and leaning close to whisper to each other during the movie. I wondered if he and Megan would have fun on their date. Probably. They were good friends, after all.

About half an hour into the movie, Carly leaned over to me. "I'll be right back. I drank too much Sprite."

A few seconds after she left, I reached into the popcorn bucket and was surprised to find my fingers already scraping the bottom. We'd gone through it awfully fast. I picked up Carly's drink. Empty. Suddenly I felt suspicious. Why had she really gone to the bathroom? Was she throwing up? She wouldn't do that in a public restroom, would she?

I told myself to calm down. Carly really might be going to the bathroom. She *had* finished off her whole Sprite, and, when were younger, we always teased her on road trips about how she had the world's smallest bladder.

Relax and enjoy the movie, I told myself. *Do not think about basketball. Do not worry about your sister, or Nate, or anything else.*

When Carly slipped back into her seat, I kept my eyes on the screen and didn't say anything.

As we left the theater, I saw Jaydon Fullmer and a bunch of his friends coming in. I glanced over at Carly, expecting her to want to talk to him or at least say hello, but she looked straight ahead. She pretended not to see him.

"Hey, fresh meat!" Jaydon called out in her direction. "Carly! Come over here!"

I looked at my sister, but to my surprise she shook her head and didn't say anything back. She kept walking, fast.

"Carly!" Jaydon called again.

"Hey, Jaydon, take a hint," I called back.

"Ohhhhh," said some of Jaydon's friends, and Jaydon opened his mouth to say something back to me. Carly and I didn't hear what he said, though, because we pushed through the glass doors and went outside.

"What was that all about?" I asked her.

Carly threw her soda cup into the nearby trash can with as much passion as I'd slammed my locker closed at practice. "Jaydon Fullmer is a jerk. He's all sweet to me one minute, ignores me the next, and then calls me 'fresh meat' in front of everyone."

It took everything I had not to say, *I told you so.* Instead, I tried to be careful. "But what's changed? Jaydon's always been kind of like that."

"You're right, okay? Are you happy? You're right, and I finally realized it."

I didn't say anything else as we walked to the car and got in. It had gotten dark while we'd been in the theater and the night felt black and icy. Winter in our town is so stark and beautiful and cold; it can either focus and calm you, or it can depress you.

I realized that Carly was crying. "Jaydon was the first guy who kissed me. I knew he was a flirt, but I thought he really, really liked me. But he's been kissing other girls all along. I kept thinking that things would change, that eventually the other girls would go away and it would just be me that he liked, but that never happened. Now I'm not even the one he pays the most attention to."

"I'm sorry, Carly."

She wiped her eyes and set her jaw. I knew that look: I'd seen it on my sisters' faces and felt it on my own. It was the look that meant she had finished crying, even if she hadn't finished being sad. "You know that last scene in the movie?"

"Yeah." It was one of those scenes where the couple finally reunites against all odds and in spite of the people and situations that have conspired throughout the movie to keep them apart. As the music crescendos, the guy takes the girl into his arms and at last, at last, at last they are together.

"Do you think that's ever going to happen to me?"

Well, no, not literally, I thought about saying. *I don't think you're going to meet the guy of your dreams at your first high school dance and then move away and wonder what could have been and then have a chance reunion at your first college party but then you have to say good-bye again because he has to drop out of college since his mother is dying and then the years intervene but you meet again, both divorced or widowed, at a birthday party to which both of your precociously adorable children have miraculously been invited.*

But I knew what she really meant. "Of course it will. Someone is going to fall crazy in love with you someday."

CHAPTER 15

I don't think any conversation that begins with the words, "We need to talk," has ever, in the history of the world, gone very well.

I know in the history of Juliet Kendall it hasn't.

But I'm getting ahead of myself.

The week before the Christmas holidays was a long one, but I had something to look forward to at the end of it: a date with Nate. When I was somewhere I didn't want to be (basketball practice with Coach Slater), or doing something I didn't want to do (homework), or feeling something I didn't want to feel (worrying about Carly), I imagined going out with Nate.

I imagined it in very specific ways: Nate holding my hand as we walked into the restaurant. The smell of the food when the waiter brought it to our table. The laughing and hurrying to the car in the cold night air after leaving the warmth of the restaurant. The music from Nate's radio playing softly in the background as we sat in his car and talked and laughed and exchanged gifts. The rustle of the wrapping paper as he opened his present from me. The pause in our conversation as he leaned over to kiss me. The kiss.

And the date went perfectly, from the moment he rang the doorbell to the moment we sat in the car after dinner ready to exchange gifts. Nate leaned a little closer, I leaned a little closer. I could almost feel the kiss that would come right after he said, "Merry Christmas, Juliet."

He said the words. We both leaned in. We kissed. Exactly how I'd imagined.

So why was something off?

I pulled away from Nate and looked at him. "Is something wrong?"

"Of course not. Why would you think that?"

"I don't know." How could I tell him what I couldn't pin down myself? "I guess I feel like something is different right now."

"I don't want to talk about this now," he said, looking uncomfortable. "We've been having a really good time."

I didn't like the way that sounded. "So there *is* something wrong."

"I guess. I don't know."

"Well, while you're deciding, let me give you this." I handed him the present, all wrapped up.

Nate, like lots of guys, opened the present before he read the card. I'd spent a lot of time on the card—not on making it or anything, but on what I'd written inside. "Thanks," he said, pulling the sweatshirt out of the box. As he looked at it, I saw something in his face that I didn't understand.

"Did I get the wrong size?"

"No, it's right. It's great." He kept looking at the sweatshirt but he didn't put it on. I started to doubt myself. Did he think I was trying to mark him as my territory or something by giving him something to wear? I silently cursed Max in my mind.

And that's when Nate looked up at me and said those fateful words: "We need to talk."

I knew it, I thought.

"Okay. What about?"

"You know how I took Megan to that student government thing last weekend?"

"Of course."

"Well, we had a good time."

"I know. She told me."

"How much did she tell you?"

"I don't know. Not a lot. She said that you guys had a good time. We haven't talked much this week." *We haven't talked much this week.*

Oh.

Realization seemed to hit my heart first. I know how stupid that sounds, but that's what happened. It's like I felt this pain in my chest before my brain finally caught on. Nate wanted to tell me that something had happened between Megan and him on their date. And no matter what it was, no matter what he said, I already knew that I was going to keep hurting when he finished talking.

Nate fidgeted, something he didn't usually do. He kept balling up the sweatshirt I'd given him and then unfolding it again, looking at it instead of at me. Finally he met my gaze. "Do you think it's possible for a guy to like two girls at the same time?"

I'm afraid I laughed in his face at that. "Um, if you're Jaydon Fullmer, then yeah."

Nate looked hurt. "It's—I like you, you know that. But on Saturday, on that date with Megan, we had so much fun. I started to realize that I might like her too. I think it's been sneaking up on me since we've been hanging out so much with student government and everything. I know this is stupid."

"So what happened?"

"Nothing *happened.* We had a good time. But something felt different. Before, when I would hang out with Megan, it was like hanging out with a friend, no big deal. But on Saturday, it felt like a big deal. I don't know how to explain it. It started to feel like I liked her. Like I felt about her the way I've felt about you." Nate wouldn't let go of the sweatshirt. He wouldn't look at me.

I wanted to grab the sweatshirt out of his hands and throw it out the window. I always prefer to feel angry rather than sad, so I went with it. "So you think you get to make a choice between us? You think you can sit back and ponder your decision and then you'll let us know?"

"No, that's not what I meant—"

"What *did* you mean?"

"I think we should date other people," he mumbled.

"We *do* date other people," I said, and then I laughed in spite of myself. "That's how this whole thing started, remember?"

"I meant, maybe *we* should stop going out for a while. You know, go back to being friends."

I sat there for a moment, staring straight ahead at the dashboard. It was kind of fitting, in a way, that everything would come to an end here in Nate's car. So many of our best moments were tied somehow to this little space. The first date, the first dance, countless good conversations and jokes and glances and kisses. We had a lot of memories here.

From now on, though, it would just be Nate's car. I would stand on the outside and wave at him as he drove past. It would be one more little place, one more person that didn't belong to me anymore.

Kendall girls have tempers. Usually we can control them, but when you combine humiliation and pain and anger, there's trouble. I'd already snapped at Nate and I knew I would do it again. And, not only that, it became crystal clear to me that I was also in danger of breaking an unwritten Kendall girl rule: We do not cry in front of people who aren't family. It was time to get out of there.

"I'll see you later," I said, opening my door.

"Wait." Nate put his hand on my arm to stop me. It was very, very unfair that I still felt tingly at his touch. "I want you to have this," he said, holding out the gift he'd brought for me. "I meant it when I said I want to be friends. I'm sorry, Juliet. I'm really, really sorry."

I took the gift. I climbed out of the car and shut the door. I walked away without looking back. With each step, I thought to myself, *Do not cry. Do not cry. Do not cry.*

I made it inside without crying. In fact, I made it all the way up to my room without crying. I didn't know where the tears had gone, but at least I hadn't lost it in front of Nate. I still held the gift that he'd given me in my hands, and I decided that I'd better get it over with and see what was inside. No point putting it off.

I untied the ribbon. *No card,* I noticed, and felt a fresh wave of humiliation wash over me as I remembered the card I made for him and the careful way I had selected each word to tell him how I felt. I reached inside the bag and pulled out . . . a sweatshirt. For the University of Tennessee.

My favorite school, the one with the renowned women's basketball program. No wonder Nate looked funny when he opened his gift. We'd given each other (almost) the same gift. We understood each other that well.

And it was over.

That was when I cried.

Maybe, I thought later, *this is totally one-sided. Maybe Megan doesn't like Nate at all.*

We had basketball practice the next morning and I played so badly I almost deserved Coach Slater's opinion of me. When practice ended I started for the car and Megan followed me.

"Are you okay?"

"I'm awesome," I told her. "Thanks for asking."

"No, really—" she began, but I broke in.

"I had a horrible practice. I probably solidified my non-starter status for life. And do you know what's even better? I found out something last night. From Nate."

She interrupted me, like she didn't want to hear me say the words. Maybe she thought if she said them first it wouldn't be so bad. "Jule, it just sort of happened. We were hanging out on that date, and then all of a sudden it seemed to turn into a real date instead of a date so that you guys could go out again. I'm so sorry."

"I don't need to hear about it," I said. "Nate told me how he feels, and now I know how you feel. It's all *very* helpful."

"I didn't mean for it to happen—" Megan began, and I broke in again. I didn't want to hear any more.

"Now that you guys are dating, there's something you should remember. You should be careful about who he dates when he's not dating you. *Especially* if you think it's someone you can trust." And then I walked off. Once again, to my relief, I kept back the tears until I was alone.

I didn't know when I'd gotten so mean.

I didn't know when I'd started crying so much.

CHAPTER 16

When I was six, I really, really, *really* wanted one of those fancy Americana Gal dolls. As in I wanted one so bad I dreamed about the dolls at night. Drew pictures of them during the day. Read the catalog as though it were divinely inspired literature.

The doll I wanted was the kind of tomboyish one, the one named Kat. She had bouncy, shoulder-length blonde hair, which I had always wanted (mine was long and brown and boring). She came with a little book about herself and a tiny baseball glove and a pack of pretend baseball cards. I didn't care much about baseball, but I could respect her dedication to the sport. She also had a pink plaid jumper and pink patent leather shoes. It was the best of both worlds: sports and pink.

My family didn't have a ton of money, and I knew it, so for Christmas I only asked for Kat, figuring that would help increase my chances of getting her. When my mom helped me write my list to Santa, I wrote "KAT" at the very top and then slid the paper over to Mom so she could read it.

"What else?" she asked.

"That's all I want."

"Are you sure? What about some—"

I interrupted. "I'm sure. Kat is all I want." To seal the deal, I picked up my pencil and signed my name at the bottom of the letter.

I wasn't playing fair, and I knew it. Maddie and Em had seen fit to enlighten me concerning the true identity of Santa Claus, so I knew Mom and Dad were really the ones who bought the presents. Still, what did I have to lose?

On Christmas morning, I went into the family room before everyone else woke up and peeked at the gifts. A doll with blonde hair sat next to my stocking, twinkling Christmas lights bathing her in a beautiful glow. My heart started to pound. But as I crept closer, I saw that she wasn't Kat. She was the cheaper knockoff version, though wearing a dress very similar to Kat's plaid one. I knew my mom must have found the closest fabric she could and then tried to recreate the jumper. Even then, my heart ached for both of us. For my mom because she'd tried so hard, and for me because the doll wasn't the one I wanted.

I was glad that I peeked because then I had time to put on a front for my family. I had time to get over my disappointment. When we all gathered around the tree later and opened our gifts, I acted all excited and didn't show my true feelings.

Which was good, because Emma and Maddie were not so sensitive. "Look! Jule got a Pretend Kat!" I never did get to call her Kat. Before long, Pretend Kat got shortened to P.K. and then to Peek. I was always loyal to Peek, though. I didn't want her to ever guess she hadn't been wanted.

"Juliet? It's your turn." Dad handed me a gift.

"Thanks, Dad." Ten years later, I was doing the same thing: Pretending to be excited on Christmas morning when I felt mostly disappointment. This time the disappointment was a deeper, different kind. I knew that I wouldn't get what I wanted because I knew that no one could wrap those things up and give them to me. For a second I allowed myself to imagine that it was possible—that I could open a box with a note that said, *Your sister is magically cured from whatever it is that is bothering her* or *You will play varsity basketball again, effective immediately* or *Things will go back to the way they were with Nate.* But no one could hand those things to me. I felt that all the gifts, as nice as they were, were empty. Empty gifts for an empty girl.

After we opened our presents, Mom glanced at the clock. "We should probably get ready for sacrament meeting."

Carly grumbled a little, but I jumped up and headed for the shower. I couldn't wait to get to church. I hoped that I would finally feel better once I sat in the chapel, singing the hymns and feeling the Spirit. Maybe I would stop feeling so empty. Maybe it would finally feel like Christmas.

And then the worst thing happened. We went to church, and for the first time that I could remember, I felt nothing.

Nothing. My parents sang happily, my dad's enthusiastic bass almost drowning out my mom's gentle alto. Carly and I both sang too, but it seemed like something was wrong with Carly, and I knew something was wrong with me. I felt bad for my parents, sitting with their two broken daughters. I looked up at the chorister as she beamed down at the congregation. I wanted to feel that overwhelming, burning happiness too. Why couldn't I?

I didn't feel the Spirit and I didn't know why. I couldn't think of any terrible sins I'd committed. I'd been busy and preoccupied with everything taking place in my life, and lately all my thoughts had been focused on Carly and Nate and basketball. Maybe I'd worried about those things too much. Maybe I'd worried my way right out of a testimony without even knowing it; let it slip away while I focused on something else. Maybe I'd forgotten how to feel the Spirit. That couldn't happen, could it? I felt sick to my stomach. I closed my eyes and tried to pray. I didn't even know what to say, except, *Help*. When I opened my eyes, I still felt empty.

I was just about to give up when we sang the closing song: "Silent Night." And there it was. For a brief moment, as the sopranos in the choir soared over the voices of those of us in the congregation, I felt what I wanted to feel. I felt something good.

It was gone too soon, though, and I didn't know how to hold onto it.

One of my presents had been tied up in a long red ribbon laced with silver threads. The glitter caught the Christmas tree lights as I folded the ribbon neatly into sections, creasing each fold sharply. I put it in the box next to all the other ribbons I'd saved from the packages.

Next to me, my mom gathered the wrapping paper into a bag for recycling. "Oops, here's another one." She detached a long golden ribbon from the paper and handed it to me.

I took the ribbon and carefully removed a piece of tape before I folded it away. Not for the first time, I was struck by how much work we'd gone to in order to present our offerings in the best light. Ribbon, bows, glittery paper. Had the Wise Men worried about the containers holding the gold, frankincense, and myrrh? Maybe. Maybe they'd spent lots of time and money carving the boxes and gilding the urns that carried the precious gifts. I didn't know.

"Are you okay, Juliet?" My mom finished with the wrapping paper. She sat down next to me and started peeling one of the ripe, oversized oranges that we always found at the bottom of our Christmas stockings. The smell of the orange peel reminded me of other Christmases.

I was grateful Mom didn't ask if I was upset about my breakup with Nate. I told my parents and Carly after it happened, of course, but I'd avoided the topic ever since, and they had taken their cue from me.

"I guess."

"What's wrong?"

"Christmas didn't seem the same this year."

But of course she didn't know what I meant. "Oh, sweetie, I'm sorry. I know you love it when all your sisters are home. I do too. We'll all be together again next year."

"It's not that. It's—" I didn't know how to explain that I felt I'd lost my grip on my testimony. Plus, how could I tell my mom that on Christmas Day? That would pretty much ruin it for her too. "I don't know."

"Sometimes we make too much of the holidays," my mom said, giving me a hug. "It can be easy to feel let down."

I took my gifts back to my room to put them away. As I hung up some of my new clothes in the closet, I glanced over at poor old Peek sitting on the bookshelf, a layer of dust on her shiny blonde hair. When I was six, she was not what I wanted. But we had good times and I ended up loving her anyway. The scuffs on her face and the mends in her pink plaid dress showed that; she still bore the scars from my childhood. Most of my other toys had long since been given away, but I hung onto Peek so that I could give her to my daughter someday. I remembered how happy my mom looked when I'd exclaimed that I loved the doll. With time, it came to be true.

Maybe if I kept trying to do all the things I was supposed to do—reading my scriptures, going to church, praying—my testimony would come back.

So before I climbed into bed, I read my scriptures and knelt down to pray. I might have been down, and maybe even a little bit out, but I was still Juliet Kendall and I didn't give up without a fight.

CHAPTER 17

December/New Year's

Five days after Christmas we had another basketball game. Once again, I didn't start. I sat on the bench watching everyone else play through the first three quarters of the game. Watching Megan as she ran up and down the court making shot after shot after shot.

I wondered how it would feel to be Megan. She had everything: a starting varsity position and Nate Carmine. She was on top of the world. Had it only been a month since I'd been in her shoes?

Coach Slater called a time-out and we gathered in the huddle. "Alisha, take a break," Coach said.

I brightened, standing up halfway in anticipation. Finally. My chance to get in the game. Maddie sat in the bleachers, watching with my parents. And I knew, even though I wished I didn't, that Nate also sat up in the stands with Max and the rest of our friends. If I didn't get to play it would be very embarrassing.

"Catherine, go check in."

Catherine smiled and ducked her head. As the only sophomore on the team, she was shy, and I knew she didn't want to hurt my feelings by showing her exultation too openly. She pulled off her warm-up jersey and ran to the scorer's table.

The buzzer sounded, signaling the end of the time-out. Catherine ran out on the court. I sat back down on the bench. I didn't look up at the bleachers where my family waited and watched. I didn't even look out at the game to see my teammates play. I looked down at the scuffed, golden surface of the hardwood floor and bit my lip.

You know that old saying about being all dressed up with nowhere to go?

That was me. I had on my uniform, my shoes, my lucky ponytail holder, not to mention my stupid knee pads, mouth guard, and ankle braces. I was ready. And not only on the outside, either. I had my muscles that I'd toned and strengthened through constant drills. My legs ached to run up and down the court, and my hands longed to dribble and pass and shoot the ball. My mind was full of plays and ideas, memories of other games, ideas for future ones. I had something to offer, I just knew it.

But Coach Slater didn't want any of it.

No one wanted any of it.

"What is going on?" Maddie fumed, climbing down out of the stands. "You had two minutes and ten seconds of playing time. *Two minutes and ten seconds!* I started timing it when you went in. And it's not like you went in there and choked! You played well!"

"I know." I didn't want to talk about it. On some level Maddie's indignation felt validating, but mostly I felt humiliated. My parents and my sister came to my game to watch me sit on the bench. Again.

"Have you talked to Coach Slater about this, Jule? She's screwing up your season!"

"I've talked to her. It doesn't make any difference. She thinks I don't score enough points."

My parents both looked sympathetic. "Maddie, keep your voice down," my mom said gently. "Everyone can hear you."

"I don't care! This is ridiculous. Anyone with half a brain can see it." She turned and glared in Coach Slater's direction, but luckily Coach Slater didn't see her.

"Let's get out of here," I said.

"Don't you have a team meeting to go to?" Maddie asked.

"Not anymore. We stopped doing that a couple of games ago. We're actually supposed to be shaking everyone's hands right now and thanking them for coming to the game."

"Even the fans for the other team?"

"Yeah."

Maddie rolled her eyes. "That's ridiculous."

"I think it shows good sportsmanship," interjected my mom.

Maddie looked around the gym. "It doesn't look like anyone is shaking hands yet."

"Watch. They will. Coach Slater will start and then we'll all have to do it too. Can't we please leave?"

"If that's what you want," my dad said, looking me in the eye.

I sighed. "Can I start by shaking your hand, Dad?"

He looked at me proudly. "That's my girl. A true sportswoman."

As I walked through the crowd, shaking hands and thanking people for coming, I decided it was nice that at least I could still make my parents proud.

I escaped that night without having to talk too much to Megan or Hanna, but the next night was New Year's Eve. Hanna called around nine o'clock. "We're all going to the big New Year's Eve dance. And maybe to some of the First Night celebration downtown before that. You want to go?"

"I think I'll stay here." If I did I would have the house all to myself. Everyone else had somewhere to go: a dinner (my parents), a party with old high school friends (Maddie), a friend's house (Carly). Being alone didn't seem like a bad idea. I could watch TV and go to sleep whenever I felt like it.

"Juliet, you gotta come out sometime. Nate's out of town. He won't even be with us."

"But Megan will, right?"

Hanna didn't say anything. I sighed. "I know, it's stupid, but it's barely been a week. It's still awkward."

"I will pick you up at ten," Hanna said in a no-nonsense voice. "I'll bring you back right after midnight. Two hours, Juliet. You can do two hours. Now go get ready. Am I right in assuming that you are wearing sweats and haven't showered yet?"

"Give me some credit," I said defensively. "I've showered. I *am* wearing sweats, though."

"You have an hour. Go!"

I walked down the hall to our bathroom. Carly was inside with the door locked. I knocked. No response. I knocked again. Still nothing. Was she throwing up her dinner in there?

I knocked again, louder this time, forcing the issue. It suddenly seemed necessary. "Let me in right now, Carly. I need to shower."

"Why? You showered this morning." Her voice sounded a little rough.

"I know, but I want to shower again. I have a date tonight, for New Year's." A lie.

"Use Mom and Dad's bathroom."

"All my stuff is in this one. Come on, Carly. You've been in there forever." I tried to keep my voice even. I didn't want her to know that there was anything more than general sisterly frustration behind my voice.

"All right." The toilet flushed and Carly opened the door. She brushed past me without saying anything, heading straight for the sink. I didn't get a good look at her face. I went inside the bathroom and locked the door behind me. On the other side of it, I heard Carly running the water and brushing her teeth in the sink.

It smelled like she'd been throwing up. And the really scary part was that I had been standing outside the door almost the whole time she'd been in the bathroom, and I hadn't heard a thing. She was getting so good at this that she hadn't made a sound.

I *had* heard a crinkle, or a rustle, I remembered. I opened up the medicine cabinet that hung above the toilet. Nothing in there besides the usual old makeup, extra contact solution, and a shriveled tube of toothpaste.

I had an idea.

I reached up onto the top of the medicine cabinet where you couldn't see and I felt around. My fingers closed on something up there in the dust and I pulled it down.

It was a pack of laxatives, exactly like the foil wrapper Carly had dropped a few weeks earlier. But this time some of the pills were still inside. So that's where Carly kept them. I felt around again and found another package, then another, and another. Where did she get them? There were so many. There was no way she could have dropped them into the shopping cart without Mom noticing, and there weren't any stores within walking distance of our house. Could she have bought this many the day we picked up the Christmas cards? I felt a stab of guilt for not following her, for purposely choosing to close my eyes.

I put the packages back. I turned on the shower spray and sat down on the edge of the bathtub, my head in my hands. Now what? I had to talk to Mom and Dad. And I would—after I had a shower that I didn't need and left the house for a date that didn't exist.

It seemed like all the good parts of my life were make-believe. Only the bad stuff was real.

CHAPTER 18

January

"Please," I begged my mom, "don't tell Carly I'm the one who found them." The two of us stood in the bathroom on New Year's Day, talking in hushed voices. Everyone else was getting ready for church. Sacrament meeting started in less than an hour.

My mom reached up and pulled down the last of the packages, her face pale and worried. "I won't." She took a deep breath. "I'm going to go talk to your dad, and then we'll talk to her."

She didn't tell me that it would be okay. She didn't say those words because she didn't *know* if it would be okay. I could see that much in her face and it scared me.

A little while later, my parents knocked on the door of Carly's room and went inside. I didn't mean to eavesdrop, but on my way down the stairs I heard their quiet voices and then Carly's voice, raised.

Maddie stood by the front door, wearing her church clothes. "What's going on up there? I knocked on Carly's door but there was this weird silence and then Mom told me they'd be down later. Is something wrong?"

"I don't know."

"You're a terrible liar, Jule."

And a terrible sister, I thought. I couldn't shake the feeling that I had betrayed Carly somehow. I couldn't betray her again by telling Maddie what I had found. "You'll have to ask Mom and Dad."

The faint but unmistakable sound of Carly crying drifted down from upstairs. Maddie raised her eyebrows at me.

"I guess we'd better go to church on our own," I said, reaching into the closet for my coat. "Do you want to walk or should I drive Old Blue?"

"We are daughters of our Heavenly Father, who loves us, and we love Him . . ." I glanced around the room to see if Carly had slipped into Young Women during the opening song. I didn't see her.

Carly's Mia Maid teacher came over to me as we all split up to go to our classes. "Where's Carly today?" she asked. "Is she sick?"

I nodded, hoping that it was less of a lie if I didn't say the words. Then again, maybe she *was* sick. She sure wasn't well. "She stayed home."

"Tell her that we hope she feels better soon," Sister Harper said, and I had to fight away the urge to laugh. I knew she meant well, but I didn't think I could relay that message, no matter how sincere Sister Harper's intent. We all hoped Carly would feel better soon. The hard part was figuring out how to make it happen.

I stood outside the door of my classroom for a minute. I wanted to walk out of the building and straight home. Inside, the other Laurels talked and laughed with each other and with our teacher. I felt separated from them—because of my fading testimony and because of what happened that morning with Carly.

"Juliet?" One of the girls waved at me. "Aren't you coming in?"

No. I'm going to stay out here. I don't belong in there with you and your perfect testimonies and your perfect lives. Even as I thought that, I knew I was being unfair. The girls in that room probably had hidden problems and doubts that I didn't know about. But it still felt very lonely when I went inside.

"I take it Carly didn't go to Young Women?" Maddie asked me in the hall after class.

"No. Did Mom ever make it to Relief Society?"

"No."

Dad came around the corner. He wore a suit and tie, but you could tell that he hadn't had time to shave. It seemed sort of shocking to see him out in public like that, although I didn't know that anyone else would notice besides us. "Hi, girls. I came for the last hour. Did you walk or drive?"

"We walked," said Maddie.

"Me too." Dad pulled on his coat. "Ready?"

We left right away; none of us wanted to stay and socialize in the halls. Dad and Maddie and I didn't say anything about Carly as we walked back home through the cold winter afternoon. It seemed that we had an unspoken agreement; we didn't want to mention what was going on at home until we were back there, safe inside the walls of our house where no outsiders could hear us.

Most of the sidewalks were clear, but there were icy footprints in front of the Carlisles' old house where no one had shoveled. Maddie had worn heels, so Dad held out his arm to help her. I crunched along behind them, putting my feet in the iced-out footprints of someone who had walked there before me. I slipped a little, but I righted myself before I could fall.

Mom sat at the kitchen table, still wearing her pajamas, a glass of orange juice and a piece of paper in front of her. When we came in, she flipped the paper over, and I wondered what she had written on it. A letter? A list of things to do to help Carly? Or was it nothing more than the little flowers and curlicues Mom doodled sometimes when she talked on the phone or daydreamed? Suddenly, I wanted to see that paper. I wanted to know if she'd been able to come up with a plan while we'd been gone.

"I'm sorry we missed church," Mom said. "We just finished talking a little while ago, and I didn't want to leave Carly alone."

"Where is she?" I asked.

"She's up in her room. She'll be down in a little while. Right now she's feeling emotional and embarrassed."

"Does all of this have something to do with her food issues?" Maddie asked.

Mom nodded. "We confronted her about what's been going on lately. The weight loss and the laxatives."

"Oh, no," Maddie said, her eyes wide. "She's been using laxatives?"

Dad nodded. "At first she denied that they were hers, but after we talked to her for a while, she admitted it."

"Admitted what, exactly?" Maddie asked. "Did she admit to the laxatives, or to more than that?"

"She admitted to using the laxatives and she admitted that she's been making herself throw up," Mom said quietly.

"Did she say how long she's been doing this?" Maddie asked.

"At least a year, but it's really escalated the last few months," Dad said. "I had no idea it had been going on so long."

"I thought it started this fall," I admitted, feeling clueless.

"She says she started at the beginning of eighth grade. At first, she would throw up once a day or once every few days." Mom shook her head. "She told me that it got better for a while this summer. But things have been really stressful for her lately, and she's gotten worse again. She said it's happening 'a lot,' but she wouldn't say exactly what she meant by that."

"So what happens now?" Maddie asked. "It's not like she can stop all of a sudden. It's not going to be that easy."

"We know that," Mom said. "She's agreed to talk to someone."

"Like who? A therapist?"

"Probably. I'm going to call Carolyn tomorrow and see if she can recommend anyone."

"Wait," I said. "You're going to call Carolyn?"

"Well, yes. It makes sense. She's a nurse. I'm sure she has a better idea than I do about who to contact."

"But Carolyn's in our ward. Are you going to tell her what's going on? Carly will hate that."

"Carolyn's a good friend, and she's a medical professional. She'll keep it confidential."

"Do you honestly think Carly will go?"

"She promised us she would talk to someone."

When I went upstairs to change out of my Sunday clothes, I put my scriptures away on the bookshelf, next to the little framed picture of the Savior that the Young Women's presidency had given me when I turned twelve. It was probably my imagination, but I could almost hear Him saying to me, *Juliet, we have to talk.*

I know.

But I was having a hard time praying. I was scared—scared that I would pour out my heart and no one would answer.

The new year started off with all of us determined to do better. Mom made an appointment for Carly with a therapist and she kept it. Mom and Dad read books and articles about eating disorders and they went to talk to the therapist, too. My parents waited until we were all home before they started fixing dinner, and we all ate it together. I worked even harder at basketball and did my homework and read my scriptures every night.

I wrote to Emma even though I didn't know what to say. When our stake president set Emma apart the night before she left on her mission, he'd promised her that her family would be blessed through her faithful service as a missionary. It seemed ironic that, instead, our family was suffering through its hardest trial to date. I put those thoughts out of my mind and wrote Em a letter that told her all of the best and none of the worst.

Everything ran like clockwork for a couple of weeks. So I was a little surprised when I came home late from practice one day in mid-January and the clock had stopped. Instead of my family sitting down to dinner when I walked in the door, I found a clean kitchen, no Carly, and no Dad. My mom sat at the table by herself, looking kind of blank and leafing through the pages of a cookbook.

"What's for dinner?" I asked.

"I don't know."

"Um, okay." I didn't want to give her a hard time, but I was starving.

I started opening the cupboards. "We've got plenty of stuff for spaghetti. Oh, wait, we had that last night. There's rice, taco shells—" I looked over at my mom.

"I know we have food, but I can't seem to figure out what to make."

Dad came into the kitchen. "What's going on? Is it my night to make dinner and I forgot?"

"No, it's my night."

"Mom can't decide what to cook," I explained.

"My mind keeps going around in circles. If I cook really healthy dinners, will Carly think I'm trying to make her thin? If I make something fattening, will she think I'm trying to sabotage her?" My mom shook her head, looking unhappy. "I feel like everything I've done is wrong, even the food I've made."

"Everything we've done hasn't been wrong," my dad said.

"Really? What have we done right?"

"We love our daughters."

While they talked, I quietly found Mom's binder, the one she'd started filling up with new, extra-healthy, extra-nourishing recipes. I flipped through the book until I found a recipe for fajitas that didn't look too hard to make; I started getting out the ingredients. I accidentally let one of the cupboards slam shut a few moments later and my parents both looked up.

"I thought I'd get started," I told them. "Do fajitas sound okay?"

"That sounds perfect," Mom said, smiling at me. "There's a recipe in the binder—"

"I already found it. You guys go hang out. I'll take care of this."

I did everything exactly according to the directions in the recipe. I cut up the peppers and onions and I cooked the chicken; I sliced limes and chopped cilantro and warmed the tortillas in the oven. I followed the directions and it turned out perfectly. My hands and the kitchen smelled like herbs and citrus, smells that seemed to me to be both hopeful and healthy.

When we ate dinner that night, I watched my family even more closely than usual. Carly only ate one single, slender fajita, but she didn't excuse herself from the table immediately afterward. She had kept her appointment with the therapist earlier that day. Mom and Dad were cheerful and supportive and complimentary. I was a good daughter and a caring, concerned sister. We were back on track and following the directions. Things were bound to turn out all right in the end.

CHAPTER 19

I think there should be a law that you have to break up by degrees.

I mean, that's how you start a relationship, right? You don't usually go from absolutely nothing to absolutely everything right at the beginning. You become acquaintances, you become friends, you become friends who flirt, you become more than friends. You become something, then something more, then something more.

And when you break up with someone, you don't just lose your boyfriend. You also lose the guy you flirt with in class, the person who sits by you on the bus for the track meets, the friend you call when something good or bad happens—the list goes on and on of what you've lost.

But you can never go back. Once you cross that line from being friends, you can't just step back across it when the romantic part of your relationship ends. And since you can't go back, you have to go on.

I used to love the time between classes. I loved walking toward my locker and hoping to find Nate waiting there for a few minutes of talking and holding hands.

Now I didn't want to see him. Or Megan. I especially didn't want to see the two of them together, talking and laughing. Since Megan and I had lockers near each other, I started carrying all my books around in my bag so that I wouldn't risk running into her between classes. I kept my basketball gear in Old Blue and ran out to get it after school. I avoided walking past the spot in the hall by Coach Giles's old classroom where Nate and I had had our first kiss back in October.

I started bringing my lunch from home. Usually I went out to my car and sat in the parking lot with the heater on, eating my bagel in a little world of my own. I wished that our high school didn't have a closed-campus policy so that I could go home for lunch. I wished that Megan and I were still close. I wished that Nate and I were still dating. I wished that my sister would wake up one morning completely cured.

I wished a lot of things, sitting in that car by myself, hiding out from people and places that might cause me pain.

On some level I was ashamed of how weak I was, how I'd do anything to avoid feeling hurt. But on another level I felt almost strong, a little proud of the way I'd cut off the parts of my life that made me feel too much sadness.

There was one painful part of my life that I couldn't eliminate: basketball. I couldn't avoid seeing Megan at practice. I couldn't avoid the embarrassed and sympathetic glances of the other girls as I sat on the bench game after game. And I couldn't avoid the fact that Coach Slater didn't think I was good enough to be a starter.

I tried to impress her. At practice, I hustled even more than usual so she could see that I was hardworking. I shoveled the snow off the patio and spent hours in the backyard practicing my shots. On the rare occasions when Coach Slater did put me into the game, I tried to score more points and play the way she wanted me to play.

I even swallowed my pride and asked her if she would move me back down to the JV team. I figured that way I could at least get some playing time. But she said no. "If I wanted you to be on the JV team, I'd put you there," she told me. As I turned away, I had a flash of my old anger, so sharp and distinct it made me catch my breath.

But I swallowed it down. I kept following directions. I kept plugging along and doing what I was supposed to do. Reading scriptures, going to practice, doing my homework. Going through the motions.

Like I said, you can't go back, so you have to go on, even if it gets kind of tiring carrying everything around with you.

A few days after Coach told me that I couldn't move down to JV, I couldn't sleep. Around two in the morning I went downstairs to the kitchen to get something to eat. As I stood in the kitchen making hot chocolate and toast, I heard a humming sound. It came from the basement and seemed familiar, but I couldn't place it. Could it be the furnace? Or someone doing a load of laundry late at night?

I looked over at the door that led to the basement. Someone had left the basement stairwell light on—I could see a strip of bright light on the dark hardwood floor. When I went over to turn off the light, I finally recognized what the sound was. The treadmill.

I walked down the stairs quietly and peeked over the banister. Carly. Running fast on the treadmill and listening to her iPod, her back to the door. She didn't hear me. She wore only her running shorts, socks, shoes, and a sports bra. I could see every vertebrae on her back. She was thin, but not so gaunt that she would stop you in your tracks. She wasn't on the very edge yet. But I knew that something was going on inside her that could take her to that edge.

It's a hard position to be in, knowing that whatever you do will cause someone pain. If I told my parents about Carly's late-night workout, they would be upset and sad and worried, but if I didn't, Carly would keep running, and running, and running, until she was gone.

"You're quiet this morning."

Carly hadn't said anything during our ride to school. She didn't really even look at me. Instead, she gazed out the window or down at her hands. "So?"

"So, nothing. I was just noticing."

"You notice a lot of things, don't you, Juliet?" She still wouldn't meet my gaze. "Sometimes I think all you do is watch me."

So she knew I'd told Mom and Dad about the treadmill. I'd hoped she might think they had discovered it on their own. Mom had promised not to bring my name up.

I didn't know what to say.

Carly finally turned and looked at me and I recognized the look on her face. It was the driven, I'm-a-Kendall-girl look that I'd seen on my sisters' faces in games or at practice, the look I knew appeared on my own face when I was determined to get something done. But there also seemed to be a sharper edge to it on Carly's face, a sort of hunger in her eyes that scared me. We were tough girls. We pushed ourselves hard but we never pushed too far. I got the idea, looking at Carly, that she would push herself until she dropped. And I wasn't exactly sure what she was pushing herself toward.

"It's okay," Carly said to me. "What did I expect?"

"Are you mad at me?" I asked.

She didn't answer.

I kept on living up to expectations.

Coach Slater expected me to mess up, and I kept messing up when I tried to play the game she wanted me to play instead of the one I knew.

Carly expected me to tell on her, and I did.

My parents expected me to hold it together, and I tried.

And then I finally did something that no one expected. Not even me.

CHAPTER 20

We had a home game that night. I sat on the bench again. As always. Hanna sat next to me, radiating frustration. She hadn't started the last few games either. She still had the energy to get angry about it, though; I was slowly drifting toward resignation. The season would be over in a month or so, and it wasn't likely that anything would change before then.

"I don't get this," Hanna said to me. "Why isn't she playing us?"

"What's to get? Nothing she does makes any sense."

"We should walk out of here," Hanna said. "Take off and not look back."

"If we did that, we'd never play again. She'd never let us back on the team."

"I know," Hanna said sadly. Neither of us spoke after that. We watched as the game continued just beyond our reach.

Something like a slow burn started inside of me. I couldn't get Hanna's words out of my mind. *I could walk out of here.*

But you're not a quitter, I kept telling myself. *You didn't join this team to quit. You have to stick this out, even if it's hard. Even if something you love has turned into something you hate.*

I looked up in the stands. Carly hadn't really spoken to me since the treadmill thing and she wasn't at the game. But really, who could blame her? I didn't get any playing time. I'd even told Mom and Dad not to bother leaving work early to come to the games anymore. Why should they go to all that trouble when I would probably be on the floor for a grand total of three minutes, if that?

Alisha dribbled the ball right into her defender, who stole it and broke down the court for an easy layup. Coach motioned for Catherine to sub in. This time, Catherine wasn't even giddy or excited. She'd taken off her warm-up jersey as soon as the other team stole the ball.

You didn't join this team to quit, I thought again. *But you did join this team to play. If you play this game because you love it, then go. Walk out. Play on the church team or something instead. You can't make Coach Slater play you more. You can't get Nate back. You can't stop Carly from doing what she's doing. You can't control anything else in your life. But you don't have to sit here if you don't want to. You can control this.*

I stood up, pulling off my knee pads. A couple of the other girls on the bench glanced over at me, but most were intent on the game in progress. I started walking and I didn't stop when I got to the end of the bench. Megan looked over at me in surprise from her spot out on the court. Coach Slater called my name. "Juliet! Where are you going?"

I'm gone, I wanted to say. I walked slowly and purposefully, resisting the urge to run until I got out of the gym. Then I ran as fast as I could. I had been holding back for too long.

CHAPTER 21

Walking out of the basketball game felt like a clean break. I should have realized it wouldn't be that easy.

I drove straight home and went out back to the basketball hoop. I wished I had someone to pass to, but at least I was playing. I made shot after shot by myself in the backyard where I used to play with my sisters and with Megan. Then my parents found me.

"Juliet?" Mom asked. "What's going on?"

Dad sounded worried. "We both came to watch the end of the game, but you were gone. Hanna found us afterward and told us you walked out."

I concentrated on lining up my shot.

"Honey," my mom said softly. She didn't sound mad. "Are you okay?"

Not really, I wanted to say, but it seemed like they'd already reached their quota of daughters who were not okay. I turned around. "Yeah. But I quit the team."

"Why?"

"I guess it all built up. I sat there today and I knew I couldn't take it anymore. So I left."

They both came closer and my mom put her arms around me. "You've had a frustrating season and you toughed it out for a long time."

"You guys aren't going to try to talk me out of quitting, are you?" I asked. "Because I already did. It's over."

Dad said, "I think we both wish you'd finished out the season, only because it might be better in the long run if you did. But in the end, it's your decision, and we'll stand behind you."

I let my mom hug me for a few moments more and then I pulled away. "I'm going to shoot around out here for a little bit. Will you—" I hesitated. "Will you tell Carly and Maddie for me? I don't really want to talk about it anymore."

Dad nodded. "All right."

The phone rang right after I came in from my own little game of one-on-none. Mom answered. "Yes, she's here." She covered the receiver with her hand and whispered to me, "It's Coach Slater. You might as well get it over with."

I took the phone. "Hello?"

"Juliet, this is Coach Slater. I'm calling to tell you that I'm going to have to discipline you for your actions today. I'm trying to decide whether I should suspend you for two weeks or for the rest of the season."

I almost laughed. She still didn't get me.

"Juliet? What do you have to say? You will also have to apologize to the team tomorrow at practice."

Why not? I thought. I did owe them that.

"Okay. I'll be there at practice tomorrow."

"I'll let you know then what I've decided. I'm very disappointed in you, Juliet." She waited as though she expected me to say something. I didn't have anything to say. She'd never listened to me before; she wouldn't listen to me now.

"Good night," I said, and hung up the phone.

Hanna called later that evening. She apologized and tried to get me to come back to the team. She felt like my decision to quit was partially her fault since she had suggested that we walk out of the gym. I kept telling her not to worry about it, that I was the one who made the decision and that I wouldn't be coming back.

After I hung up with Hanna I felt exhausted and I decided not to answer any of my other calls. I didn't want to talk to anyone—not Maddie, because I worried that she'd think I'd let her down. Not Megan, for a lot of reasons. And not Nate. I was surprised when a text message from him popped up on my phone, but I deleted it without reading it.

I couldn't avoid Megan completely, though, so I wasn't surprised when she found me in the hall the next day. "I can't believe you quit! We're playing Hillyard in two weeks! And then there's region playoffs, and state . . ."

"So? I don't ever play."

"Is playing time the only thing you care about? Doesn't being part of the team mean anything to you?"

"You know what, Megan? It doesn't. Not anymore. Coach Giles left. Coach Slater doesn't let me play, so I contribute exactly nothing. And you know what makes it even easier to walk away? The fact that my best friend on the team stabbed me in the back."

"I didn't stab you in the back! Except for that one date—which you knew about—I never went out with Nate until after you guys broke up!"

I didn't say anything. To tell the truth, I missed Megan. She and I had been best friends for years, and it felt strange and painful to have her disappear from my life. If things with Carly hadn't been so bad, I probably would have tried harder to work through the fallout with the Nate-and-Megan incident. But as it was, I had my fill of hurt and of strained relationships.

It reminded me of the time I'd dropped my grandmother's antique vase, the one made of almost paper-thin white glass with delicate pink flowers along the side. When it fell, it shattered into pieces so quickly that I was almost convinced it had broken before impact. Feeling horrible, I bent down and tried to gather up the pieces.

"Don't worry, Juliet," my grandmother said, putting her hand on my shoulder. "I'll get the broom and we can sweep it up."

"I think we can fix it," I insisted anxiously, gathering the larger pieces into a pile. "I could try to glue it back together."

Grandma reached out and took one of the biggest fragments from me. "I'll keep this one to remember the vase. It's all right, honey. It would take too much time for you to fix, and it wouldn't ever be quite the same anyway."

That's how I felt about Megan. Our friendship had so many pieces—basketball, dress shopping for homecoming, birthday parties over the years, middle-school crushes, a million inside jokes and shared experiences—but I didn't have the time to fix it, and I felt like even if I did, I would always see the cracks and remember that it had been broken before.

"Look, I'm really sorry," Megan said. "But I told you, I didn't mean for it to happen! What was I supposed to do? What do you want me to do now?"

"Nothing," I told her. "Just leave me alone."

As the end of the school day drew closer and closer, I started to feel nervous. I tried to think of what I would say, hoping to find the right words to explain to my team *why* I walked away from them.

Even though less than twenty-four hours had passed since I'd been a full-fledged member of the team, I already felt like an outsider when I walked into practice. The other girls all wore their jerseys and shorts; I wore my jeans and sweater from school. They sat on the bench as a team; I stood in front of them, alone. It would have surprised me how quickly you can go from being part of something to being a total outsider, but I'd had experience with that kind of thing lately.

"Juliet has something to say to all of you," Coach Slater said by way of introduction. She and I hadn't exchanged a single word since I arrived in the gym. She stood off to the side as if to make it clear that I was completely alone.

"Coach Slater asked me to apologize to all of you for what I did last night."

The gym was silent. Everyone looked at me and waited.

"I do owe you an apology. I shouldn't have walked out on the game. That was lame. I'm sorry for quitting that way." I took a deep breath. "I still know that quitting the team is the right thing for me right now." I didn't look over at Coach Slater to see her reaction. My apology and explanation weren't for her. They were for my teammates. "I still love basketball, and I still love you guys. I promise I'll come back and cheer for you from the stands. But it's hard for me to feel like I don't have anything to contribute. I asked to be moved to the JV team so that I could try to contribute there, but I guess that wasn't an option. I don't care where I play. I just want to play. I'm going to miss you guys, a lot, but I can't sit on the bench anymore. I hope you understand."

It was harder this time to walk away, especially when, led by Hanna, they all started cheering my cheer:

"Pride, Honor, Panther Spirit

"Come on team, let's hear it

"GO, PANTHERS!"

And then they added: "We love you, Juliet!"

Without basketball, I had a lot of free time. Too bad I didn't have a guy to spend it with or a best friend to keep me company.

It didn't take long to make a new routine for myself. I left school, went home, and shot around for a while in the backyard. Then I did some homework. Then, around dinnertime, I went back to the school to pick up Carly, who was either cheering at a game or at practice. I became the chauffeur for *her* life instead of the driver for *mine*.

One night I timed it wrong and got there too early, before she had finished cheering for the freshman boys' basketball team. I climbed up into the stands to watch the end of the game. So far, she'd held up her end of her bargain with my parents: she could keep cheerleading as long as she made her therapy appointments and came home with me straight after cheer practice and games.

There were only a few minutes left and the game was close. Carly jumped and danced. The boys ran up and down the floor and took shots.

The spectators yelled and clapped. It seemed like I was the only one not in motion.

I pulled off the beaded bracelet that Maddie had brought me from Costa Rica and started twirling it around in my hands, a nervous habit I'd developed recently.

The other cheerleaders hoisted Carly into the air for a lift. The crowd cheered. Some freshman boy whose name I didn't know scored a basket and the crowd shouted again, louder this time.

Shoot. I'd dropped the bracelet. It had landed right near the crack in the bleachers. As I reached to grab it, it slipped out of sight.

I climbed out of the bleachers and went underneath them to find it among the other things people had dropped—popcorn, a baby's pacifier, a sock. The floor was sticky with soda in one spot. I looked up through a crack and tried to figure out where I was.

I heard a squeak and the sound of feet. A couple of the varsity cheerleaders sat down right above me. I could tell by their shoes. They giggled and snapped open their pop cans.

I figured they were sitting almost where I had been; my bracelet must be close. Peering down at the ground, I took a step forward. Then I heard them say my sister's name and I froze.

"Carly Kendall is the best dancer on the freshman squad," one said.

Another one laughed.

"What?" the first one asked, sounding defensive. "She is!"

"Oh, I know she is," said the one who laughed. Payton North, I was willing to bet. "But haven't you heard about her little *issue?*"

"No." Slurp on the soda. "What are you talking about?"

Payton's voice lowered, and I could see the other cheerleaders' feet slide along the bleachers as they moved closer. "She has an eating disorder. Like, a really bad one."

"Oh, she does not," scoffed one of the other girls. "So what if she's skinny. I'm skinny, and *I* don't have an eating disorder."

"No, I'm serious. She has one for real. I heard her throwing up in the bathroom one day before practice. I waited until she came out of the stall and she seemed all surprised to see me. She didn't think anyone was there. Later I asked Savannah what was up with Carly."

"And Savannah told you?"

"Not in so many words, but you should have seen her face. She tried to cover, but I could tell a lightbulb went on in her mind. I think she had noticed something wrong but didn't put it all together until then."

"I still don't believe you."

"Really? Then how about this. Carly left her bag open a couple of weeks ago and I walked past. And guess what was in there? A whole box of laxatives. I saw the corner sticking up so I pulled it out a little more to make sure."

No one spoke. "So should we tell someone?"

"Her parents already know," Payton said smugly. "I told my mom about it and she called Carly's mom and Carly's mom thanked my mom for her concern and said they were taking care of things."

"It's sad. Some people can't take the pressure."

"It must run in the family. Did you hear about Juliet quitting the basketball team? She walked right off the court in the middle of a game." Payton laughed. "It's actually kind of funny. For years, everyone's talked about the Kendall girls like they're so amazing, and it turns out they're even more screwed up than the rest of us."

"You guys!" I heard the voice of another cheerleader in the distance. "Ms. Hanover wants to talk to us before the next game."

The cheerleaders left. I stood in the dark under the bleachers. I wanted to do something, but I didn't know what I could possibly do that would make things better instead of worse. I felt sick. For my mom, who had to field that phone call from Mrs. North, for myself because I'd overheard the conversation, but most of all for Carly.

The buzzer sounded to end the game and I took a step. Underneath my right foot, I felt the beads of my bracelet snap. One more broken thing. I bent down to pick up the pieces.

CHAPTER 22

February

"It's only for one night," Mom said. Her eyes looked worried, and she pulled her wedding ring off and on, off and on. It reminded me of the way I twisted my bracelet before it broke, and thinking of that reminded me of the conversation I'd overheard. I felt a stab of pity all over again for my mom as I pictured her talking to Payton's mom on the phone. It didn't take much to imagine Mrs. North's voice—sugary and sickeningly sweet, full of mock concern and barely hidden elation at knowing someone else's life wasn't picture-perfect.

For months, Mom and Dad had planned an overnight trip to celebrate their twenty-fifth anniversary. They almost called it off before Carly's therapist gave them the go-ahead. The therapist said that they needed to trust Carly.

"Go, already," I said. "You guys deserve a break."

"We could ask Maddie if she'd drive home for the weekend," Dad suggested. "Then you'd have her around, too."

"We'll be fine. We can handle it."

Still, when they got in the car to leave, they kept looking back.

At first, Carly and I had a decent night. We ate dinner, we watched a movie together, and then we both said we were tired and wanted to go to bed early.

One of us lied.

I'd almost fallen asleep when I heard the very gentle thud of the screen door closing. I recognized it immediately—my room was right above the back door and I'd heard the sound many times. I sat bolt upright, my heart pounding. Was someone coming inside? Did we forget to lock the back door?

Then I realized that I had it all wrong. I didn't need to worry about someone coming *in*. I needed to worry about someone getting *out*.

I hurried across the hall to my parents' room and peeked through the blinds. As I watched, a dark figure climbed into a car waiting in front of our neighbor's house. Carly.

A thousand thoughts raced through my mind. I could call Mom and Dad. I could call Maddie. I could call Savannah. I could lock the back door so that Carly would have to call me to get back in. I could get in Old Blue and drive around and try to find Carly myself. I could cry. I could pray. I could scream as loud as I wanted because no one would hear.

I didn't do any of those things. I climbed back into my bed and listened.

My secret, awful wish had come true: I was finally alone.

It seemed that hours passed before I heard the screen door thud again. I heard Carly tiptoe up the stairs and then I heard her throw up in the bathroom. She wasn't as careful as usual because she thought I was asleep and not listening. But I heard everything: the sounds of her brushing her teeth, washing her face, and closing the door to her room. The room that we had shared before there was so much empty space in the house.

Through all of that, I did nothing and said nothing.

What did she want me to do? I was only a kid. I was only sixteen. Suddenly sixteen years seemed like nothing. A fraction of what my life would be. A fraction of what I would know. The most overwhelming feeling of exhaustion came over me.

And here is what I decided to do: I rolled over and fell back asleep.

"Mom and Dad should be home soon," Carly said at breakfast. "Do you think they'll be surprised to see that the world didn't fall apart?"

Her tone was light and unconcerned, almost joking, and it made me livid. How could she talk like that after what happened last night? There was a huge, deep disconnect between the way she saw things and the way things actually *were*.

Suddenly, I wanted to slam her reality and ours together and I didn't care about how loud a crash it made.

"Didn't it?" I said, and my voice sounded shaky, out of control. I took a deep breath. "I heard what you did last night. You promised you wouldn't go out; you did. You promised you wouldn't make yourself throw up; you did."

"How do you know?"

"I saw you. I heard you."

She didn't bother denying it.

"You're sitting there acting like nothing happened. Like Mom and Dad are wrong to be worried about you. We're all stressed out of our minds about you, and you don't even seem to care."

"I'm so sorry if *my* problems are stressing *you* out," Carly said sarcastically. "Can you ever forgive me?"

"What else are you doing that you're not supposed to be doing?" I stood up from the table and stormed upstairs, practically radiating anger. I'd never felt so much rage before, and I didn't stop when I got to my room. I kept on going down the hall to Carly's.

She was right behind me. "Where are you going?"

"Where do you think?" I threw open the door to her room.

"You have to respect my privacy!" Carly screamed.

I went straight to her desk and opened the bottom right-hand drawer, where she always used to keep her special stuff when she was little. "Why? *You* don't respect anything. You don't respect any rules or anybody's feelings. And the worst part of all is that you don't even respect yourself." My hand closed on what I was looking for. The package of laxatives. But there was more.

"What else are you keeping in here?" I asked. Carly ran across the room to try to stop me, but I pulled out a container of the diet pills I'd heard about on the news. The ones that could be really dangerous if not monitored closely.

"Where did you get these?"

"It is none of your business! *Get out of here!*" Carly was practically hysterical.

"What is going on?"

My parents stood in the doorway.

For some reason, I felt as though I were the one caught doing something wrong. Maybe because I was. All the fight went out of me and I just held out the pills and laxatives. "Carly threw up again last night. I couldn't stand it anymore. I came in here and found these."

Carly tried to grab the packages out of my hand. I threw them over the top of Carly's head, and my dad caught them as though we were playing some sick, twisted form of keep-away. This was *all* like some twisted game, where none of us knew the rules, where no one could ever win, where walking out wouldn't do one bit of good because you could never really quit being part of a family the way you could quit being part of a team. I pushed past Carly and my parents and ran out the door.

I couldn't even run away effectively. Ten minutes into my drive on the freeway in Old Blue, I pulled off at an exit and texted Mom: *I went for a drive. I'll be back soon.*

I sat in the car and stared out at the emptiness around me. I'd driven away from the city, out into the middle of nowhere. Bits of trash and leaves blew in the wind and everything was brown and gray and black and white. My eyes ached for color. For a minute I thought I saw a splash of red, some late fall leaf or early spring flower, but it was only the plastic bag from a hamburger wrapper blowing past.

The ugliness of the whole day caught up to me and I felt sick. I laughed to myself at the irony. If I actually threw up, would Mom and Dad think that I had come down with bulimia too? As if it were some kind of contagious disease that could run rampant through a family? Bulimia wasn't contagious, at least not like a virus. But unhappiness seemed to be.

I sat in the car until I got too cold and then I drove back home. Initially, the house was so quiet that I thought everyone was gone. But when I went upstairs I heard hushed voices coming from behind my parents' door. And worst of all, I heard Carly crying in her room.

Every time I walked out, I ended up with an apology to make. I knocked gently on Carly's closed door. "Carly. It's me."

She stopped crying. I expected her to tell me to go away, but she didn't.

"I did everything wrong today. I'm sorry."

Silence.

"I'm sorry," I said one more time.

CHAPTER 23

When the dust settled after Mom and Dad's ruined anniversary trip, things changed again in the Kendall house.

Everyone lost something that weekend. Mom and Dad lost the ability to trust Carly. Carly lost the privilege of going out until she earned back their trust (but she could still do cheer, thanks to her therapist's recommendation). We all lost a little more of our certainty that our family was whole and healthy and fixable.

And I lost something else. I couldn't quite tell what. Part of Carly's trust? My parent's belief in me that I could handle anything? My own sense of identity? I didn't think I was the kind of person who barged into her sister's room.

A few days after the blowup, Mom told Carly and me at dinner that the three of us were going to a fireside that night. "It's for all the young women and their mothers in the stake. The speaker is going to be talking about body image and advertising and some of the challenges our young women face in today's world. It seems . . . relevant."

I expected Carly to get upset and to refuse to go, but she surprised me.

"Fine," she said, and she went upstairs to put on a skirt.

In the car, Mom made the mistake of thanking Carly for her compliance. "Thank you for agreeing to come, Carly. You too, Juliet."

"I'll do anything to keep doing cheer," Carly said acidly. "Even this."

At the stake center I ended up in the middle again, sitting between Mom and Carly. I didn't glance around to see if I knew anyone else. Payton North lived in our stake, and I especially didn't want to see her. I looked straight ahead at the pulpit or down at my program, which had a picture of the Savior on the front. Carly, my mom, and I sat quietly in our pew. None of us knew what to say to each other anymore.

"I'm very grateful for the opportunity to speak to you young women this evening." The speaker was poised, polished, and after the first line of her talk, I didn't hear much of what she said. I watched my sister instead. Carly got more and more tense. Every muscle in her body seemed to tighten, one by one. Her back, her arms, her neck. She kept her eyes locked on the woman's face as she spoke.

I caught another line of the speaker's message: "Your body is a temple. When you do things like starve or hurt yourself, it weakens that temple."

My own body started to respond to the tension in Carly's. Carly couldn't look away from the speaker; I couldn't look away from Carly. I wanted to reach out and touch her arm or whisper something in her ear—anything to distract her from the way she internalized the speaker's words. But I didn't dare. I could imagine her lashing out or snapping at me.

My mom, sitting on the other side of me, couldn't see Carly. Mom listened earnestly, leaning forward slightly. She and Carly listened to the same speech, but I knew they heard different messages—one inspiring, one accusing.

After the closing prayer, Carly slid out of the pew and started to leave, so my mom and I both followed her.

"That was pretty good, don't you think?" Mom asked as we skirted around a cluster of giggling teenagers. Carly was far ahead of us. I saw the double glass doors swing open and shut as she headed for the car.

"Yeah, I guess."

When we reached the car, Mom and I climbed into the front seats. Carly sat in the back with her arms folded.

"Well," Mom said, "what did you think?"

Neither Carly nor I answered. I glanced at my sister in the rearview mirror and was startled to see her looking straight back at us, her eyes full of anger. I looked away. This wasn't my fault, not this time. I didn't suggest coming to the fireside.

"Do you feel like some—" Mom paused, looking at Carly's face in the rearview mirror. I finished the sentence in my mind: *Do you feel like some ice cream?* In the past, that's what we always ate after a fireside or the Young Women's broadcast. Now, getting ice cream seemed like a potential minefield none of us wanted to cross.

My mom waited for a moment, then she started the car. She didn't know what to do and for some reason that made me mad. If she didn't know what to do, who did? She was the mom. Dad was the dad. It was their job to know what to do.

Carly spoke up a few blocks later, her voice acidic. "Was that supposed to cure me?"

"What?"

"All that stuff about how your body is precious and if you mess with it, you're a horrible person. Do you think that makes me feel better? Do you think that makes me able to stop?"

"Carly, that's not the important part. The part that mattered was the part about how much Heavenly Father and Jesus love you—"

Carly interrupted. "And that makes me feel even more guilty! If I could stop, I would, but I can't! I don't need more guilt on top of everything else. Is that all the gospel is going to give me?"

"No, no, no," Mom said. "That is *not* what the gospel is about. Heavenly Father loves you and does not want you to feel guilty. He's not angry with you. He wants you to see yourself as the wonderful person that you are."

"What are you, Mom, His personal spokesperson? Just like the speaker thought she was? Do you have anything else to tell me? Any other messages from God?"

"Of course not." My mom stayed calm. "You can hear Him yourself. You can have your own revelations and promptings."

"The only voice I hear in my head is one that tells me that I'm never going to be good enough," Carly said. "Where is the voice I'm supposed to be hearing?"

"It's there, Carly. I promise. But you have to keep listening."

"You make it sound so easy. It's not easy."

The thing that really scared me was that I kind of understood what Carly was saying. Lately, I struggled to hear that voice too.

When I was younger, I thought of Joseph Smith the way he appeared in Church movies: handsome and confident. Only when we studied his life in seminary did I realize that his story could be seen as the worst tragedy ever. Lately, I couldn't stop thinking about him and everything he'd been through.

Near the end of the Prophet's life, the Church was fragile, and the members of the Church were being driven from their homes. If he hadn't had faith that he had been doing what God wanted him to do, it would have looked like a pretty terrible mess.

So did he see a vision of how it would all turn out? Or did he only *believe* that it would be all right? In that last, falling moment, when he called out to Heavenly Father, did Joseph Smith know that he'd been heard?

"Carly, I know what you mean," I began. "I don't always feel everything I want to feel at church, but I keep going because—"

Carly didn't let me finish. "Because Kendall girls go to church. Kendall girls are good girls. Kendall girls play basketball and act perfect and they definitely *don't* do disgusting things like make themselves throw up."

"That's not what I wanted to say." I felt slapped, stung, embarrassed.

"Oh, yeah? I already know how all our conversations will end. With everyone talking about how I've let them all down. How I don't do this and I don't do that and how I disappointed everyone by not playing basketball . . ."

That was so unfair. I hadn't mentioned basketball in months, not since that time in the fall when she'd told me not to bring it up anymore.

"Carly, Maddie and Em and I never cared what you did. Yeah, we were surprised when you decided to be a cheerleader, but it's not like it bothered us or anything."

"But it bothered *me!*" She almost screamed the words at me. "Because no matter what I do, I can't get away from it! I can't get away from what you and Emma and Maddie have all done!"

"Are you trying to say that it's *our* fault you're bulimic? Are you trying to blame that on *us?*"

Mom said something, but neither of us heard her.

"What?" I snapped at her.

"Please stop. Both of you. Please."

Carly and I both fell into a cold, brittle silence. I rode the rest of the way home with my fists clenched and my teeth ground together, holding everything in. If any of my anger leaked out, I worried I would cause another explosion. I didn't want that.

Here is what I did want: I wanted us to have a normal interaction like the ones we used to have all the time. I wanted to go to a fireside, to feel the Spirit, to discuss things over ice cream with my mom and sister. I felt angry, but I also felt something more.

I felt hungry.

I was starving for the way things used to be.

CHAPTER 24

If we had written a creed about what it meant to be a Kendall girl (which we hadn't, no matter what Carly believed), it might go something like this:

Kendall girls are good girls. They excel in sports. They like to date, but none of them have a reputation for being boy-crazy. They don't look exactly alike, but they are on the tallish side, with long brown hair (eye color may vary). They like to laugh. They like to dance. They respect their elders. They go to church. They don't cause trouble at school.

At first, when I got the note to go to the counselor's office during lunch, I thought it had something to do with Carly. But it didn't. *I* was the problem. I wasn't on track to graduate.

When Ms. Santos told me the news, I almost laughed. Could anything else go wrong? "Are you serious?"

"I'm afraid so," Ms. Santos said sympathetically. "We've caught the problem in time to fix it, but as it stands right now, you won't have enough P.E. credits to graduate next year."

"How can that be?"

"Coach Slater didn't give you credit for basketball, since you didn't . . . complete the season." I had to give Ms. Santos credit for her diplomacy.

"But I played every day for almost the whole year! Can't I get partial credit or something?"

"You could, if you were able to talk to Coach Slater—"

I shook my head. "That's not going to work."

"Well, then, you'll need to sign up for an additional P.E. class your senior year." She looked at my transcript. "Or you could participate in track again this season."

"Oh. Right."

"That would be the easiest way to take care of it. Why don't you go talk to Coach Walker?"

"Okay." I only said it to get Ms. Santos off my back. I didn't want to do track again—not with Nate and Megan on the team.

"Great," Ms. Santos said. "She has a free period right now. I'll call her and let her know you're coming."

Oh, well. At least I could talk to her during my lunch hour instead of sitting alone in Old Blue eating my bagel.

Coach Walker seemed thrilled to see me. "Juliet! I'm so glad you're going to high jump again!"

"Well, I'm not really sure yet. I'm kind of busy after school. I have a lot of homework." A lame excuse. I loved track practice last year, but I didn't know if I could face it this year. Not only did it mean seeing Nate and Megan on a regular basis, it also meant being part of a team again. I didn't want people depending on me. I didn't want to let anyone down.

"That's no problem," Coach Walker said brightly. "I'm afraid that we still don't have an official coach for you anyway, so you can practice whenever you want. Evenings, mornings—whatever works for you."

Well, in that case, why not? I had to do something to graduate and this might just work. No crazy coach. No set practice times. Come when you want. Do what you can. No pressure.

What more could I ask for?

The early morning February air bit my fingers as I pulled the covers off the high-jump mats. I hadn't brought any gloves, so I tucked my fingers up inside the sleeves of my hoodie for warmth.

I'd hoped that the track would be deserted on a freezing Saturday morning, and it almost was. The only other people I saw were two older ladies in sweat suits walking around the outermost lane of the track. I didn't see a single person my age. Perfect.

I pulled the last cover off and stood back, sizing things up. No bar, but that was all right. I could jump without it. You don't always have to have the bar; you don't always have to take your measure. Sometimes you just need to remember the form, the feeling, the way you need to move before you start calculating how well you've done.

I stretched out for a few minutes, bending over and bending back. Then I started to run in that bouncy lengthy stride that's best for the high jump; I accelerated, gaining momentum for the last explosive step. I jumped, leaning backward, arcing my body.

The mats smacked cold against my shoulders when I landed. I always forgot that part, the way it felt to land. I rolled automatically into a backward somersault and onto my knees.

I decided to try again. I had no idea what my jump looked like, but I could tell that my form was definitely rusty. This would take some time. I ran and jumped until I was the last one left on the track.

My plans to practice again on Monday were thwarted by the biggest storm of the year. It came in the night and turned everything into rounded hills and mountains of snow. It blanketed streets and sidewalks and reminded us that winter wasn't finished just yet.

"I'll drive you girls to school today," Mom said at breakfast.

"Oh, Mom. I can handle it. How do you think we've been getting to school all winter long?"

"None of the other snowstorms were this bad, and Old Blue doesn't have all-wheel drive. No arguments." Resigning ourselves to looking like middle-schoolers getting dropped off by their parents, Carly and I climbed into Mom's minivan. I sighed and looked over at where Old Blue hunched under the snow in the driveway. Hopefully we could take her out of hibernation before too long.

We were only about two houses away from our own when the van started to slide. It slid right into a snow bank, hood first. "Shoot," my mom said in a tone that sounded close to swearing.

We got out to assess the situation: good and stuck. The drift was deep, and the back of the minivan poked out into the middle of the road.

"Our car is in everyone's way," I observed helpfully.

"Who's going to get us out?" Carly complained. "Dad's already at work."

"No one's going to get us out," Mom said. "We'll do it ourselves."

We walked back to the house to get our snow shovels and gloves. Mom and I worked on digging out the front of the minivan. Carly chipped away at a patch of ice near the back wheels, a sour expression on her face.

"Can I make a comment about how ironic this is?" I asked. "That you expressed concern about *my* driving and now we're digging *you* out of the snow?"

Mom gave me a look. "You can. But I think you're too smart for that."

"Right." I dug a little harder, even though I wasn't in any hurry to get to school now that we were guaranteed to be late. It would be nice to miss the entire day. I could go back to bed and curl up and sleep.

Snowflakes landed on my hands, face, and eyelashes, making it hard to see. I wiped them away and glanced over at Carly. She had given up even the pretense of shoveling and had her face turned to the sky and her eyes closed. The snowflakes landed on her like butterflies or flower petals and melted away almost instantly on her warm skin.

It had been so long since I'd looked at her as Carly, and not as the Sister I Worried About. Bundled up in her coat, with snow falling all around her, she looked like the Carly I remembered from other winters— the Carly who dragged her sled up the hill over and over, even when the rest of us got tired and collapsed at the bottom, the Carly who loved digging snow caves with Dad, the Carly who fell backward into the snow with her arms wide open to make snow angels.

When Mom finally got the car to move, she didn't drive toward the high school, to my surprise. Instead, she made a slow and careful seventy-five-point turn and went back to our house. In the few minutes we'd been gone, the driveway had already been covered again with soft white snow.

"Um, Mom," Carly said in her snottiest voice, "the school is the other way."

"We're not going to school. Or work. The three of us are taking a snow day." Mom turned off the minivan. "We're staying home and watching that miniseries Dad gave me for Christmas. *North and South.* I think you girls will like it."

Carly and I stared at her in disbelief. "Isn't that thing four hours long?" I asked.

"Isn't it, like, British television?" Carly added.

Mom ignored us. "Obviously, the roads are too dangerous; we didn't even make it down our street. I think viewing a classic film is enough of an educational experience for today. I've wanted to watch this with you girls for months. We'll change into our sweats and curl up on the couch." She smiled at us.

I started to grin. "Sounds good to me." It sounded much, *much* better than going to school. Now I didn't have to worry about where I would eat lunch without Old Blue or how to avoid Nate and Megan in the halls or any of it. It was as though Mom gave me a Get Out of Jail Free card for the day.

When we got inside the house, Carly tried to go upstairs to her room. "I'm going back to bed."

"No, you're not," Mom said firmly. "You can fall asleep on the couch next to us if you want, but you have to give this a try. The love story is a classic and it's based on a famous novel. I'm *sure* you're going to like it."

Carly groaned but sat on the couch.

We did like the movie, almost in spite of ourselves. The first hour went kind of slow, but then, as Carly said, the main male character really started to smolder. By the time we were halfway through, Carly stopped complaining entirely.

We took an intermission and made homemade salsa and chips, which used to be Carly's favorite snack. She ate them without any drama and without excusing herself to hide out in the bathroom afterward. When my dad came home for lunch, he looked a little surprised, but then he sat down and started making fun of the hero's cravat until we all threw pillows at him and told him he had to leave if he couldn't keep his mouth shut.

When the movie ended, none of us went off to our own rooms. Instead, we watched the whole thing again during that long, quiet, snowy afternoon. Carly and I both fell asleep at different parts the second time through but neither of us left the couch.

That day was like an island. A little island of good in a whole sea of bad. Or maybe it was like stepping stones in a river, and we made it to one little safe stone in the middle of water that was so cold and so fast it could kill us if we slipped. I wanted to stay in that day and stand on that stone forever.

CHAPTER 25

I sat in Old Blue and debated whether or not to keep my promise to the basketball team. Then Hanna texted me: *You're coming, right?*

I sighed and texted her back: *Yeah. I'll be there.*

"There" was Eastview High, where the South High Lady Panthers had their first-round state play-off game. The game against Eastview might be my last chance to make good on my word to come cheer for the team. The play-offs were single elimination: if South lost, their season ended.

I didn't want to watch the team play without me. I'd managed to avoid it since I walked off the court back in January. But I cared about the girls and especially about Hanna. I should go.

It took only a few minutes to drive across town to Eastview, which is a lot fancier and newer than South. You can tell that as soon as you walk through the doors. Everything hasn't had as much time to get worn out and used up, and their school has skylights in the halls, so it all feels a little brighter.

Plus, their gym has state-of-the-art everything and their fans are rabid, even for their girls' teams. I stood at the bottom of the bleachers for a few seconds, hunting for a place to sit.

A guy waved at me and called out, "Juliet!" It took me a few moments to realize that the guy was Max and that he wanted me to come sit by him. I hesitated because Nate sat next to him, but then Nate saw me and waved too. No way out of it. I climbed up into the bleachers.

"Hey. What have I missed?"

"Not much," Max told me, gesturing toward the basketball court. "Hanna didn't get to start. She's going to be mad."

At first, watching the game seemed like kind of an out-of-body experience. I almost expected to see myself out there playing (or, more accurately, sitting on the bench). It felt weird to sit in the stands of the rival high school with my old boyfriend watching my former team play. It was kind of like watching my previous life pass before my eyes.

Max must have been thinking along the same lines. After Megan made a shot, putting South up 4–0, he turned to me and said, "Is it weird to watch them winning without you?"

"*Max,*" Nate said. He sounded exasperated.

But I didn't mind too much. Max was Max. He said what he thought, and if I was honest with myself, I had to admit that I'd wondered the same thing. "Yeah, a little bit."

But as the game went on, things changed. I might have thought that it would be hard to watch the team win without me, but I soon realized it was much, much worse to watch them lose.

Things went well for the Panthers at first, but it turned into a rout at the end. Alisha made her shots; Megan played great; Hanna spent too much time on the bench but played solidly when Coach put her in. No one choked, but they didn't play effectively as a team. What they really needed was a guard who ran the plays well and who could see the open girl and make the right passes at the right time.

They needed me.

It's okay, I told myself. *You couldn't make a difference. Coach Slater wouldn't have you out on the floor anyway.*

But I still wondered about what might have been.

The buzzer sounded. Coach Slater gathered the girls and they dispersed into the stands to shake everyone's hands. Megan went over to find her parents and I saw her mom give her a comforting hug. Hanna made her way through the crowd to us. I stuck out my hand to shake hers, but she didn't even notice. "Well, I guess our season is over. That's it."

"You played great."

"*When* I played. Maybe I should have quit like you did."

"No, you shouldn't have. You did the right thing."

"Well, either way, it's over now." Hanna looked around the gym. The Eastview team still celebrated out on the floor and little knots of friends and family surrounded the dejected South players in their blue jerseys. Coach Slater stood alone, looking at her clipboard as if to figure out what went wrong. The season was officially over.

I put my arm around Hanna. I knew she'd hoped for different things out of her senior year of basketball. "You did a great job, Hanna. You stuck it out until the end, and now you won't have any regrets."

"I guess." Hanna changed the subject. "Hey, we should hang out tomorrow night. I won't have practice anymore."

"That would be great, but I can't tomorrow. I have something I have to do."

"High jumping?"

"No, something else." I glanced around at the crowded gym. "I'll tell you about it later."

"Welcome. We have a few new people this evening, so let's all go around the circle and introduce ourselves." Amy, the counselor in charge of the family support group, smiled at me. "Just to make sure everyone's in the right place, this is a support group for teenagers who have a sibling, a parent, or a friend with an eating disorder."

I was in the right place, but it still felt strange. However, I doubted I felt as strange as the boy sitting next to me. There were only two guys in the room. The rest of the people were girls, and I had a guilty feeling of relief about that. *See, other girls besides you have failed their sisters,* I thought to myself.

The closer they got to me, the more nervous I became, which was stupid. All I had to do was say my name and why I was there. Two sentences, less if I consolidated them like the girl who started us out: "I'm Mallory, and my sister has an eating disorder."

A couple of girls had moms with eating disorders, which kind of freaked me out. That would be really hard. I'd never thought of a mom having an eating disorder before. If my mom fell apart like that, I don't know what I'd do.

My turn. I copied Mallory but inserted my name for hers: "I'm Juliet, and my sister has an eating disorder."

After the introductions, Amy broke us up into pairs. She paired me with the guy next to me, who introduced himself as Jonah. When we turned our chairs to face each other I got my first good look at him. He had spiky brown hair and brown eyes, and he was tall.

"So, Juliet," he said. "Where are you from?" He had a deep voice and his tone was friendly, but with a reserved quality about it, too.

"Here. I go to South. What about you?"

"I'm from here too. I go to Eastview."

I didn't know what to say, so I tried to make a joke. "Oh, *Eastview*. I don't know if I can be paired with you." The moment the words were out of my mouth, I wanted them back. When you were at a family support meeting for people whose loved ones had eating disorders, you didn't make jokes about something as supremely unimportant as school loyalty. I flushed.

He was nice enough to joke back. "Me either. *South?*"

Thank goodness he didn't call me an insensitive jerk. "Sorry. That was kind of lame. I guess I'm nervous. Are you new too?"

"No. I've been coming for a while."

"So what do we do now?"

"Talking in pairs is supposed to give us a chance to talk about things that we might not want to say in front of the whole group. I think the theory is that it's not as intimidating."

"Oh."

"Amy usually has us do this when we have new people. Then when we get back in the big group, everyone feels more comfortable."

"Do we talk about ourselves or about our family members?"

"Either. Both." Jonah paused. When I didn't say anything, he took a deep breath. "Okay. I'll get us started. I'm here because my sister is in the residential treatment program. She has anorexia."

"My sister's in the outpatient program. She has bulimia." Now I paused. "Am I supposed to tell you how that makes me feel or something?" This all seemed kind of forced, although Jonah was nice enough.

"If you want to."

"Okay." Even if I wasn't very good at this, and even if I couldn't see how it would help me, much less Carly, I had to do it. "I'm worried about her. I feel like I dropped the ball. She's my little sister, and I should have taken better care of her."

"How long has she been having trouble?"

"For about a year, but it's gotten a lot worse the past few months."

"It's good you caught it so fast," Jonah said.

"Fast? She's been doing it for a year."

"Well, fast compared to us, I guess. My sister's been anorexic for three years." His voice was sad. "She's not doing very well. This is her second time through the residential program. I don't know what we're going to do if it doesn't work."

"I'm really sorry."

"Yeah." We both sat there for a second, and then Jonah spoke again. "So tell me about you. What do you do? Basketball?"

"What made you guess that?"

"Your keychain." I'd been playing with my keys and twisting them around over and over, the same nervous habit I once had with my bracelet. My keychain said *South High Lady Panthers* and was shaped like a basketball. Duh.

"Oh, right."

"So do you play?"

"I used to. I don't anymore. It's a long story. What about you?"

"Not me. I like to shoot around and stuff, but I've never been on a team or anything. I was only five-nine until my junior year."

"You're kidding me." He had to be at least six-two now.

"Nope."

"So what's your thing? What do you like?"

He shrugged and smiled. "I don't know. Everything."

"That's pretty broad."

"Sorry. I like lots of stuff. Running, playing guitar, work."

"Where do you work?"

"For a landscaping company. It's called Green Machines. I mow lawns in the summer, but right now we shovel snow."

"Really? I didn't think people who went to *Eastview* shoveled other people's snow or mowed other people's lawns." *Awesome, Juliet.* I tried to fix it. "Sorry. I guess today's my day to make sweeping generalizations."

"It's okay. Maybe *some* people who go to Eastview don't mow lawns. But I do."

"And you like it?"

"Yeah. I love it. I've been doing it for a while." Neither of us spoke for a second—I didn't dare open my mouth in case something else stupid came out. Finally Jonah asked, "You want to know why?"

"Sure."

"I like the extra money. That's part of it. But it's really because of Claire. My sister. When everything first went down with the eating disorder and she came here for the first time, I wanted something to get me out of the house as much as possible. Something physical. I liked working hard and not having to think too much. Work was my best escape."

I nodded. "That makes sense."

"What about you? Have you found a way to escape yet?"

I thought of the freezing-cold practice at the high-jump pit. "I'm not sure yet."

Jonah nodded as though he understood. It was nice to know that he probably did.

Jonah and I walked out together after the meeting. While we'd been inside, night had sharpened and darkened. I shivered and zipped up my coat; Jonah grabbed a hat out of his pocket and pulled it on. We stood talking underneath one of the parking lot lights for a minute before we went our separate ways.

"So what did you think? Will you be back?" Jonah waved to the other guy from the group and then shoved his hands back into the pockets of his jacket.

"Yeah, I will. It was better than I thought it would be."

"Then I'll see you next week."

"Sounds good."

I tried to see which car was his, but he disappeared into the darkened parking lot. Still shivering, I went to Old Blue and climbed inside. I'd told Jonah the truth—I'd be back the next week. It felt good not to feel alone, even if it lasted for only an hour.

Hanna called before I left the parking lot at the center. "So how was your mysterious meeting?"

"Good."

"What was it, anyway?"

"I went to a support group for people who have family members with eating disorders."

Silence.

"Obviously, that's just between you and me."

"Is it Carly?" Hanna asked softly. Before I could answer, she said, "Never mind. Sorry. Is everything okay? Do you want to talk about it?"

"You know what, I really don't," I said. "It was fine. But I don't want to talk about this for a while."

"Okay," Hanna said, unoffended. "I won't ask."

"You can ask. But don't get bugged if I don't want to answer." I paused. "How was your last team meeting?"

Hanna groaned. "Don't get bugged if I don't want to answer."

When I got home, I could tell that everyone had been waiting for me. They acted like they were doing homework (Carly), and sorting out the family budget (my parents), but I knew they wanted to find out about the meeting. Carly was in therapy; my parents were in therapy; I was finally doing my share and going to meetings too.

"Hey," I said.

I guess Mom decided that we might as well have things out in the open because she went ahead and asked, "How was the meeting?"

"Pretty good, actually."

My parents smiled in relief. Carly didn't look up from her homework.

"That's great. What happened?"

Normally, I didn't love giving a play-by-play to my parents, but I figured that our family could use all the good news we could get. I didn't mind sharing mine. "Well, the counselor started us out with introductions and then we talked in pairs. I met this guy named Jonah who seemed really nice—"

"Wait a minute," Carly interrupted. "You met a *guy?*"

"Yeah. Jonah. He's been coming to the meetings for a while. Anyway—"

Carly interrupted me again. "Doesn't anyone else have anything to say about this?"

I stopped and looked at my parents. My confusion was reflected in their faces. "About what, Carly?" my mom asked.

"About what Juliet did."

What? "I didn't do anything—"

"I think it's sick," Carly said. "You're meeting a guy because of me. You're basically getting something out of this whole my-having-problems thing."

"That's not what it is at all," I protested. I'd barely said two sentences. How could I have possibly messed up so quickly? "The counselor *assigned* him to be my partner, Carly."

"It's still sick." The veins stood out on her neck.

"Carly—" Mom began.

"No, I'm serious. This is disgusting. My own sister is benefiting from what you are all doing to me."

"From what you're doing to *yourself,* you mean," I snapped, unable to stand it anymore.

"Juliet—" my mom said at the same time that my dad said, "Carly—"

Everyone stopped talking.

"Fine," I said, all my anger suddenly gone. "I won't talk to him again outside of the group meeting. If he asks, I won't hang out with him or go out with him. But we weren't even close to that. It wasn't what you think." I thought I might have found a friend, someone who understood about eating disorders and sisters and escape. How could I explain that to Carly?

Carly looked a little surprised, but then she narrowed her eyes and said, "Good."

"And I won't even ask if you're happy now because I know you're not. I know that nothing and no one in this world can make you happy." I turned to leave the room.

"Juliet," my mom said, but I kept walking. It was like walking off the basketball team two months ago, except that this didn't feel clean or therapeutic. It didn't feel like a break. It felt like I was ripping away at something, and I knew I was still attached to all that pain in the room behind me.

CHAPTER 26

March

"Juliet! *Juliet!*"

Something was wrong.

I turned around to see Savannah dodging around people in the hall, her face white and worried. My heart started to pound and my mouth went dry. I couldn't move. I stood there until she reached me and grabbed my arm. "Carly just passed out!"

"Where is she?"

"By her locker. You have to help her."

I have to help her. I wasn't frozen anymore, but there were too many people in my way. "Excuse me!" I yelled, pushing my way through, grabbing someone's backpack and shoving them aside without apologizing. Savannah was close behind me. "What happened?" I called back over my shoulder.

"I don't know. She came out of that bathroom near our lockers and saw me. She said 'Hey,' and then she collapsed."

I rounded the corner and saw a cluster of students gathered around a spot near Carly's locker. Faces turned our way and people moved back so that I could see Carly, lying in a crumpled, awkward position on the floor, her long brown hair pooled around her head. Her eyes were closed, and her face was pale and still.

I dropped to my knees next to her. One of the history teachers had arrived before me and was taking Carly's pulse. She was unconscious but I could hear her breathing fast, in and out, in and out. *She's still breathing.* That had to be a good sign, didn't it?

"Has she ever passed out before?" the teacher asked me.

"No, never." I reached for Carly's other hand. "We have to do something!"

"I called the paramedics," the teacher said. "They're on their way. It might be overkill, but she doesn't look good and I don't think the school nurse is in today."

People murmured around us, watching the scene play out before them. They didn't know how little they mattered. Only Carly mattered.

The paramedics arrived and cleared the hall of students. They even made Savannah leave. But they let me stay. That was when I started to betray my sister.

I told her secrets to anyone who asked, anyone who would listen. I couldn't stop telling them.

She's bulimic. She's made herself throw up for months. She's never passed out before. She had been in the bathroom right before she fainted. We thought she wasn't throwing up as much, but obviously we were wrong. Please help her.

I told the paramedics while I held Carly's hand in the ambulance.

I told the nurses and the doctor at the hospital when they hooked her up to an IV and started running tests. Carly drifted in and out of consciousness, looking dazed and faint.

"She is severely dehydrated," one of the doctors said. "And from what you've told me, I expect the results of her blood work to show that her electrolyte levels—like her potassium level—are way off. We need to rule out things like organ damage and kidney failure. How long has she been purging like this?"

"Over a year," I said. "But we thought she was getting better."

The doctor put his hand on my shoulder. "I'm sure your parents will be here soon." I know he meant for that to make me feel better, but it didn't help much. The truth was that my parents didn't know what to do either.

It seemed to take a long time for my mom and dad to get to the hospital. While I waited, I looked at my sister. Carly's eyes were closed. She still looked pale, except for the red, irritated patches on her arms and hands where the nurses had had trouble finding a vein for her IV. "It's always harder in dehydrated patients," one of them murmured to me. "I'm sorry."

Just hurry, I'd thought. *Hurry and fill her up with electrolytes and whatever other magic potions you have on hand.* Once they placed the IV, I followed the path of each pristine droplet from the bag down the IV tube. The crystal-clear liquid dripping into Carly's IV seemed almost beautiful to me because it did something I couldn't do. It helped my sister, at least for the time being.

I heard the sounds of other tragedies and emergencies going on around us, and then, once, I heard the incongruous sound of laughter. A few minutes later the nurse poked her head behind our curtain and told us that they would have a room for Carly soon.

We'd be here for a while, I realized. I felt thankful and scared at the same time. Maybe they could fix this. But if they could, wouldn't they send everyone with an eating disorder to the hospital right away?

Maybe no one knew how to fix this. They couldn't leave Carly hooked up to an IV forever.

I wished that I could call Jonah. At our last meeting he'd mentioned that his sister had been hospitalized before. He'd also entered his number into my phone in case I ever wanted to call. I wanted to get out my cell phone and dial his number and ask him what happened next. Where we went from here. But that would betray the person lying in the bed next to me, so I couldn't. I'd already done that enough for one day.

A few hours later, while my parents were out in the hall with the doctors, Carly began to talk to me. She let me hold her hand but she didn't look at me. She stared up at the ceiling and the words came out, words that were part of a whole that only she could see.

"I wanted this to be the best year ever. I wanted it to be the year that I was finally good enough. I thought, if I can get a senior guy to like me, then that means I'm popular. And then when Jaydon stopped liking me, I knew I wasn't good enough or thin enough. I needed to be better, lose more weight. It made sense."

"None of this makes sense," I said. Her logic was everywhere and nowhere at the same time.

"I knew he had a reputation as a player, but I thought that if I was the one to change that, it would prove something about me."

"Nothing about Jaydon Fullmer proves anything about you, Carly. You're so much more than that."

She wasn't listening, of course. "I'm so messed up. I'm so messed up," she kept saying, over and over. "I'll never get fixed. Do you think even Heavenly Father can fix me now?"

She started to cry, a sound like the shatter of glass. It was the sound of something breaking. I knew that sound—but this time it was something more precious than a vase, something even more precious than a friendship. It was the sound of a person flying to pieces after holding herself together for too long.

Is it lying when you tell someone things that you feel like you *should* believe, that you *used* to believe, but that you don't *know* anymore?

But looking at Carly's face, I didn't have any other choice.

"He can help you." I hoped that if in fact He did exist, He would understand. "He loves you."

Carly finally looked at me.

"*I* love you," I told her. I tightened my grip on her hand and prayed that He would help me hold on long enough.

CHAPTER 27

Carly stayed in the hospital for two days while they got her system back in balance and made sure her kidneys and other organs were functioning okay. She'd become severely dehydrated from throwing up and from using so many laxatives, and that was what had caused her to faint.

I had thought things might get better because we were all trying so hard. Instead, they'd gotten worse.

"Did we cause this?" my dad asked the doctor. "Did we make her try to hide it more? She didn't throw up at school before."

"You can think that way if you want to torture yourself," the doctor said bluntly. "But I'd think of it like this. If she had passed out like this late at night, at home, it might have been a few hours before anyone found her. Damage would have certainly occurred. If something like this was going to happen, and it seems that it was almost inevitable, this is one of the better scenarios."

I could see what he meant, but it was hard to think of Carly passing out in the hall at school as one of our better options. Maybe later I would be grateful. But for now, all I could think of was the fact that we were sitting around my sister's hospital bed. That we hadn't been able to help her, so we'd taken her to a place where we had to put our trust in machines and strangers to do a better job than we had done.

Carly fainted on a Friday. Saturday was spent at the hospital; and Maddie drove up from college for the day. She had to go back that night, and when we hugged good-bye at the hospital I almost couldn't let her go.

On Sunday, I went to sacrament meeting. I slipped into the chapel right before the meeting started and sat alone on the long pew at the back. I didn't want to talk to anyone around me, so I crossed my ankles and looked down at my feet until the opening hymn started. Then I looked up. While I sang, I looked at the rock wall behind the pulpit, searching for the familiar face in the pattern there. I looked at that spot on the wall until I bowed my head for the sacrament prayer.

The little plastic cups filled with water reminded me of the liquid in Carly's IV bag. That had saved her; this could save me. I closed my eyes and let the feeling of prayer wash over me. Even though I didn't have an answer yet, the act of praying wasn't hard that day. Someone had to be listening. Someone had to love Carly as much as we did.

I couldn't face my Young Women's class, though. I couldn't go without Carly. So I went home instead. I was surprised to find my mom in the kitchen waiting for me. She hadn't left the hospital since that first day.

"Is Carly back?"

Mom sat down at the counter. "Juliet," she said. "We have to talk."

I've said that I hate those words. When I heard my mom say them, I hated them so much that I shuddered as I stood there, and the peace I had felt at church seemed to fade away. Something bad was going to follow those words. I knew it. I didn't sit down.

"When is Carly coming home?"

"We've decided to check her into the residential program at the treatment center."

The guilt settled down on me, dark and heavy enough to take my breath away. In some weird way, I felt like I was the one responsible for getting my sister sent away from home. I'd told her secrets to anyone who would listen. I'd sobbed them out in the emergency room underneath the fluorescent lights and among the strangers wearing scrubs and name tags. I'd laid them bare when they weren't my secrets to tell.

But what alternative did I have? Some secrets can't be kept and shouldn't be kept. I knew that, but the guilt was still there. We were the Kendall girls. We looked out for each other. We all took care of each other. But now I knew the truth of something I'd suspected all along. I was the weak link in the chain. I let Carly break.

"When is she coming home?"

"It depends on her. There's a sixty-day program, and one that lasts ninety days—"

"So we're going to pay someone else to fix her?" The moment I said the words, I wanted them back. "I'm sorry. I didn't mean that the way it sounded. I meant—I don't know. I wish we could help her. I wish she didn't have to go away."

"I don't know what else to do," Mom said, her eyes full of tears. "I don't know what else to do."

On Monday morning, I drove over to the hospital to say good-bye to Carly before I went back to school. Once she started her treatment program, she wouldn't be able to have contact with us for a while.

Carly stood by the window of her hospital room wearing jeans and a sweater. There were no IVs in sight. She looked out the window, just like she'd looked out the window of Old Blue so many times when we drove home from school together. My mom sat in a chair next to her, and my dad filled out some paperwork. No one looked up when I came in, and I was tempted to slip back out again and let it all happen without me.

Then Carly turned her head and saw me, and I couldn't avoid saying good-bye.

Afterward, I drove Old Blue to South High, where people in the halls whispered behind my back because they didn't know what to say to my face.

Carly had passed out at school. Everyone knew. That didn't matter as far as I was concerned. I didn't care about what people thought of me, and I didn't have any shame or embarrassment on behalf of our family. We hadn't been the perfect Kendall girls since the day I walked off the basketball court. I was the one who ruined that, not Carly.

But I couldn't stand to think about what their whispers and gossip meant for Carly. I couldn't stand to think about some of those cheerleaders nodding their heads and saying that they'd been right all along. I did not want people to give Carly the label of the Cheerleader with the Eating Disorder. Because she was more than that. She was beyond any label, and so was every other human being.

"What do we tell people?" I'd asked my mom on Sunday. "What if they ask?"

She looked me in the eye and said, "You don't have to answer unless they love Carly. And if they do, we tell them the truth."

I'd felt a little better, but not much. I still knew that people are too quick to label. I knew that from personal experience: I'd been ready and willing to slap the Kendall Girl label on myself. And I'd made the mistake of labeling other people too.

The Evil Coach. The Boyfriend-Stealer. The Ex-Boyfriend. Did I have what it took to strip off those labels and see people for what they really were, flawed children of God walking around and making mistakes?

How does He do it? How does He see all our truth and love us still?

CHAPTER 28

Megan found me the next day as I tried to escape to Old Blue for lunch. I planned to turn on my music and eat my bagel and spend a half hour in the capsule of my car without anyone around me. I didn't even want to talk to Hanna about what had happened, not yet.

"Juliet, wait up."

I stopped, but I didn't turn around to face her. "What?"

"Are you okay?"

I didn't answer. I waited.

"You don't even seem like yourself," Megan said awkwardly. "I know we don't hang out or anything anymore, but you're so different. Even though I only see you in the halls and at church, I can tell. I know there's a lot going on with Carly—"

"I don't want to talk about it." I turned to meet her eyes for the first time in a long time. "You are not the person I can talk to about these things. So I appreciate your concern, but there's nothing to say."

"Nate and I aren't really dating anymore."

"Okay." I waited for her to see that that didn't change anything. I was so far past caring about Nate.

"I want to be friends again, Juliet. We need each other."

I tried to look past the label; I tried to do the right thing. Tears welled in my eyes. "I can't right now, Megan. I'm sorry."

My dad used to joke that living in our house was like living in a girls' dorm. When all four of us girls lived upstairs at home, it was crowded and loud. Music blared; hair dryers buzzed; we fought and yelled and laughed.

After Carly left, I got in the habit of standing in the doorway of her room and taking in what I could from there. I knew she would hate it if I went inside and snooped around while she was gone, so I stayed in the hallway. When I thought about it, Carly's room was a pretty apt metaphor for the way things had been going between the two of us. I was shut out of someplace I used to belong. I didn't belong in "my" room anymore; Carly didn't confide in me anymore.

Now when I got ready for school in the bathroom in the morning, no one knocked on the door telling me to hurry up. I had plenty of hot water for my shower, and no one asked to borrow my clothes. The lid to the toothpaste never got lost. With Carly gone, I missed Emma and Maddie even more. I was alone.

When someone is gone, they usually leave something behind. A message on a cell phone, a ponytail holder in a drawer, a lost flip-flop under a bed, their handwriting noting an item on the shopping list on the fridge, a tube of lip gloss in the glove compartment of a car. It's almost impossible not to; and I think in a way that's kind of nice. I liked finding an odd sock of Maddie's in the laundry after she moved out. It seemed like a reminder that she could never remove herself from the house completely.

Because I found these things comforting, I became kind of a Carly archaeologist. I tried to piece together something about her from the things that she'd left behind. Not from anything in her room—that was too personal—but from the things left outside. Those, I figured, were fair game.

So I used the lip gloss in the glove compartment, and the ponytail holder. When I found an old shopping list with "rosemary-mint shampoo" and "trash bags" written on it in her handwriting, I picked up the shampoo at the store and put it on the bathtub ledge, ready for her to use when she got home. I hunted around in the summer clothes box in the basement until I found the other flip-flop, and then I broke my own rule about going into Carly's room so I could set the matched pair right inside her door. I listened to a message she'd left earlier in the winter on my cell phone, and at the end of the thirty days when it was time to delete it or save it, I saved it.

I learned a little. I learned that I liked the shade of pink lip gloss that my sister used and when her tube ran out, I bought my own in the same shade. I realized that she must have been conscious of the trash bag supply because she always had to reline the trash cans to remove evidence of her bingeing or laxative boxes. I realized that her ponytail holder was the exact shade of her hair because she liked it to blend in and that the bottoms of her flip-flops were worn on the sides because she walked with her feet slightly turned out, the way I did. I'd never noticed that before. Listening to her recorded voice as she called for a ride home, I heard something in it that I'd missed the first time I'd heard the message. Loneliness? Hurt at the way Jaydon had treated her? Had she been worried about getting home fast enough to get rid of any of the food she'd eaten at the party? There was definitely something.

Sometimes, though, those little bits of knowledge were worse than nothing at all because they reminded me how little I really knew Carly.

And sometimes one of the little things she'd left behind caused me a sharp stab of actual physical pain and loss. Like the little wooden disc with her name on it on the family home evening board. I felt a pang every time I saw it hanging there in the kitchen under Lesson.

One Monday night I couldn't take it anymore. I couldn't stand to see her name there, frozen, nothing changing, time standing still. My hand hovered over the disc, but I didn't know where to put it. On the extra hook at the end, with Emma and Maddie's discs?

I took the whole board off the wall and decided to take it down into the basement and hide it away in the storage room. No one would notice.

"What are you doing?" Dad asked. Startled, I turned to face him. He stood in the doorway of the kitchen.

"We've outgrown this," I said, echoing Carly. "I'm putting it away in the basement."

"We've outgrown family home evening?"

"No, not family home evening. The family home evening board." A thick layer of dust covered the top of the board and it left a mark on my black T-shirt. I put the board down on the counter and reached for a rag to clean myself up. "See? It's all dusty. I'm the only one who ever changed the names anyway. And it's not like we don't know who's doing what. There's only three of us left now."

"All right." Dad turned and started rummaging through the mail on the counter, and I went down to the basement. In the storage room, I found a place on a shelf between some cans of food storage and a bin of our old clothes. I felt a touch of anger. My family tried hard. We prepared for the future and didn't throw away too much from the past. We followed the rules and played fair. Maybe that was why I was so angry that the world didn't seem to be playing fair back.

Dad wasn't in the kitchen anymore when I came back up from the basement, but I heard a very familiar *thunk, thunk* sound out in the backyard. I went to the kitchen window and looked outside, out into one of those nights when the clouds are patchy and white against the dark sky and you don't know if they're going to gather into a storm or blow on past.

Dad dribbled the ball. He faked left, then right, and then he pulled up and shot. It was good. He ran forward to grab the ball and shot again. The invisible opponent didn't have a chance, not playing against Dad on the court he'd built himself.

I heard my mom come into the room behind me. "He needs some light, don't you think?" she asked, and she flipped the switch near the window that controlled the back porch lights. Dad turned around and shielded his eyes. When he saw us in the window, he waved.

"Should we make him some lemonade?" Mom asked me.

"I think hot chocolate would be better. It's freezing out there."

Mom warmed up some milk while I found the cups. I got out two blue ones and one yellow one—yet another Carly artifact. The yellow mug was the only one left from an old stoneware set we had years ago and Carly always drank out of it.

Mom poured the hot milk; I stirred in the chocolate powder and dropped a single plump marshmallow into each mug. "Do you want to tell Dad to come in?" Mom asked.

"Why don't we go out? It's cold, but it's a really pretty night." I didn't want to sit in the kitchen to drink our hot chocolate. I didn't want Mom to notice that I'd been redecorating and that the family home evening board was gone.

Mom and I put on our winter coats and carried the mugs outside. Dad dribbled the ball back and forth and he didn't see us as we sat down on the back steps.

"Dad," I called. "We brought you something." I held out the yellow mug to him.

The three of us sat together, watching the stars come out and the clouds drift in the wind above us. I curled my hands around the warmth of the cup and it helped to make the cold all around me bearable. As family home evenings go, it was one I would always remember, even though it lasted for only about ten minutes before we went inside. I remembered it because of the ache I felt for those who were missing and the solace I found with those still there.

CHAPTER 29

The days were getting warmer and the light lasted longer each evening. I might not have noticed if I hadn't been outside practicing the high jump, but I paid attention to each extra minute. I needed every bit of light that I could get.

Jonah stood waiting for me outside the doors as I left the center. "Hey. How are you doing?"

"I'm okay." I'd told the group when Carly had entered the residential program at the center, but Jonah and I hadn't really had a chance to talk about it yet. We hadn't been paired up at group therapy or had a conversation recently—just hello and how are you. My guilt wouldn't let me do anything more than that. I'd made a promise to Carly after all.

But now he was waiting for me. I couldn't ignore him.

"It's really hard when they first go in, isn't it?" Jonah's voice was empathetic. He knew how it felt. He'd already been through it before. And it hadn't worked.

"Yeah." I wanted to ask him about his sister's experiences with the residential treatment program, but I was afraid of what I'd hear. If it hadn't worked for his sister, what made me think that it would work for mine?

"Hang in there. The beginning of the stay is the hardest part for everyone."

Amy came out of the doors behind us. "Hey, you two," she called out, and we waved as she walked to her car. I was glad she didn't stop and talk. I liked Amy, but right then I didn't need more counseling. I needed to talk to Jonah.

"You know what's the easiest part?" Jonah asked me.

"What?" There was an easy part to all of this?

"Having a break from being in charge. Don't you feel that way? Like if something goes wrong now, at least it's not on our watch. We don't have to blame ourselves for this one." Jonah looked at me, searching my face for understanding.

I wanted to deny it and tell him that I didn't feel that way, but I knew what he meant. "Yeah. Although if something bad does happen, I'm sure we'll still feel guilty."

Jonah shook his head. "I know what you mean, but you can't let that happen. You can't get sucked down, too."

I drove over to the track instead of going straight home. It was dusk—my favorite time to high jump. Once I'd uncovered the mats, I pulled on my shoes and started to jog around the track.

I liked the repetition of my workout routine. I ran a few laps, slowly, to warm up. Stretched my legs out. Got ready for the first try. Then I ran again, taking big steps. I picked up speed. And then . . . the jump. Sometimes I cleared it, sometimes I didn't.

Almost every evening, at around the same time I started jumping, a girl would come to run laps. She was overweight with long, dark hair, someone I semi-recognized. She definitely went to South High—but was she a freshman, a sophomore? I kept trying to place her. She jogged a little, then walked a little, then jogged a little again, on and on and on.

The first night she came onto the track she didn't see me standing there stretching. She almost ran into me. "Oh," she said, sounding embarrassed. "Sorry. Usually there isn't anyone practicing this late—I'll come back later."

"No worries," I'd said. "You're totally fine. The rest of the team already left and I'm high-jumping, so I won't even be on the track. I'll be over there." I pointed to the pit.

"Oh, okay." She smiled at me and jogged away.

When I finished warming up, I got ready to jump. The girl came around the turn and I waved. She waved back. I heard the sound of her steps as she passed me. Then I started to run and I could hear only the wind and the sound of my breathing.

Later that night, the house was too quiet. I called Hanna but she didn't answer. My parents were attending a therapy session. I wanted to see Carly, but I couldn't. So I decided to do the next best thing. I hunted around in the media cabinet until I found the home movies.

When we were little, our parents recorded a lot of the minutiae of our lives. There were hours and hours of us coloring, swimming, wandering around in the yard, building towers and knocking them over, blowing out candles on birthday cake after birthday cake after birthday cake, singing random church songs at the top of our lungs for whoever was behind the camera. Somewhere along the line we became either less interesting or more reluctant to be recorded. Now we had only the big events documented. I looked at the labels. BASKETBALL: MADDIE AND JULIET. SUMMER/JULIET'S SIXTEENTH BIRTHDAY PARTY. *No, thank you.* SPRING/CARLY'S CHEER TRYOUTS. *Perfect.*

Mom recorded all three rounds of tryouts, so I started with the first one. I'd missed that round because of a track meet. But I had remembered to leave Carly a good-luck note on the bathroom mirror that morning. When she made callbacks, she was convinced that the good-luck note was part of it, so I had to make sure to leave a note on the bathroom mirror on the mornings of the other rounds, too. She'd teased me about being superstitious during basketball tryouts, but she was just as bad as the rest of us.

On-screen, Carly ran out onto the floor. My mom cheered too loudly into the microphone on the camera. "Oops," she said. I smiled.

There were five other girls in Carly's tryout group, and even if you hadn't planned on watching Carly, you couldn't avoid it. Everything she did was clear and sharp. Her hair flew out behind her as she spun. Her eyes seemed to find yours as she looked out into the audience. It was impossible not to see her. And I couldn't help but notice the difference between the Carly on-screen and the one I'd seen last, in the hospital. It reminded me of when we compared our present and former selves with the Christmas card, only now the difference in Carly was even more pronounced.

I watched her run out on the floor for the second round, as bright and bouncy as she'd been in the first. Even then, I reminded myself, even then, it had already started.

It was so hard to believe.

I was watching the final round of cheerleading tryouts when my parents came home. It sounded like they were arguing on their way up the stairs. Hadn't they seen Old Blue parked in the driveway? Didn't they know I was home and could hear them? Maybe they were so upset they didn't care.

"One in five women struggle with an eating disorder," my dad said. "We have four daughters. Statistically, this isn't—"

"Don't talk about statistics!" my mother yelled, and I drew in my breath. My mother never yelled. She rarely even raised her voice. "We failed. That's what this all amounts to. We failed!" I heard their bedroom door slam shut.

I wanted to follow my parents up to their room, knock on their door, and say, *You haven't failed.* But I couldn't intrude. This was their argument, and even in the middle of it they still had each other.

I remembered the night when my parents went out of town and Carly snuck out. I'd been so glad to be by myself for a change, but I didn't feel that way anymore. Now I wished that I had Emma, or Maddie, or Carly, but I didn't have anyone. I was alone.

On the screen in front of me, Carly finished her routine and ran off the floor.

CHAPTER 30

"You all have an assignment this week," Amy told us at our next meeting. "I want you all to go out and pretend that you're your sister or your mom or your friend. Or your brother," she added. A new girl had joined us, one whose brother was bulimic. "I want you to walk through the mall or a shopping center and take a good look at the images and advertising you see. Think about how those things would affect you if you had an eating disorder. One of the hardest parts about recovering is that you still have to have food to survive. You can't just quit, like alcohol or drugs. You have to deal with food every single day."

Jonah waited for me again when the meeting ended. He wore a pair of dark jeans and a bright green T-shirt from work with a picture of a smiling lawnmower and the words "Green Machines" written on the front. Not everyone could wear that shirt without looking silly, but Jonah could.

He must have noticed me looking. "You like the shirt?"

"Very professional."

"You should see the truck I drive when I'm at work. It's green too." Jonah smiled at me. In spite of myself, I loved his smile: always sudden and quick and accompanied by a crinkling around his eyes that brightened his usually thoughtful expression. "Hey, do you want to go to the mall together this weekend? You know, for that assignment Amy gave us?"

"I can't." How could I explain to him that Carly saw my friendship with Jonah as unfair and twisted? "My sister made me promise not to hang out with anyone from group therapy."

"Really? When did she say that?"

"Before she went in."

"She might not feel that way anymore."

"I know. But I promised her I wouldn't, and I haven't been able to talk to her since."

"You have my number though, right?" Jonah asked.

I nodded.

"Good. In case she ever lifts that ban and you want to call."

"Okay. Thanks."

My first track meet of the season lasted less than half an hour. In high jumping, you get three tries to clear a height. Three times, I hit the bar. I didn't even clear the opening height.

I went over to the edge of the pit, picked up my warm-ups, and pulled them on. Then I walked toward Old Blue before anyone could stop me. I didn't feel sad and I wasn't discouraged, but I didn't want people to come and try to tell me that I'd done a good job when I obviously hadn't. I also didn't want them to tell me I'd do better next time.

Because who knew if there would even be a next time? I took things one day at a time. All I knew was that I would keep high jumping as long as it helped.

On Saturday I drove to the mall alone to do my assignment. *Try to see things the way Carly might see them,* I told myself, remembering Amy's words.

I started by walking past the clothing store that always had huge posters of male models out front. The good-looking guy in the poster wore jeans but you could see only about two inches of them. The rest of the picture showed his chest and abs. I wondered what Carly would have thought about it. Maybe she would have seen the guy as someone perfect and unobtainable. Maybe she would wonder if she had to be a super-skinny model to get someone like that. Maybe she wouldn't think anything at all except that he was hot, and then she would walk on. I didn't know. It was hard to be someone else.

It did get easier as I went along. The lingerie store, of course, had women plastered in each window wearing next to nothing on their perfect, airbrushed, surgically enhanced bodies. That was a no-brainer. It was easy to see how that might have affected my sister. It even affected me, and I've always been pretty confident. I looked at the girls in the pictures and wondered what it would take for me to look like them. Surgery, definitely. Starvation, probably. I'm not fat, but I have a lot of muscle.

Almost every single store had a message about appearance, which was obvious, since the whole point of stores is to sell things, but it still kind of shocked me when I thought about it. There were nutrition stores that were filled with diet pills, entire stores dedicated to skin and makeup, and, of course, plenty of clothing stores with teeny tiny skinny mannequins in the windows wearing teeny tiny skinny clothes. In one of the big department stores, I saw a grainy-looking ad for perfume that pictured a skinny woman wearing a low-cut designer gown and smudged eye makeup. She reclined on a bed as though she'd been thrown there. I didn't like it. There was something scary about the whole thing, and about the fact that a lot of the ads I'd seen were similar: sex and violence and victimization tied up with a pretty bow.

A girl and her mom stood at one of the makeup counters, both of them peering into one of those big round mirrors that reflect back every flaw in great detail. "See those lines around my eyes?" the mother said to her daughter. "That's what you don't want to have happen to you." The daughter nodded, and the woman behind the counter turned to select a product from the shelf behind her.

I left the department store and wandered into a store I liked: one that carried the kind of stuff I wore (jeans, hoodies, sweaters, T-shirts). Music videos played in the background. Once again, all the girls were pretty and skinny. Once again, the guys had a lot more clothes on than the girls did.

Hoping for a reprieve, I ducked into my favorite sports store. More television monitors with music videos. Even if you moved away from the screens, the speakers blasted the music into your ears. The whole mall was full of images and refrains that seeped in through your eyes and your ears while you thought that you were just looking at a shirt or a pair of running shoes or a jar of lotion.

And, of course, there was the food. Candy stores, greasy hamburgers, oily pizza, swirls of ice cream, and twisted, doughy pretzels with salt on top—all the things that you're not supposed to eat if you want to look like the women in the ads. All the things that, to Carly, were the enemy, because she couldn't eat them without guilt.

I began to see why my irate sophomore English teacher had once said that all culture had become junk. It didn't seem like anything in the entire mall might actually be good for you.

Except, maybe, for the piano store. A girl and her father stood looking at a piano and I stopped to watch them. The girl sat down on the bench and played a few measures of a song I recognized as a Bach piece, one I'd never learned to play. Carly could play it, though. She was the only one of us who'd stuck with piano lessons for more than a couple of years and the only one with any true musical ability. But it had been months since she'd sat down at the piano in our house. I turned away.

We're taught about temptation in Young Women—how it can sneak up on you. That day in the mall, I also realized that Carly's temptation was blared loud and clear in radio ads, in full-color pictures hanging in store windows, and on television screens. It was literally written in the sky in the neon lights of restaurant signs and spotlighted billboards, so out in the open that we didn't even notice anymore. We looked at it and took it in and walked on by without realizing what it was and what it meant.

It made me realize how strong Carly really was. How strong all of us teenage girls really are. We walk this gauntlet every time we go to the mall, turn on the radio, or listen to people talk. Almost no one tries to lift us up. Almost everyone wants to bring us down. It's amazing that we stay standing as long as we do.

Something needs to happen. Something needs to change. But what?

I felt kind of depressed. No wonder Carly never felt good enough. Even though Amy told us that media and culture weren't the entire problem, it was easy to see how they were a huge part of it. A line from a talk I loved by Elder Jeffrey R. Holland came to mind: *"The world has been brutal with you in this regard."* All day, every day, women and girls are told that they're not good enough. Is it any wonder that sometimes even the strongest of us believe it, even for a minute?

CHAPTER 31

Spent and tired, I rested my head against the edge of the bathtub next to the toilet. The cool hard edge of the porcelain pressing into my forehead brought relief: it felt solid, and I felt shaky. I thought about Carly. How many times had she done this? She made herself throw up, but did she ever get used to it? Or to the feeling afterward?

Thanks to the stomach flu, I was really going the extra mile in my assignment to imagine what it might be like to be my sister.

Mom knocked on the bathroom door. "Are you okay, Juliet?"

"I think so." I stood up slowly and opened the door. "I think I have the flu. I just threw up."

"I know. I heard you. Let me get you back into bed." After I flopped back into my bed, Mom pulled my quilt snug around me and smoothed back my hair. I closed my eyes and heard her leave the room. I wanted to disappear into sleep.

Before I could, Mom came back into the room. "I brought the thermometer, Juliet. Let's take your temperature."

When the thermometer beeped, I handed it to her to read and closed my eyes again. "It's 103.2!" she said. "Do you think you could keep some Tylenol down?" I heard both worry and relief in her voice.

"Probably." I pretended not to notice the relief. Had she really been worried that I might be bulimic too? Probably not, but it was easy to worry these days. As I finally sank into sleep, I had one last thought: *It's nice to be taken care of again.*

My flu didn't last long, and soon I was back out at the high-jump pit. Now that the days were longer, I could practice more. I wanted to do better at the next meet instead of failing to clear even the very first height. When I practiced, I cleared the bar easily at the opening height, and I could clear heights a lot higher than that, too. Once, to my complete shock, I made five feet. Now I had to figure out how to do it when it counted.

"Hey, Morgan," someone called out to the other evening regular, the girl who jogged every night. *Morgan,* I thought, relieved to finally know her name.

"Hi, Savannah," Morgan called back.

"Savannah?" I turned around.

Savannah walked toward me, looking uncertain. "Hi, Juliet. Morgan told me that you practiced here after the rest of the team went home."

"Yeah, I do. What's up?"

"Um, I wanted to talk to you, but I didn't want to do it in the hall at school. I've been wondering how Carly is doing."

I felt horrible. Hadn't anyone told her anything? "She's staying in the residential program at that center for a while. Did you know that?"

"Yeah, your mom called and told me when Carly first went in. But I haven't heard anything since then. Carly can't call out or anything, right?"

"No. They think it's a good idea to limit her contact with other people right at the beginning. I haven't talked to her either. Only my parents have so far."

"I really miss her." Savannah was trying not to cry.

I put my arm around her. "Me too."

"Nothing is the same without her, you know?"

"I do." My heart went out to Savannah. I hadn't thought much about how Carly's friends were dealing with this. Payton North was poisonous, but most of the cheerleading squad, like Savannah, were good friends with Carly.

"What have you heard lately?" she asked.

"Well, not much. She told my mom that she has a new friend named Sophie. Mom thinks that's really good for Carly because it sounds like Sophie is determined to get better. She's a senior now and she feels like she's wasted too much time in high school on bulimia."

Savannah looked sad. "I'm glad Carly has someone who understands. I wish I could have helped her."

"So do I."

"Do you think the treatment will work?"

"I sure hope so." I wanted the program to work with every fiber of my being. I didn't want Carly to have to go through this again. How many girls—like Jonah's sister Claire—had to go through the program more than once? My parents didn't talk much about money, but I knew our insurance didn't cover all of Carly's treatment and that they'd had to use some of their savings. I didn't know if they could afford another round of treatment, although I knew they'd do anything to help Carly.

"I have a letter for her. Will you give it to her when they start allowing stuff like that?"

"Of course. And I'll try to keep you more in the loop, Savannah. I'm sorry."

As Savannah walked away, I thought about all the times I'd wanted to help Carly and failed. I thought about that time at the movies with the popcorn. I thought I was doing something fun with Carly and that the popcorn filled her up the way it did me, but it wasn't the same. She ate it and got rid of it and was still hungry.

I knew all about hungering for something. I read and read the scriptures and didn't feel anything. I sat in my Young Women's class with the other girls and tried and tried to feel the feelings they were feeling, and I felt nothing. When my seminary class had a special testimony meeting after learning about the martyrdom of the Prophet Joseph Smith, I listened to the testimonies and wished my heart would fill with fire and my eyes would fill with tears and my soul would fill with knowledge.

Feeling discouraged, I stood alone at the edge of the high-jump pit and tried to clear my mind before I jumped. I stretched my arms as high as they would go and then leaned over to touch my toes. When I stood up, I leaned forward and then back, visualizing my approach one more time before I started to run. I picked up speed and got ready to jump, but I pulled up short and jogged past instead.

No one saw me, but I felt shaken. I'd failed the approach, something I hadn't done in more than a year—not since I first learned to jump. What happened?

It's okay, I told myself. *No big deal.* In the high jump, a failed approach won't automatically count against you as a failed attempt. You can try again as long as you haven't broken the plane of the bar, which means that you can't let your hand or any other body part go under (or over) the bar.

But still . . . I didn't like the way I'd lost my focus. If you want to clear the height, you have to be committed. Somewhere in my mind I hadn't been committed to that jump.

At the edge of the pit I took a good long look at the thin silver bar suspended above the bulky blue mats. *You* will *jump,* I told myself. *You* will *go for it. So what if you don't clear the bar. You'll never get better at this unless you give it everything you have.*

The only thing I could cling to, the only thing I had that looked like faith anymore, was this: Both Carly and I had once felt full. She looked in the mirror and liked who she saw. I sat in church and knew that the truth was there. I believed that with effort and practice and commitment those things would happen again. It was all I believed, and I hung on to it as tightly as I could.

Deep breath. Lean forward, lean back. Eyes on the bar. Run. Run. Run. *Jump.*

I held my breath as I sailed over the bar.

CHAPTER 32

April

My next track meet coincided with my parents' first meeting with Carly at the center. I was glad that they could go see her, and I was glad that no one in my family would see me jump.

Half the track team had gone to a bigger meet at another school, so the meet at South was particularly low-key. There were even fewer people than usual scattered throughout the stands and only a couple of team buses in the parking lot. Prime Juliet Kendall jumping conditions.

I cleared the initial height. *Thank goodness.*

Then I cleared the height after that, and the height after that, and soon I was the only one left. Not that that meant much at such a small meet, but still. I was the last girl standing.

The official in charge of the high jump set the bar at five feet and smiled at me encouragingly. "If you clear this one, you'll qualify for state," he said.

On my first attempt everything felt right, and I thought I might have it until my heel touched the bar and it fell to the mat. On the second attempt, I psyched myself out and I wasn't even close—I hit the bar with my shoulders on my way over.

Before the third attempt, I closed my eyes. *It's dusk, and you're all alone on the South High track. Morgan is running around the turn at the other end, and no one is watching. No one is watching.*

I almost cleared the height. I thought I did. My heel brushed the bar so lightly that I almost didn't even feel it. Then I heard the bar hit the mat as I landed.

Shoot, I thought, *I almost qualified.*

Then I thought, *Wait a minute. Why do I care?* I never planned for high jumping to be about the competition. It was about what happened at practice: those moments out on the track under the sky where I worked through my fears and my uncertainties and remembered how to pray. When I played basketball, my prayers happened before each game. With high jumping, it felt like I prayed through every practice. It was different, unspoken—more a clearing of my mind—but something about it felt like prayer all the same.

"How did your meet go?" Dad asked me when I got home.

"Pretty good."

"Did you clear the opening height?"

"Yeah." I decided not to mention the fact that I'd almost qualified for state. I was scared enough about raising my own expectations; I didn't want to raise anyone else's. Besides, I needed to find out about something much more important. "But that doesn't matter. Tell me about Carly."

"She seems . . . good." Mom smiled. "It's still early. It hasn't even been a full month yet. But it was so wonderful to see her in person. She looks better. I think the worst part of the stay is behind her."

Dad added, "You can come with us next week to visit. Carly's really excited to see you."

"Oh." Even though I wanted to see Carly, the idea of visiting her made me nervous. I didn't want to do anything wrong. I didn't want to mess anything up.

"Carly gave me a letter to give to you."

"Really?"

Mom nodded and handed it to me.

"I don't think I've ever gotten a letter from Carly before."

"Writing is part of her therapy. Something about this letter is part of her recovery."

I took the letter up to my room to read it. I knew my parents wanted to know what it said, but they let me go and I was glad. Sometimes you want something to be yours for a little while before you share it.

Hey Juliet,

One of the things we're supposed to do here is think about who we've hurt (besides ourselves) and apologize to them. I think that you're one of the people I've hurt the most, and I feel really bad about that. You've always looked out for me and been a great sister. I want you to know that I know that, even if I haven't been good about showing it the last few months. I owe you a lot of apologies.

I'm sorry for getting mad at you for telling Mom and Dad about the laxatives and everything. I know you were trying to help me. I couldn't see that at the time.

I'm sorry that I told you it was sick that you were becoming friends with that guy from therapy and that I made you promise not to hang out with him. You should be friends with whoever helps you. I know how important it is to have a good friend to help you get through stuff. I've made a friend here who has helped a lot.

I'm sorry for lying to you and telling you guys that I was doing okay when I really wasn't.

There are probably more things that I should apologize to you for, but this is a start, right? I hope you understand. I'm not very good at this letter-writing thing. Hopefully I'll get better. I love you and I miss you.

And I'm sorry for all the pain I've caused. I really am.

Carly

I read the letter about fifteen times, and each time I felt a little more encouraged, a little more absolved for all my mistakes and missteps. And Carly sounded like she was doing better. When I read, I looked for hope in her words, and I always found it. Maybe this could work after all. Maybe things were going to be okay. I'd thought that before and it hadn't worked out, but I couldn't help but think it again as I looked at my sister's writing, firm and clear, on that piece of paper.

All Carly really needed to write was that one sentence at the end of the letter: *I love you and I miss you.*

So I started my letter back to her with the same lines:

Dear Carly,

I love you and miss you too. And I'm sorry too...

I waited until the next day, Saturday, before I called Jonah. As soon as he answered his phone, I said, "The ban has been lifted."

"Juliet?"

"Yeah, it's me."

"So you're saying we can hang out now?"

"Yeah. Like right now, if you wanted."

Jonah laughed. "I'm working right now. But I can come over to your house in a couple of hours. If that's okay with your parents."

"I'm sure it's fine. They'll be here." I gave him my address.

"I'll bring something for you. It's the closest thing to guaranteed therapy that I've found, next to shoveling snow."

"I can't wait."

I kept looking out the window to see if Jonah had arrived yet. Finally, I saw someone pull into our driveway. It had to be him. I opened the door and then I did a double take. The car was a Land Rover. It was an old one, but still. Did *Jonah* drive a Land Rover?

He did. He climbed out of the car, wearing jeans and his work T-shirt.

I opened the door for him and he grinned when he saw me. "Hey," he said, climbing up the porch steps. He handed me a CD. "This is for you."

"Thanks." I glanced down at it. Through the clear plastic cover, I saw that Jonah had written ESCAPE MUSIC in blocky letters on the shiny silver surface of the disc. What songs were on there? Would they really help me escape?

Jonah stood there, waiting. "Come on in," I said, opening the door wider.

He gestured to his feet. "I should probably leave my shoes outside. They're filthy."

"Oh, it's okay."

"No, really. I'm not going to make a good impression on anyone if I track mud through your house." Now that Jonah stood closer to me, I could tell that he was already getting a little tan from working outside, and he smelled like grass and dirt and gasoline. He pulled off his shoes and came inside. "Hey, would it be all right if I asked you for a glass of water?"

"Of course. The kitchen's right in here," I said, guiding him through the family room where my dad sat watching an NBA game. I steered Jonah behind the couch, hoping to stay out of my dad's line of vision so that he wouldn't take it upon himself to hang out with us. Unfortunately, there's no such thing as being out of Dad's line of vision if you're a guy hanging out with a Kendall girl. As I'd anticipated, Dad caught sight of us and wandered into the kitchen right as I handed Jonah a glass of ice water. I sighed inwardly.

"Dad, this is Jonah. Jonah, this is my dad."

Jonah put the glass down on the table and shook hands. "It's good to meet you, Mr. Kendall."

"You too, Jonah." Dad sat down at the table. "Tell me a little bit about yourself."

It took us fifteen minutes to get rid of my dad. Jonah's glass of water sat on the table, ice cubes cracking and melting, while Dad asked Jonah about what his parents did, what he liked to do, what his favorite sports teams were, what classes he liked in school, what his blood type was, etc., etc. I almost said something to tease my dad about giving Jonah the third degree but I didn't. Dad was still upset with himself for not knowing much about Carly and Jaydon until it was over.

Finally, Dad decided to go back into the family room to finish watching the game. "Feel free to join me, you two," he said.

"Maybe in a little bit," I told him.

Once he was out of earshot, I blurted out, "I didn't know you had a Land Rover." The minute the words left my mouth, I grimaced in embarrassment. What was with me? I thought I'd stopped making those kinds of blunders. It didn't matter what kind of car he drove, even if it was the polar opposite of Old Blue.

What I said next was even worse. "I mean, I didn't know you were rich." I clapped my hands over my mouth, wishing the words back. And I'd thought my dad had embarrassed me!

"My *family* is rich," Jonah said. Luckily, he looked amused.

"Sorry," I apologized. "That doesn't matter. I don't know why I brought it up."

"It doesn't matter," he agreed. "My family may have money, but we're still messed up."

"But at least you guys can pay for treatment and therapy and everything." I couldn't seem to stop myself.

"That's true. We are really lucky that way. But I think my parents would sell everything they owned to get help for Claire." He sighed and took a drink from his glass. "They have all this money put aside for her to go back to college. I wonder if she'll ever be able to use it."

"How old is she?" I asked, surprised. Jonah always spoke so protectively of his sister—I'd assumed she was younger.

"She's twenty-one. Everything started when she went away for her freshman year at Stanford. That's how we missed it for so long." Jonah cleared his throat. "Anyway. Let's listen to that CD. Do you guys have a CD player in your living room or somewhere?"

"Yeah," I said, counting my blessings that it wasn't in the family room with my dad.

"Great. Let's go listen to the first song. Here's the thing, though—if you want to really hear what's happening with the music, you have to close your eyes."

"Yeah, sure," I said, teasing. Then I saw he meant it. "Oh. You're serious?"

"Well, I *was*." He gave me an embarrassed grin. "But now that you're mocking me I'm not so sure."

"No, I'm willing to try it," I said, trying to make him feel better. But still, part of me thought, This *is your guaranteed therapy? Seems kind of cheesy to me.*

We went into the living room and I slid the CD into the player. Then we sat awkwardly on the couch. To my surprise, Jonah reached over and took my hand. He raised his eyebrows at me as if to ask if it was okay. I decided that it was and smiled at him.

"Okay, now close your eyes," Jonah said, as the first notes of the music drifted across the room. I glanced over to make sure that he really did close his eyes (yup) and then I followed suit, hoping that my parents wouldn't come into the room right then. What would they think if they saw us sitting on the couch, holding hands in broad daylight and listening to emo music or something? They'd think I'd lost my mind. I laughed a little in spite of myself.

"Juliet. Listen."

"Okay." I tried to quiet down.

The music swelled out of the speakers. It wasn't emo at all. After a few seconds, I could name the song. "Abide with Me; 'Tis Eventide" by the Mormon Tabernacle Choir. *So Jonah is probably LDS,* I realized. He'd made a few comments in our meetings that made me think he might be, but I'd never asked.

"You brought MoTab?"

"Yeah. What were you expecting?"

"I don't know. I guess I didn't expect you to find an escape in something like this."

"I find it where I find it," Jonah said.

And that, I thought to myself, *is rather appealing.* I tried to focus on the music instead of Jonah, but it was hard. Carly hadn't been entirely wrong. I liked Jonah because he understood how I felt, but didn't I also like Jonah because he was a good-looking guy?

Pay attention to the music, I told myself, and I did. At first, I couldn't figure out how the words applied to what we were going through, but then the choir sang the chorus:

> *O Savior, stay this night with me;*
> *Behold, 'tis eventide.*
> *O Savior, stay this night with me;*
> *Behold, 'tis eventide.*

Exactly. I felt like our family was in the middle of an eventide—a darkening evening that was cold and frightening. There was nothing I wanted more than for the Savior to stay with me as we stepped into a place where I could not see.

Partway through the song, it happened. What Jonah had promised. I started to feel differently. Jonah's hand no longer sent little thrills up and down my spine, but was instead a strong warm current that held me to the moment and to the words of the song. I realized that Jonah wasn't so much holding my hand as a boyfriend would, but, instead, it was as though he wanted to tell me, *You are not alone in this.* I held on tight, kept my eyes closed, and listened. As I did, the song and the connection filled an empty place inside of my heart and I did not feel alone.

Later, after Jonah left, my mom knocked on the open door to my room.

"I saw you and Jonah in the living room," she said.

I didn't turn around. I kept my head bent over the quote I was copying onto a piece of paper. "He brought me a CD to listen to. He said it would be therapeutic."

"Is holding hands part of the 'therapy'?" Mom's voice was teasing.

But I didn't want to let her laugh at us. "I guess. That was really nice, too, but not like you're thinking. It was just—" I finally turned around in my chair to look at her, and her eyes softened. She could tell that I'd been crying. "Good," I finished. "It was good."

"So it *was* therapeutic. It worked." Mom's eyes searched my face.

"I don't know what you mean by 'worked,' but it helped."

After she left, I looked at the piece of paper in my hand. On it, I'd written another portion of Elder Holland's talk, a part that came to mind as I held Jonah's hand and tried to remember and believe that I was not alone: "Your Father in Heaven knows your name and knows your circumstance. He hears your prayers. He knows your hopes and dreams, including your fears and frustrations. And he knows what you can become through faith in Him."

Later that night, I went downstairs to get the CD. As I got closer to the living room, I heard the strains of "Abide with Me; 'Tis Eventide." Had we left the CD player on? As I reached for the light I noticed a dark shape on the sofa.

"Mom?" I said softly.

All I heard was a long, shuddering sob.

I went to sit next to her. I reached out and held her hand like Jonah had held mine earlier. Her fingers tightened around mine as the voices of the choir sang to us.

When they sang the final verse, my eyes filled with tears again. That verse seemed to be exactly about me and what I was going through with my testimony:

> *Abide with me; 'tis eventide,*
> *And lone will be the night*
> *If I cannot commune with thee,*
> *Nor find in thee my light.*
> *The darkness of the world, I fear,*
> *Would in my home abide.*
> *O Savior, stay this night with me;*
> *Behold, 'tis eventide.*

I realized that the words of the song were the same ones I'd said over and over to Carly in the hospital. *Abide with me. Abide with me. Don't leave. Stay here.*

We always want the people we love to stay. We don't want them to leave us. It's not so much that we don't want them to grow and change; it's more that we don't want the time together to end. I didn't want my sisters to leave, I didn't want Nate or Megan or Coach Giles to leave. Most of all, I didn't want Carly to leave.

But, I realized as I listened to the song, there is only One who can always stay. So I prayed to Him: *Stay with me. Stay with me.*

CHAPTER 33

"How long before Carly comes in?"

Mom put a hand on my shoulder. "Not long. The last time we came, we only waited for a minute."

I could tell that the people who ran the center had gone to a lot of trouble decorating the family meeting room where we waited for Carly. The furniture seemed homier than I expected—armchairs that actually looked comfortable, a polished wooden coffee table with a few dents and scars along the side. There were carpets and paintings and plants instead of linoleum and medical charts and hand-sanitizer dispensers.

But there was only so much they could do. The carpet was industrial strength. The paintings on the wall were the kind of washed-out, innocuous prints that you see only on the walls of hotel rooms: a bowl of flowers, a woman holding a straw-brimmed hat and looking out to sea. It was a place somewhere between a hospital and home.

A row of African violets lined the windowsill. The purple of the flowers was so bright that I thought they must be fake, so I pinched one of the leaves. "Oops," I said, embarrassed. The plant was real, and I'd ruined the leaf.

The door opened and I shoved the fragment of green into my pocket and turned.

Carly came into the room, smiling at us and wearing a T-shirt and jeans that I'd forgotten about but remembered immediately. *What else have I forgotten?* I wondered. She looked a little nervous, and she was still thin, but mostly she seemed okay. I felt relieved. In my worst-case scenarios, she had looked glassy-eyed and out of it, or had been upset and begged us to take her home.

Mom and Dad told me that the first two weeks had been hard for Carly, but she was doing better now. They'd told me that the counselors were pleased with Carly's progress. It had sounded almost too good to be true, but I could look at Carly and see that something had changed.

No one came into the room with her, which surprised me. I don't know what I'd expected—nurses with white caps following her around with notepads, like in a scene from an old movie or something. Carly didn't look around at anything, and it reminded me that she'd been here before. She had spent hours and days in a place that I knew almost nothing about and weeks in rooms I couldn't even picture. That was strange.

My parents both hugged her, and then it was my turn. I put a big smile on my face, ready to be supportive and wonderful, ready to act like a sister who had it together and who didn't destroy plants in the family meeting room.

"Hey," I said, throwing my arms around her.

"Hey, Jule." She hugged me back.

When we pulled apart, we both smiled and looked around, not sure where to begin. Mom and Dad sat back down on the couch. At first, I sat next to them, but then that left Carly alone in an armchair facing the three of us. It looked like we were interviewing her as a prospective member of our family or something. I didn't like it. I stood up and started dragging another chair over next to her.

Everyone watched me. "Don't mind me," I said. "Just rearranging the furniture."

Carly looked amused. "You'll have to put that back. They're really particular here."

"I'll put it back," I promised.

"So what's new out there in the free world?" Carly asked.

No one laughed.

"That was a joke." Carly rolled her eyes.

"Let's see," Mom said. "Emma's doing well. She's closing in on her one-year mark. She sent a letter for you, and so did Maddie. Maddie's going to try to come up for the next family meeting if she can get away from school." Mom put the envelopes with Emma and Maddie's letters in them on the end table next to Carly.

"I have a letter for you from Savannah too." I pulled it out of my pocket and added it to the pile. "She found me at the track. She really misses you."

"I should write to her," Carly said. "It's hard to know what to say."

"The letter you wrote me was good."

She smiled at me. "Yeah? I'm glad you liked it." There was a pause. "So, have you been on a date with that guy yet?"

"Not a date. But he came over to the house once to bring me some music."

"What kind of music?"

"Um, some Mormon Tabernacle Choir."

"You're kidding."

"Nope. I liked it."

"What's his name again?"

"Jonah."

"He has a name from the Bible *and* he listens to MoTab?"

"Yeah."

"He'd better be cute," Carly teased.

I was determined to change the subject. For one thing, I didn't want to get teased about Jonah, and more importantly, we were here to talk about Carly, not me. "But I want to hear about you. Mom says you've got some good friends in here."

"Yeah, I do. Especially Sophie. She's a couple of years older than I am and she's been like a big sister to me."

Ouch. That hurt, but I tried to hide it. "Oh, really?"

"Yeah. She's really motivated to get better, and she keeps telling me to do it now so I don't waste my life. She's been bulimic for six years, and she says she'll never get those years back." Carly looked down at her hands. "I don't want that to happen to me."

Mom reached forward and patted Carly's knee.

"We don't want that to happen to you, either," Dad said.

It was quiet again, which made me uncomfortable. It felt like those moments in fast and testimony meeting when no one gets up to speak and you think, *Somebody say something! This time is going to waste!* We only had an hour with Carly. I didn't want to squander one second of it.

Carly looked back up. "So what else is new? Are you still high-jumping, Jule?"

"Yeah, and that reminds me. Do you know someone your age named Morgan?"

"Morgan?" Carly thought for a second. "Yeah, I do. Morgan Carpenter. Really long, dark hair, kind of short and shy."

"That's the one."

Carly was surprised. "How do you know Morgan?"

"We both go to the track when everyone else is finished practicing."

"Is she high-jumping too?"

"No, she runs and walks around the track. Mostly runs, now. She's getting better and better."

"I bet she's trying to lose weight. Some of the people in our class were really mean to her because she's overweight. Do you remember when she tried out for the cheerleading squad last year?"

"*That's* why she looked familiar," I realized, feeling ashamed of myself. Morgan had been on the video, but only for the first round of tryouts. She'd been on the back row and I'd glanced over her and then moved on almost immediately. I was looking for Carly. Morgan had registered only as, *Short chubby girl, isn't going to make it, not my sister.*

"It was really bad after she tried out. People had been calling her 'Moo-gan'—like a cow—for a while, but after tryouts, things got even worse. Some of the other cheerleaders were horrible. They were sort of mad that she'd tried out because they thought it was ridiculous that someone like her would even think she could be a cheerleader. They were merciless."

My heart ached for Morgan.

"You didn't do that, did you?" my mom asked, a look of horror on her face.

"No, Mom," Carly said, weariness in her voice. "Most of us are nice. It was only one or two of the girls. I wasn't mean to Morgan. I'm only mean to myself."

The room was quiet again. Carly broke the silence herself this time. "Actually, that's not true. One of the things I have to own is that my bulimia is hard on you guys, too."

We talked for a while longer, about what Carly was doing in the center and the things she'd learned. She told us about the people she'd met. I asked her if she knew Claire, Jonah's sister, and she paused.

Before she could answer, we heard a gentle knock on the door and a woman opened it a little. "You have about two minutes of your visit left," she told us.

We all stood up to hug each other. I promised myself that I would not break down, but when it was my turn to hug Carly, I lost my resolve and my voice wavered when I spoke. "I'm so excited for you to come home."

I expected her to say, *Me too,* but she didn't. She gave me one last hug and then walked away.

I turned on Jonah's CD again. "Abide with Me; 'Tis Eventide" finished playing, and for once, I didn't hit repeat. I let it go on to the next song.

I'd gotten kind of hung up on "Abide with Me." I listened to it everywhere, in my car and in my room and in the living room. It had become the soundtrack for my week. After so many times through that one song, I knew all the verses by heart and I sang along. When I was in the halls at school or out practicing at the high-jump pit, I repeated the words over and over to myself.

The choir started singing "O My Father."

I smiled. "O My Father" had always been one of my favorite hymns. I loved the references in the third and fourth verses to a Mother in heaven. It was nice to know that there was a woman who cared about us too and that the celestial kingdom was a place filled with families.

I liked picturing men and women, couples and families, hand in hand throughout the eternities.

But that time, the line that stood out to me was a different one: *Yet ofttimes a secret something whispered, "You're a stranger here."*

Exactly. I felt like a stranger in my own life. I felt like I had lost who I was and what it meant to be Juliet Elisabeth Kendall.

I used to know. I was a South High Panther. I was a varsity basketball player. I was Nate Carmine's almost-girlfriend, and Megan Gelty's best friend. I was a good student. I was a good sister. I was a Kendall girl, and all that that meant. I was a team player. I was a girl with a testimony.

It didn't seem like I was any of those things anymore.

I felt like I was flying, but it didn't feel good. It didn't feel the way flying is supposed to feel, because I wasn't sure I could get back home. I felt like I was looking back down at the person I used to be, at the place I used to inhabit, at the life I used to have, from a height farther and farther away. I worried that if I couldn't get back down to the ground, back down to something to anchor me, I would drift away into nothingness.

After the song was over, I went back to "Abide with Me." As the music washed over me, I sang along. *Abide with me. Abide with me.*

At dinner, Mom and Dad and I talked about the visit. We all had the same opinion—that it had gone well—and we all felt cautiously optimistic.

"Did you hear what she said at the end, though?" I asked. "I said I couldn't wait for her to come home, and she kind of blew it off. I thought she'd be counting down the days."

"I think it's a little scary to think about leaving the center," Mom explained. "She feels safe in there. In some ways, I'm sure it's nice for her to have all the distractions removed."

Even though that made sense, it still made me feel a little defensive. Living with us had to be better than living in the center, right? "But at first she hated it, didn't she? She missed us."

Dad nodded. "It was rough at the beginning. Now she's got a lot of friends who understand exactly what she's going through."

"Don't feel bad about Sophie," Mom added. She knew me too well. When Carly had said that Sophie was like a big sister, that hurt my feelings more than I wanted to admit. "I know it's hard to feel like other people are helping her when we can't. But as long as she's getting the support she needs, that's the important thing. Right?" She sounded as though she were convincing herself as well as me. I knew this was hard on her too.

"Right." When I thought about the visit and took my own feelings of hurt out of it, there were a lot of things to be happy about. Carly hadn't thrown up in several days, something she was very proud of. She looked better. She seemed more like the take-charge Carly, the one who made things happen. I dared to think that things were looking up.

Later that night, I rummaged around under the bathroom sink trying to find the nail polish remover and pulled out a plastic bag with something inside it. It was the box of Carly's red hair dye from back in the fall. She'd never used it. Underneath the label Awesome Auburn, a model beamed up at me. Her shiny, red-tinted swirls of hair covered the rest of the space on the box.

A little while later I stared at myself in the mirror. Staring at my long reddish hair. My face looked paler than it had with the natural brown and my eyes looked wider, but maybe that was because I was surprised at what I'd done.

I definitely looked different. I wondered if Carly would approve.

"Juliet? Before you go to sleep—" Mom stopped short at the sight of me. "Oh."

"My hair's red," I told her unnecessarily.

"It looks—different." She hurried to add, "It looks good, honey. I'm just surprised."

She wasn't the only one. At school the next day, one of my teachers asked me if my new hair color indicated feelings of rebellion. Another teacher thought I was a new student. Max passed me in the hall and didn't say hello.

Hanna stopped me before my third-period class. "Oh, nice. Is this a sign of rebellion?"

"No. Why does everyone keep saying that?"

"It's kind of drastic. Good drastic. You've even got a little of your Kendall swagger back."

"I don't swagger!"

"*Sure,*" Hanna said, and then she walked off down the hall, swinging her hips exaggeratedly to make me laugh.

Jonah noticed it too. When he picked me up to go to our meeting, the first thing he said was, "Hey, nice hair."

"It's a sign of rebellion."

"Really?"

"No. But everyone seems to think it is."

"What is it, then?"

I thought for a second. "I think it's a sign of change."

"You look good."

"Thanks."

I didn't know if it was the hair, or the fact that Carly was doing better, or that Hanna had told me I was getting my swagger back, or that Jonah said I looked good, or what, but things were different at the next track meet.

I warmed up by myself like usual and sized up my competitors. None of them paid any attention to me. They didn't think I was a threat. Until that day I would have agreed with them.

Or maybe they didn't recognize me with my red hair. I smiled to myself. It felt good to be incognito.

When we started doing practice jumps, I ran fast and jumped high and it felt exactly right. I heard a couple of the girls murmur to each other. All of a sudden I felt that old fire, and I looked over at my competition and thought, *Bring it.*

I cleared the first height with plenty of room to spare. I could feel it.

They kept raising the bar. I kept clearing it. The murmurs grew louder, and a few people started clapping in the stands.

It didn't take long before the bar was set at five feet. Qualifying height. *I can clear this height in practice,* I thought to myself. *I can clear it here and now if I want to. And I do* want *to.*

I cleared it easily, just like when I was alone on the track at dusk. Piece of cake.

Grinning fiercely, I jumped off the mats and beamed at the official, who smiled back. "Congratulations," he said. "You've qualified for state." I heard a couple of people clapping right there in the pit, and I turned around, surprised. Were my parents there? I'd told them not to come for a while and I'd thought they understood. But it wasn't my parents. It was Coach Walker and Megan.

"Great job, Juliet!" Coach Walker slapped me on the back. "You're going to state! It's been years since South has had anyone qualify in the high jump."

"Way to go, Jule," Megan said quietly.

"Thanks."

I cleared the next height, still riding my wave of elation, but then I missed the one after that. Reality started to sink in. What had I done? I was right back where I didn't want to be—in a place where people counted on me and expected something from me.

I could kind of understand why Carly might be nervous about leaving the center.

So I didn't tell anyone at home that I'd qualified for state. Just in case I decided to walk away again.

CHAPTER 34

Jonah called to tell me the news that his sister Claire had completed her stay and was coming home. "Tomorrow's the day. It's official now."

"That's great." Silence. "I mean, isn't that great? I'm sorry. I guess I assumed—"

"I hope it's great. Her counselor is still worried about her. She's not sure Claire really wants to change. My mom and dad are worried we're going to have to take the next step."

"Which is . . . ?"

"Inpatient medical care. Treatment in a hospital."

"Oh."

Jonah sighed. "But maybe it's going to be fine. None of us wants to doom her before she even has a chance. Maybe she's better this time. Who knows? We'll have to wait and see."

"Good luck." That didn't seem like enough. "I'll be praying for you guys." With anyone else, I would feel weird saying something like that, but not with Jonah. He'd brought me a CD of hymns, after all. He knew what it was like to worry about your sister and how it felt to watch your family fall apart. We were more than friends, in a way I'd never been with anyone before. We were people who understood each other.

"Thanks."

My phone call from Jonah wasn't the only important one of the day. Later that evening Mom came into my room. "Carly's counselor called me a few minutes ago."

"Oh?"

"Today wasn't a good day for Carly. She'd been doing much better about not purging, but things were rough for her this morning."

"Oh, no."

"The counselor said that it happens to a lot of girls. They'll be doing well for a while and then have a relapse like this."

"How? I mean, how do they throw up there in the first place? Don't they make sure the girls can't do that kind of thing?"

"They do monitor the bathrooms and the showers, but the girls can still find a way if they really want to." Mom sighed. "I guess they have some plants at the center and she threw up in one of them after lunch. She hoped no one saw her, but Sophie did. Sophie told the counselor and the counselor asked Carly about it, and Carly admitted it and said that she'd thrown up after breakfast as well. She's really upset."

So I wasn't the only big sister figure who told on Carly. Mom put her arm around me. "You could write her another letter. I'm sure she would love to hear from you right now."

"What do I write about?"

"Whatever you want. I think what she needs most is to know that we love her."

Sitting at my desk, I wasted too much time as usual on worrying about what *not* to say. Finally I decided to stop worrying and start writing:

> Hey Carly,
>
> It was good to see you last week. I've missed you so much. I've read the letter you sent me about fifteen times.

I told her that I loved her and was proud of her. I told her a couple of stories about things that happened at school. When I finished up, I added one more thing:

> P.S. Do you want to know a secret? No one else knows, not even Mom or Dad or Maddie. I qualified for state in the high jump.

The next morning we woke up to more than six inches of heavy, wet, spring snow. "Are we taking another day off to watch *North and South*?" I asked my mom, and she smiled at me.

"I wish," Mom said, and I knew that she didn't just wish that we could skip work and school again. She wished that Carly was there with us. Mom peered out the window. "It's already started to melt. It won't be around for—oh, *no*."

"What?" I went to stand at the window next to her. "Oh."

The flowering plum tree at the front of our house had been covered in thousands of gorgeous pink blossoms. The new growth, combined with the weight of the snow, was too much for the tree. Several of the biggest branches had torn off, leaving bright white, gaping gashes along the dark wet trunk of the tree.

When the branches crashed to the ground, the blossoms had scattered. Even in the midst of the destruction, the delicate pink on pure white was so beautiful that I drew in my breath. It reminded me of something. The vase of Grandma's I'd broken? Maybe a little, but I didn't think that was it.

"Is the tree ruined?" I asked.

"I don't think so," Dad said from behind us. We turned to look at him. "I'll saw those branches so that the cuts are clean and we'll hope for regrowth."

As I drove to school, I noticed other trees in other yards had lost branches in the night. Some of the trees had even been uprooted completely by the weight of the snowfall and their tangled roots dripped dark earth onto the snow. I wondered what would happen to those trees. It didn't seem like they could be saved.

I'd driven all the way to school before I realized what the pink blossoms reminded me of. They were the same color as the dress Carly tried on back in the fall when she and Megan and I went dress shopping together. In fact, the trees themselves reminded me of my sister, and other girls like her: beautiful, blossoming, and then broken by the weight of too much snow, too much pressure.

By evening, the sun had melted almost all of the snow. The track was clear and I didn't even have to shovel off the mats before I jumped, although there were little puddles of water on the surface. While I dried them off with an old towel I found in the equipment shed, I thought about Jonah and planned to call him once I finished practicing. I wanted to know about Claire's homecoming. As I finished drying off the mats and started to set the bar, I heard someone call my name. This time it wasn't Savannah.

It was Jonah. He walked over toward the pit with his hands in his pockets and his shoulders slumped.

"Hi," I said, sliding off the mats.

"Your mom said I'd find you here."

"Yeah. I was going to call you, actually."

Jonah looked around. We were the only two people on the track. Morgan had already finished up her laps and gone home. A spring breeze blew across the infield, rustling the high-jump covers on the ground and ruffling Jonah's hair. The pulleys on the flagpole clanged against the metal and it sounded like the tolling of a bell. Jonah watched the flag snap and shake in the wind for a second, and then he gestured to the high-jump pit. "So, you're shoveling snow. Mowing lawns."

"What?" At first, I didn't get it, but then I realized what he meant. "Yeah. Yeah, I guess I am." High jumping was my escape.

"Go ahead. Don't let me bug you. I'll wait on the bleachers until you're done." Without waiting for me to answer, Jonah started toward the bleachers. I had a sinking feeling in my stomach. His face was so sad, so tired. Things must not have gone well with Claire.

I changed my shoes and put the covers back on the mats. Then I climbed up into the bleachers to sit with Jonah. He looked over at me as I sat down and I looked back.

Another boy, another evening out on the track. But it was completely different. Instead of the electric feeling of I-like-you-and-I'm-pretty-sure-you-like-me that I'd felt when I was with Nate, Jonah and I shared a feeling deeper and more difficult to define.

"So . . ." I didn't quite know what to say, or whether or not I should ask him about Claire directly. I settled for something vague. "How did it go?"

Jonah looked away from me again, this time toward the mountains. "Not good."

"I'm so sorry."

"She came home and it was okay for a little while. Like an hour." Jonah took a deep breath, but didn't continue.

Neither of us said anything for a moment and then Jonah pointed to the highest peak. "Have you ever climbed up there?"

His change of subject surprised me, but I went with it. "Yeah, with my family. What about you?"

"Yeah, with Claire. She used to be good at things like that. She enjoyed them. Now if she went hiking, it'd be a death march."

He looked at me again, his face gray. "Everything went fine at first. Then my mom started dinner. Claire was helping her and she brought up going away to college. My mom said they'd talk about it later. Claire said she wouldn't eat dinner unless my parents promised she could go. Well, you know that's not good. She hadn't been out even a day and she was already making threats. My mom got really worried; Claire freaked out and said this was her life and if she wanted to be thin, that was her choice. I left when she started screaming and my mom started crying and my dad was trying to calm them both down. I went to work for a while, but we're finished for the night. So I thought I would try to find you. I don't want to go back."

Jonah had thrown me a lifeline with the music. I tried to think of something I could do in return. Before I could think of anything, though, he turned to me with tears in his eyes, and I knew what kind of tears they were. The kind that had been a long time coming. The kind that hurt to hold in, but hurt to let out, too.

There, in the empty bleachers, I put my arms around Jonah and he put his head down on my shoulder and just cried. As I looked out at the lonely track, I tightened my arms around the tall senior boy from a different high school who knew my pain as I knew his. I held on tight so that he would know he was not alone.

It was evening, eventide. The light on the mountains was pink: the pink of sunsets and dresses and blossoms against the snow.

CHAPTER 35

"I'm getting worried about you, Jule. Do you have a date for prom yet?"

I sighed. "No, not yet." Hanna was determined to make sure I went to junior prom. I didn't know how to convince her that I would be all right if I didn't go. I had so many other things to worry about.

"This is your *junior prom,* Juliet. You *have* to go!"

Junior prom at our high school is a very big deal. For decades, South High has held their prom at the old library building downtown. The library has high ceilings and carved railings, huge columns and elegant flat marble steps out front. On prom night, at exactly nine o'clock, a red carpet is unrolled and there's an actual promenade down the steps. They announce each junior's name and the name of their date and every couple has their turn in the limelight. Parents gather outside with their cameras waiting to capture the moment. Although I felt a little sad that I didn't have a date to the biggest dance of my high school life, I knew I'd survive. It was only one more way that my sixteenth year wasn't going according to plan.

"I don't *have* to go. The world won't end if I don't."

"I could ask my cousin to take you. I'm sure he wouldn't mind."

"*No,* Hanna." I didn't want to be someone's pity date. I'd thought about seeing if Jonah wanted to go, but then everything happened with Claire. I didn't want to bother him with something as dumb as prom when he had so much going on at home.

"Well, can you come up with a better idea?"

"Maybe I could ask Stewey Simpson," I joked.

"Too late. He's got a date."

Maybe I really *was* the only junior who wasn't going. "Honestly, it's okay, Hanna. I have other plans anyway."

"Really?" Hanna sounded dubious.

Before she could say anything else, I explained. "Carly's earned her first trip out of the center. Mom and Dad and I get to pick her up Saturday night and hang out for a couple of hours."

Hanna's face softened. "Oh. Wow. That's great, isn't it?"

I nodded. "Yeah. It's a good sign. They don't let people do this kind of thing unless there's been a lot of progress."

"Good for her. Well, if you change your mind, let me know."

Ding-dong. Dong . . . dong . . . dong . . .

"Stupid doorbell," I muttered under my breath. "Stuck *again*." The sound of the bell ringing through the house was enough to make anyone crazy, particularly if your nerves were already a little on edge like mine. I wondered if Carly felt worried at all about leaving the center tonight. If she didn't, I was worrying enough for both of us.

"Juliet, can you take care of that?" Mom called from her bedroom.

"I'm in the middle of getting ready—"

"Please—"

Before I ran down the stairs, I grabbed a pair of tweezers so that I could fix the doorbell. The last thing I needed was a constant ringing in my ears.

I opened the door. To my surprise, Jonah stood there wearing a suit and trying frantically to stop our doorbell from ringing. A bouquet of cellophane-wrapped flowers rested on the top step.

"Um, hi," I said loudly.

Jonah looked at me with a sheepish expression on his face. "Hi. I think I broke your doorbell."

"Try these." I handed him the tweezers. He reached into the doorbell with them and pulled the button back out. The ringing stopped.

"Thanks," he said, handing the tweezers back to me. "Sorry about that."

"No problem. It happens all the time." Now what? I couldn't figure out what he was doing here and I didn't know how to ask. Why the suit? Had he been to an event at church? Why didn't he call first like he usually did when he was coming over? "So . . ."

Jonah reached down and picked up the flowers. Still flushed a little with embarrassment, he held them out to me. "I'd like to take you to your prom."

"Oh, Jonah." I took the flowers—pink and red roses—from him. "Thank you. They're beautiful." I felt a little rush of gratitude that he hadn't gotten lilies.

"Don't look too closely at them. This is kind of last minute, and I had to get them at the grocery store."

I didn't know what to do. The last time someone surprised me with a date was the day after my birthday. It felt like years had passed since August, and yet it seemed like it had just happened. I could still taste the Powerade and feel Nate's kiss on my cheek.

"So are you going to say yes?" he asked with a smile.

"I don't—" I moved back and held the door open. "Come on in."

His face fell as he came inside. "You don't have a date, do you? I called your mom earlier this afternoon and she said you didn't."

"No, I don't."

"But there's someone else you'd rather go with?"

"No. Definitely no. If I went with anyone, I'd go with you."

"I should have thought of it sooner," Jonah said. "I didn't figure it out until a couple of hours ago, when we were working on the grounds at that fancy Italian restaurant and all these people in tuxes and dresses kept going in. I asked one of the guys what was going on, and he told me that South's prom is tonight." He gestured at his suit. "I didn't have time to get a tux. Sorry about that."

"That doesn't matter."

"Then why don't you want to go?"

"Jonah, I'd love to go with you, but Carly's earned her first break from the center, so we were going to go get her tonight, and—"

My mom had apparently been eavesdropping because she broke into the conversation from the stairs behind me. "Carly won't mind at all." I saw a mischievous glint in Mom's eyes, and I wondered how she'd kept the secret all afternoon long. It must have almost killed her. "In fact, I've talked to Carly personally about this, so I can speak with some authority on the matter."

"I don't have a dress—"

"You can borrow one of Maddie's," my mom said.

I looked at Jonah and couldn't help but smile. He was being so sweet. "You are such a nice guy."

"So is that a yes?"

"Yes." I wanted to hug him right then, but I had an armload of grocery-store roses, plus I suddenly felt a little shy. I turned to say something to my mom but she'd disappeared. "Um, do you mind waiting for a little while? I'm going to need to get dressed and all of that."

"No problem," Jonah said. "What time is the promenade? I hear that's the most important part."

"It's at nine. We'll definitely make it."

A few minutes later, my mom found me frantically going through the dresses in Maddie's old room. Mom put her arm around me and gave me a squeeze. "This is so exciting! Let me help you find a dress."

"Shouldn't you and Dad be getting Carly?"

"We've had a change of plans," Mom said, shoving hangers aside.

"Oh, no," I said, instantly worried.

My mom saw my anxiety. "It's okay. I called the center and talked to Carly. Dad's going to pick her up, and I'm going to help you get ready. I'll meet up with them as soon as I'm done."

"Are you sure she's okay with all of this?"

"Positive." Mom smiled. "She is really, truly, happy that you're going. Oh, that reminds me. I'll be right back. She told me where to find her makeup and said to make sure that you used it."

I laughed, feeling reassured. "That sounds about right."

My mom left the room and I looked back into the closet. Maddie's dresses hung next to Emma's, and behind those were the ones that belonged to my mom back when she was in high school. We used to love dressing up when we were little. I started clicking the hangers along the rack, looking carefully at each of my mother's dresses.

Some of them were flat-out hideous but I found a light green one that looked retro in a good way. I tried it on. It fit, and I knew that Maddie had some silver jewelry and shoes that would go with it perfectly.

I was in the middle of raiding Maddie's jewelry box when my mom came back. She stopped in the doorway and gasped, "Oh, sweetie."

I turned around. "Is it that bad?"

"No, you look beautiful. So beautiful. I can't believe that you're wearing my dress."

"It fits perfectly. I think Maddie's and Em's would all be too long."

Neither one of us knew how to do a fancy updo or anything, so we hurried and curled my hair into waves and pinned a little of it back. We got the giggles imagining what would happen if I stole Maddie's homecoming queen tiara and wore it to the dance. It felt so good to laugh with my mom and to do a normal sixteen-year-old-girl thing like getting ready for prom while a cute boy waited downstairs.

But when my mom started to help me with the makeup, I knew we were both thinking of Carly. "I forgot to take a before picture," I told my mom. "Do you think she'll forgive me?"

Mom laughed. "I hope so. You should have heard her on the phone, honey. She's so excited for you. And she's so *bossy*. She told me to tell you that you're not going anywhere without eyeliner."

The last little bit of guilt I had about going to prom went away and I laughed. The girl in the mirror in the light green dress with the wavy red hair and the borrowed slippers laughed with me. She looked like someone who was going to have a wonderful time.

As Jonah pulled into a parking spot near the library, I saw all the parents gathered around the front steps already waiting for the promenade.

"I think we made it," Jonah said, opening the car door for me.

"I think you're right." We walked along the brick pathway toward the side entrance of the building. All around us, other couples climbed out of other cars. The sounds of laughter and high heels tapping and doors shutting filled the air.

"Sorry I didn't rent one of those tonight." Jonah said as we passed a limo parked right next to the entrance. "At least I traded the Green Machine for the Land Rover before I came to get you."

"You could have driven it," I teased. "Then everyone would notice us. We could make a grand entrance and park right behind the limo."

"We're already standing out a little because I'm the only guy wearing a suit."

"Are you kidding? It's fine. I'm probably the only girl here wearing her mom's prom dress, so it all works out."

"You look great."

"You too."

"Juliet!" Hanna waved at us from the doors. "You're here! You came! Come get in line with us." She was practically jumping up and down.

I glanced at Jonah and grinned. "There's no going back now."

Jonah grinned back. "As if I would want to."

"Oh, you look so lovely." Ms. Santos said the same thing to every girl in line, but I knew she meant it each time. "Juliet Kendall," she said, writing my name on the card to give to the announcer. "And your date's name?"

"Jonah Waite. Make sure to put down that he's from Eastview High," I teased.

Ms. Santos brightened. "You go to Eastview? How wonderful that you're here tonight!"

I tugged him away before she started talking about rival schools becoming friends. We weren't the star-crossed lovers from *West Side Story*. We weren't Romeo and Juliet. Well, technically I *am* Juliet, but you know what I mean.

Jonah was thinking along the same lines. "Have I ever told you that I like your name?" he asked me. "It's got that whole tragic-romantic thing going on." I must have given him a funny look, because he started to laugh. "So, does anyone ever call you Julie?"

"No way. Jule sometimes, but never Julie."

"That's good to know."

"I like your name too. It's got that whole biblical, swallowed-by-a-whale thing going on."

Jonah laughed again. I caught a couple of girls near us checking him out, probably wondering, *Who's the cute guy with the great laugh?*

I saw Megan lining up with Nate a few couples behind us. Hanna had told me that Nate and Megan were dating again. As I looked at Megan, she turned and our eyes met. I smiled at her—a little smile, a sincere one—and then I turned away before Nate could see me and before I saw whether or not Megan smiled back.

During the promenade, the couples usually walked out very formally with their arms linked precisely together. Jonah must not have noticed or didn't care, because when it was our turn, he reached for my hand and held it. "Here we go."

We went out into the night together. Families crowded around the bottom of the steps with their faces upturned and waiting, cameras at the ready. I knew no one from my family would be watching for me. But that was okay. I was dressed in my mom's dress and Maddie's shoes and I had Carly's blessing.

When we walked into the spotlight they announced my name: "Juliet Kendall, escorted by Jonah Waite, from Eastview High."

I laughed and turned to Jonah to say something about the fact that Ms. Santos included the name of his school, but Jonah was looking somewhere else. "Look, Juliet," he whispered. I followed his gaze to a spot in the crowd where I saw three familiar faces beaming up at me.

Mom. Dad. *Carly*.

My sister had used her free time to come and see me at my prom. She lifted her hand in a wave, and I beamed at her, my eyes filling with tears. Jonah squeezed my hand. I realized that I'd stopped in my tracks there on the red-carpeted stairs, and the announcer was calling the names of the next couple in line. Our moment in the spotlight was already over.

I wanted to walk right out of line and back to where my family stood and give Carly a giant, bone-crushing hug. But I followed the path we were supposed to take down the rest of the stairs and around to the side of the building. Then I turned to Jonah.

"I can't believe Carly was here!"

"You want to try to find her?"

"Yes!"

We went back to the spot where we'd seen my family in the crowd, but we couldn't see Carly or my parents anywhere. "They must have gone to the car," I said, turning to Jonah. "Do you have your cell phone with you? I left mine at home."

He shook his head. "No, I left mine in my car. I'm sorry."

My face fell and Jonah walked faster, pulling me along. "Let's run. We might still be able to catch them."

Still holding hands, we ran toward the parking lot. I felt like Cinderella, running in a ball gown with time slipping away. I had to catch Carly before she left.

We made it halfway through the parking lot before I saw my parents' car pulling into the street. They had to get Carly back to the center before her curfew. She'd probably used up most of her time driving to the library and waiting for me to walk in the promenade.

Jonah and I ran faster, trying to catch up with the car at the stoplight. I kept my eyes focused on the car and on Carly's head, which I could see through the back window. She turned her face to the side and I saw her profile, but she didn't look back and see us.

"Wait," I said, out loud. "We're coming!"

We almost made it.

The stoplight turned from red to green, and they were gone. I was out of breath and out of time. Next to me, Jonah said, "It's okay. She knows that you saw her."

"Yeah." I'd been greedy to wish for another miracle when I'd already had two in one night. A date appearing unexpectedly on my doorstep. A sister appearing unexpectedly in the middle of a crowd.

As Jonah and I walked back toward the building, I tried to pat my hair back into place so that I'd look more like a girl at the prom instead of someone at a track meet. The promenade had just ended, and music drifted out the open door and down the marble stairs.

"What do you think?" Jonah asked. "Should we dance?"

"Of course," I said, smiling at him. He took my hand and we walked up the stairs together into the darkened ballroom. I stepped into the circle of Jonah's arms.

CHAPTER 36

May

"I can't believe you wore Mom's old dress!"

"I know. It didn't look too weird, did it?"

Carly shook her head. "Not at all. You looked gorgeous. And it was complete genius."

"How's that?" I grinned and leaned back in the armchair. "I mean, I *know* I'm a genius, but go on."

"Well, by wearing her dress, you basically guaranteed that no one else would have one like it. Do you know how many girls I saw wearing the same dress?"

"Don't tell me you counted."

If I closed my eyes, I could almost pretend that we were back at home, talking about prom in Carly's room instead of in the family meeting room at the center. My parents were letting me have one of the one-hour family visits with Carly all to myself, just the two of us. It had been months since she and I had talked one-on-one.

"It was impossible *not* to notice. Three different girls were wearing identical black dresses with rhinestones on the neckline. I don't want that to happen to me!"

"So how *do* you picture your perfect prom night?" I teased.

Carly suddenly became serious. "I want to *have* a prom night."

"What do you mean?"

"You know Sophie, that friend of mine I'm always talking about?"

I nodded.

"Sophie never went to her prom."

"What happened?"

"It's a long story."

"I have time. Unless you think she wouldn't want you to tell me."

"I'm sure she wouldn't mind as long as you didn't tell anyone else."

"I won't."

"Everything started out fine. Sophie got asked by a really nice guy and she got a great dress and everything. She was excited about it. But then as prom got closer, she got more and more worried about her weight. She kept thinking about the dinner part of the date. She didn't want to seem rude by not eating, but the idea of all those calories stressed her out. So she planned ahead and threw up more than usual all week long."

I felt awful for Sophie. Prom preparations should be things like remembering to order the boutonniere, not making yourself throw up.

"Everything went fine until they served cheesecake for dessert, precut in really big slices. Sophie ate her whole piece. She tried hard not to purge, but she kept thinking about the cheesecake and all those calories. She couldn't concentrate at the dance because she kept thinking about purging. Finally, she decided to just go to the bathroom and get it over with so she could stop worrying about it.

"Sophie knew how to throw up without making a mess or too much noise, of course, but while she was in the middle of it, some girls came in to the bathroom and startled her. She got puke all over her dress." Carly paused.

"Oh, no."

"There wasn't anything she could do. Her dress was ruined and she had nothing else to wear, of course. She called her mom on her cell phone and told her she was sick and to come pick her up. Then she asked some girls to go out and tell her date that she wasn't feeling well and had to go home. Sophie didn't even say good-bye to him herself. She snuck out of the bathroom and waited in the back of the building for her mom. After that night, her date wouldn't speak to her again. He thought she decided that she didn't like him and he felt totally humiliated because she left him at the prom. Everyone was talking about it."

"Wow."

"He was one of the people Sophie apologized to when we started writing letters. She told him the truth about what happened that night. He wrote her a really nice letter back."

"Did her parents know what really happened?"

"They figured it out. They'd had suspicions before, but when Sophie's mom saw the puke on Sophie's dress she knew something was really wrong, and she confronted Sophie. That's when Sophie started therapy, but she kept having relapses. Finally, she and her parents decided they had to try something like this. They brought her to the center and then drive up from their town every week for therapy."

"Wow," I said again.

"I know." Carly's voice was soft and serious. "You know what's scary? I could picture myself doing the same thing that Sophie did."

"You could?"

Carly nodded soberly. "Oh, yeah. Easily. There's a lot of gross and a lot of ugly that happens with eating disorders, Jule. And it's hard to remember that you were anything but gross and ugly. It's hard to believe that anyone can love you once you've done all this stuff. You can't believe that anyone could know everything you've done and still love you."

"You know we still love you, Carly."

"I know. And I don't want to spend my prom night hiding out in the bathroom and lying to my parents and hurting my date. Or spend my time at college sneaking around my roommates so I can binge. Or find out someday that I can't have kids because of everything I've done to my body. I don't want any of that."

After prom, people asked lots of questions about Jonah. Who he was, whether we were together, how I met him, why I kept him a secret for so long. Hanna was particularly merciless.

"You could have told me the truth, Jule," she said. "I didn't know that

'I don't have a date' is actually code for 'I have a super-hot, super-secret prom date that I'm not going to tell anyone about, not even my nearest and dearest friends.'"

"I didn't know he was going to ask me until the very last minute."

"So what's going on with you guys? Are you dating?"

I didn't answer her right away because I wasn't sure how to explain Jonah. Yes, he was a guy, and, yes, he was a guy who could potentially be someone I had a crush on, but he was also much more than that. He was the person who had been in the right place at the right time and done the right thing, and who cared about me in the right way. He was a part of my healing and no matter what happened or didn't happen between us, he would always matter to me.

Finally I said, "We care about each other."

"Okay." Surprisingly, Hanna let me leave it at that.

A few days after prom, I decided that it was stupid to keep hiding out in my car at lunch. What was there to hide from anymore?

Still, I had to take a deep breath as I carried my lunch into the cafeteria and looked over at my old table. If I'd wanted to, it would have been easy to pretend that everything was still the same. The sunlight still slanted through the windows onto our table. The same people were there: Nate, Megan, Max, Hanna, Chelsea, Aaron, and a few others who hung out with our group from time to time. Nate and Megan sat next to each other. Thankfully, they weren't doing anything like feeding each other bites of ice cream or kissing or something like that. Hanna was laughing, her face open and animated and her bright blonde hair glinting in the sun. Max was acting like Max: throwing fries into the air and catching them in his mouth. The table was covered in napkins and milk cartons and scuffed blue plastic trays. Everything seemed the same.

But I forced myself to look more closely—to see how things had changed.

When Megan spoke, Nate turned to her with the look on his face that used to be for me. That was all right; I'd expected that. It didn't hurt me to see it anymore, except to give me a little stab of remembering how things used to be—which, I had learned, isn't the same thing as wanting things to go back to the way they were. Looking at Megan, I remembered how people used to mistake us for sisters. I remembered all the little ways she'd reached out to me over the past few months: trying to talk to me in the hall, cheering for me at a track meet.

And Hanna. I saw her differently now, too. She'd always been a good friend, but in the past few months she had shown her true colors as a person I could count on. When I'd lost Megan, in some ways I'd gained Hanna.

Maybe, I thought as I looked at Hanna, *you don't have to have a best friend. Just enough good friends. Enough good people who take turns stepping up at different times when you need something, and to whom you feel safe giving back when it's your turn.*

And Max. Well, maybe not that much had changed about Max.

As I walked closer and closer to the table, my heart pounded like crazy and I had a death grip on my lunch bag. The moment of truth had arrived. Did my friends still have a place for me? There was only one way to find out.

"Hey, is it all right if I sit here?" I asked.

Max turned to me in surprise. The fry he'd thrown in the air came back down and hit him in the eye. "Ouch," he said.

"Of course," Megan said, and Nate nodded.

Grinning, Hanna pulled out the chair next to her and I sat down. My hands shook a little as I put my food on the table and I concentrated on setting out each item: sandwich, apple, cookie, chocolate milk. Finally, I looked back up at my friends. "So. What'd I miss?"

To my relief, everyone laughed. And if the tension and awkwardness didn't completely vanish, it lifted enough to make things livable. It felt good to be back.

While I sat there, I noticed one more difference: the light streaming through the windows was the strong, bright light of spring instead of the weaker light of winter. I pulled my chair right into the middle of that patch of sun and let it warm me, even though it was so bright it made me blink.

Finally, with only a week and a half left until the state meet, I told my parents about qualifying. Of course, they wanted to come and watch me jump.

I told Jonah too.

"That's awesome. Can I come cheer you on?"

"Um, let me get back to you on that. I don't handle pressure very well."

Jonah laughed.

"What?"

"Juliet, I think you handle pressure *very* well. Look at what you've been through this year."

Once I committed to jumping at state, I practiced even longer, using every minute of daylight. When I needed a break, I ran a lap or two with Morgan. She hardly ever walked around the track anymore.

"You can go forever," I said one evening. "How long have you been running tonight? It's got to be an hour, right?"

She smiled. "Yeah, finally. It's taken months. My goal was to be able to run for an hour, and I've finally made it."

"That's great."

"Thanks. You're jumping higher now, too."

"I guess all our hard work is paying off."

"Are you going to keep jumping once the track season is over?"

"I don't know. Maybe. You'll still be running, won't you?"

"Yeah. After all the work it took to get here, I'm not quitting now."

"I know what you mean."

After Morgan left the track, I jumped for another half hour. When I finished, I pulled the covers back over the mats and zipped them up. The evening was beautiful, like prom night the week before. I didn't want to go home yet, so I went to my car and called Jonah.

"Hey."

"Hey. I'm finished jumping. Are you at work?"

"Nope. I just finished." Jonah sounded tired, and his voice was heavy.

"Is everything okay?"

"Yeah. I've been trying to decide about school. I've been thinking about it all night."

"Oh." I wished that I could help. Jonah had always wanted to experience living away from home before he went on his mission, and he'd always planned on going to the state university a few hours away. But now, he wasn't sure what to do. He worried about leaving Claire.

"Anyway. I'm ready to escape. You want to escape?"

"Sure. What are we doing?"

"Whatever you want."

"I want—" I paused. What did I want? "I think I want to play basketball in my backyard."

"All right. Give me twenty minutes to get there. I won't waste you, though, because I know you have a big meet coming up."

"Oh, Jonah, Jonah," I said. "You have no idea who you're dealing with here. *I'll* try not to embarrass *you*."

He laughed.

It was dark by the time we met up at my house, so I flipped on the back porch lights to illuminate the basketball court in the corner of the yard. I felt a little tingle of anticipation as I grabbed a ball and dribbled it. It had been a long time since I'd played.

"This is great," Jonah said, taking in the basketball standard and the cement pad. "You guys must spend a lot of time out here."

"Yeah. My dad built it himself when we moved in ten years ago. It used to be a rose garden. When he tore it out, one of the neighbors gave him grief about it and said he ruined the yard. It *was* a really beautiful garden. But my dad told them he was growing girls instead."

"How old were you when you did these?" Jonah looked at the spot on the basketball pad where there were four footprints, each labeled with a name.

Emma's footprint was first. Then came Maddie's. Mine should have been next, but Carly had thrown a fit about always being last, so I'd given in and let her go before me. Emma and Maddie's names were printed much more neatly than mine and Carly's.

"I was six. Carly was four. She didn't know how to write yet, so I had to write her name for her. The cement was wet and Carly kept telling me how to spell her name as if I didn't know." The memory made me smile, but I didn't want to get too sentimental. I passed Jonah the ball. "Let's see what you've got."

Jonah acted nonchalant and threw the ball over his shoulder toward the hoop. It missed by a mile. I grabbed the ball and teased him, "Do you need me to lower the rim?"

In response he grabbed the ball out of my hands and hit a three-pointer that was nothing but net. He turned back to me with a huge smirk on his face.

"That's it. It's on." I started to go for the ball, but Jonah beat me to it.

"You'll have to steal it first." He dribbled the ball in front of me.

When I reached for it, he snatched it away and held it right against his chest, wrapping his arms around it.

"No fair, you cheater." I reached to take the ball away from him.

He turned and my hands closed around the pebbly surface of the basketball and the warm roughness of his fingers. Our eyes locked, and his grin became even more mischievous.

We played one-on-one for a little while and then, out of breath and laughing, we decided to play HORSE. At first we did simple shots and a few outside jumpers, but then we got more creative. That's when I made what may have been the most spectacular shot of my backyard basketball career. Eyes closed, facing backward, granny-style three-pointer.

Swish.

"Did you *see* that?" I shouted.

"Not bad," replied Jonah, pretending to yawn.

"I'll bet you a million bucks you can't make that shot."

"I *own* that shot, Kendall." Jonah turned around, took a deep breath, and closed his eyes.

Right before he released the ball, I leaned in behind him and whispered in his ear, "Don't miss."

Jonah missed. Badly. As he stood there in disbelief, I bumped my shoulder into his and teased, "Either I'm amazing or you totally choked."

Jonah turned to face me. He put his hands on my shoulders and looked me in the eyes. "I'd go with the first one."

When we danced at prom the week before, I'd wondered what Jonah felt. We danced, our hands touched, and I caught myself looking longer at his eyes, his mouth, listening more closely to his laugh and the tone of his voice. I felt something and it seemed like he must have felt something, too. But I wasn't sure.

That night on the basketball court, I didn't have to wonder anymore. I knew.

CHAPTER 37

"First call, girls' high jump. First call."

The announcer's voice boomed out over the university stadium, over the track and the high-jump pit and the bull pen. It boomed into the very corners of the complex, into the girls' bathroom, where I stood in front of the mirror pulling my hair into a ponytail. My hands shook as I tried to pull back some flyaway strands and I dropped my elastic on the cement floor.

I picked it up and started over. If I took too long, I would miss the event. They'd start without me, and I'd be disqualified. The state meet was huge. The officials couldn't go around and find every single person. You either showed up for your event on time or you missed it.

When my hair was finally in place, I still didn't leave. Girls came in and out of the bathroom all the time, nervous and excited and talking about their events. One girl sobbed to someone on a cell phone. She'd hit the hurdles too many times and had been disqualified in her heat.

I stood off to the side at the small bank of mirrors, waiting for time to run out and trying to avoid looking in the mirror. I didn't want to see myself letting this experience go past, forever beyond my grasp.

"Final call, girls' high jump. Final call."

Closing my eyes, I said a brief prayer for strength. When I opened them, I looked right at my reflection: my worried face, my blue-and-gold South High track uniform, my hair pulled up in a ponytail like Carly's. I met my own gaze in the mirror for a moment. Then I bent down and grabbed the bag with my spikes and slung it over my shoulder. My sister could battle an eating disorder day after day and meal after meal and hour after hour. I could do this. Time to jump.

I was Juliet Kendall and I did not walk away. Not anymore.

I made it to the bull pen just in time. "You cut it close, kid," the official said good-naturedly, putting a check on his list next to my name. "Okay. Juliet Kendall. Everyone's here."

They led the twelve of us across the track and into the infield toward the high-jump pit. The sun shone down hot on the stands full of people. Brightly colored awnings dotted the grass around the outside of the track and athletes huddled underneath in the shade. The announcer's omnipresent voice called out our names, telling the crowd that we were the finalists in the high jump. There was nowhere to hide, not anymore.

All of my life I'd dreamed of hearing my name announced to the crowd at state. And now it was happening, but in a different sport than I'd planned. Still, they called *my* name and I was right in the middle of everything—not sitting in the bleachers, not waiting on a bench.

While we warmed up, I searched the stands for my cheering section. Sunlight glancing off the silver bleachers made it hard to see. The crowd was huge. I wondered if I'd be able to find them.

I shouldn't have worried. Maddie and Hanna stood up and screamed my name so loud that I heard them clear out at the pit. When I waved back, they sat down next to my parents and Jonah. Carly couldn't be there, but she had only another week left until she would finish her program. And Emma had sent an e-mail just for me: "I'll be praying for you. I've been praying for you all year long. Last week, I had the chance to go to the temple and I sat in the celestial room for a long time thinking about you and Carly and Maddie and Mom and Dad. I miss all of you.

It's hard to be so far away sometimes. All I really have is my faith and service and prayers to offer. I hope they help."

We all gave what we had to each other. I hadn't been alone after all, not even when I'd thought I was.

The end of Emma's letter was just like the one she'd sent me before the basketball game earlier that year: *Play hard. Give it your all.*

Those were still the things the Kendall girls did best.

One thing I usually like about the high jump is that, even at state, there is always something else happening; some race or other field event taking place at the same time. People seem to notice the high jump only when the announcer draws their attention to the pit. The crowd in the stands watched us walk out to the infield, but most heads almost immediately turned back toward the starting line to watch a race.

Even without much of an audience, I still felt jittery. Right as I made my first attempt, an official fired the gun to start the 100-meter dash. I flinched a little, my leg hit the bar, and I knew before I rolled back onto my knees that the bar had fallen.

I took a deep breath. No worries. Two more tries.

On my second try, I cleared the opening height. I heard a little burst of applause from my cheering section in the stands. I smiled.

The sun climbed in the sky, the runners went around the track, and the twelve of us became eleven, then ten, then nine, until eventually we were down to two. Somehow I was still left. I was still jumping. Along with last year's state champ, a girl from Hillyard.

The announcer's voice boomed across the field: "Ladies and gentlemen, we'd like to direct your attention to the high-jump pit, where Juliet Kendall from South High and Laura Kramer from Hillyard High are jumping for the girls' state championship. The bar is currently set at five feet, six inches."

Five feet, six inches, I thought, staring at the bar, not daring to look at all the faces now turned in our direction. I'd never cleared that height before, not even in practice, not even close. *No problem,* I told myself. *There's a first time for everything.*

I tried not to think too hard and I tried to let my muscles do what I'd trained them to do. I tried to trust my body, to trust myself, to have faith.

The moment I jumped, I knew I would clear it. It all felt so good. My foot hit the ground exactly right, my legs had spring, my back arched, and I sailed over the bar fast and smooth and graceful. The crowd went wild.

Laura, the girl from Hillyard, cleared it on her first attempt, too, and the crowd went wild again.

"We're going to move it up another inch," the official told us. "Five feet, seven inches." I glanced over at Laura. She'd cleared that height to take state the year before.

We both missed on our first try and then I missed again on my second attempt. *It's okay,* I told myself. *Whatever happens, you've done your best. You've jumped again and again and again and never once walked away.*

Laura cleared the height on her second attempt, sailing neatly over the bar. The crowd cheered, and she smiled and turned and looked at me, waiting to see what I would do. Many of the faces in the crowd watched me too. Could I clear it?

Time for my third and final attempt. I took a few deep breaths, and then I ran.

I almost made it. I thought I had—and so did the crowd—but the bar came down at the very last second. I didn't feel my back or my foot brush the bar but something invisible happened, some motion of mine moved the bar and it fell down without my knowing what caused it. I had no attempts left.

The crowd sighed and I felt a twinge of disappointment. Second place.

The official raised the bar another half inch. I stood over to the side, watching Laura as she got ready to jump. She looked determined to make the height. She didn't even pause for very long before her jump; she looked at the bar, she started to run, and over she went, clearing the bar.

And when she did, I clapped with everyone else at her accomplishment. It was amazing what the human body could do, and I wished

Carly were there to see it all. The running, the jumping, the hurdling. Everything.

When Laura failed to clear the next height, the event officially ended. "Great job, ladies," the official told us. He shook our hands.

"Congratulations," I told Laura. "That was amazing."

"You too," she said. "See you on the medal podium later."

As I collected my gear from the corner of the pit, I looked back up into the stands. They were still full of people, all cheering for someone. Even though the bright light of the sun hurt my eyes, I couldn't stop looking at all the colors. I couldn't stop looking at the people sitting in the warm May sunshine, watching those they cared about fail and succeed and win and lose.

"Thank you," I whispered, to my family in the stands and to Carly in the center and to Emma in Spain and to my Father in heaven. I hoped they were proud of me. I'd jumped higher than ever before.

And you know what was crazy? I felt like I still had it in me to go higher.

CHAPTER 38

Carly came home on a Friday afternoon six days after the state meet. We all waited for her in the backyard. When she walked through the back door with my parents, it seemed to me that she took in everything with a single look—Maddie and Savannah and me smiling uncertainly at her, the bouquet of yellow welcome-home roses on the picnic table, the sidewalk-chalk flowers we'd drawn on the patio to pass the time while we waited for my parents to bring her home.

Once everyone had a turn hugging her, Carly went over and picked up a piece of chalk. "You didn't leave me any room," she said, looking at all the flowers.

"There's plenty of room over there," I said, gesturing to the basketball pad. "There's lots of space for you."

"To be honest, the first day I was in there I was really judgmental." Carly leaned back and surveyed the blue flower she'd sketched on the cement near the basketball hoop. "I kept looking around at the other girls and thinking, '*They're* the ones who are messed up, not me. I'm going to do what I'm supposed to do and get out of here. I don't belong here.'"

The rest of us listened. Mom and Dad sat on lawn chairs near us on the grass; Maddie and Savannah and I sprawled on the concrete next to Carly, our hands smudged with chalk. Drawing gave us something to do while we listened to Carly talk. Mom had suggested that we go inside, but Carly wanted to stay in the backyard. "I've been inside so much lately," she'd pointed out.

"I thought I didn't belong there," Carly continued. "There was a girl who did triathlons but only ate a few hundred calories a day. One day she was riding her bike in a race and she passed out and fell right off onto the road. She hit her head and had to get stitches. Some of the other bikers couldn't stop in time and they ran over her. She had some terrible injuries."

I shuddered.

"There was another girl who was in college and who was so anorexic that she had to come home from school. She tried to start over, but she couldn't. She couldn't stop starving herself." Carly glanced over at me and a look of understanding passed between us.

Jonah's sister, Claire, I thought.

"And there were some other girls with worse stories than those. They kept going and going, until it was my turn." Carly filled in the blue petals on her flower while the silence filled the air. I thought of my sister sitting in that room surrounded by strangers, waiting to tell her story, wondering if she should.

"I started talking. Just to get them off my back. I realized that my story sounded every bit as bad as theirs. I tried to downplay it so that it would sound less extreme. I kept stopping and pausing while I talked and finally the group leader said, 'If you aren't ready to tell us yet, Carly, that's fine.' And that made me mad because then it seemed like my story was even crazier than it was. So I blurted the whole thing out, and while I told it, I realized that I *was* like the other girls. I mean, I made myself throw up at school, and I passed out in the hall and ended up in the hospital. My story sounded like their stories."

My heart ached as I remembered that day in the hall at school and the days that followed.

"That's when I knew I was one of the group. I had problems too.

I think that was the start of me realizing I didn't want to be that girl anymore. I wanted to not be that girl even more than I wanted to keep throwing up. I wanted my life back, and I knew I needed help. I read every scripture I could find about the Atonement and I prayed like crazy."

I knew how *that* felt.

"I definitely had setbacks. You know. I can't promise you guys or myself that I'm going to be perfect, but I promise that I'll keep trying."

That Sunday we went to church together as a family for the first time in months. It was fast Sunday, and I closed my eyes as I took the bread and water. *Please,* I prayed the way I prayed every week, *help me find my faith again.* I had had moments of faith recently, especially when I listened to the hymns or prayed my way through high-jumping. But, as beautiful as those moments were, I wanted more. I wanted to live constantly in that full stream of light and faith and belief.

Carly sat next to me. I saw her hesitate as she reached for the water and I put my arm around her. We were in the right place. We were trying. Surely something good would follow.

After the sacrament, the bishop bore his testimony and then opened up the meeting for everyone else to speak. I listened to the members of my ward share their thoughts. The heavens did not open yet, at least for me, but I knew I was where I needed and wanted to be.

My heart jumped when Carly stood up. She slid past me out into the aisle and started up toward the podium. "Oh," my mother said, like a little sigh, and I looked over at her. Her eyes were fixed on Carly's face and in my mother's eyes was an expression of pride and hope and fear. My father put his arm around my shoulder and squeezed me tight. I knew he wanted to protect both me and Carly with that embrace.

Carly stood at the pulpit and looked out at the congregation. A baby cried and a toddler complained somewhere near the back. I was grateful for the little distracting noises that somehow made the moment more real.

Carly began to speak. "I know that Jesus and Heavenly Father live. I know that they love me. I know that Jesus went through our pain for us, so we do not have to be ashamed to ask Him for help in overcoming it. He knows every way we can hurt and every way to heal."

Suddenly, in a rush as pure and physical as the adrenaline I'd felt when I was about to jump, I felt the beautiful steady warmth of light and belief flow through me. The belief was not mine. It was Carly's. But I couldn't deny that what she was saying was real and true. She *knew* those things.

Jonah came over to play basketball a few days later. He stopped short when we went into the backyard. "Whoa. What's all this?"

The tangles and twists of our chalk flower garden covered almost all of the cement. "Maddie and Savannah and Carly and I did this the night Carly came home."

"It's amazing," Jonah said. "It looks like some kind of street art or something. Did you take a picture?"

"No."

"You should. It's supposed to rain this weekend."

"Yeah, maybe we should."

Jonah looked at me thoughtfully. "Or not. Sometimes it's nice to live it and keep it in your memory, right?"

"Yeah. Exactly."

We looked at the drawings together. After a few moments of quiet, I asked Jonah, "So, did you decide what to do about going away to school?"

"Yeah. I'm going. I have to go. I can't stay for her or I'm going to end up hating her." He took a deep breath. "Do you think I'm a jerk for saying that?"

"No. Not at all. Plus, you'll be here for her this summer."

Jonah nodded, lacing his fingers through mine. "I'm not going anywhere this summer."

Jonah was right. It rained that weekend, and our flowers washed away. I never did take a picture, so the chalk garden disappeared forever. But it's okay for something to live on only in memory. Jonah was right about that, too.

When I went out and looked at the rain washing the chalk away, I noticed our footprints again. The colors and water pooled in the indentations of our toes, in the hollows of our heels, in the letters of our names: EMMA. MADELYN. CARLY. JULIET.

I am Juliet Elisabeth Kendall. I am a daughter of heavenly Parents who love me, and of earthly parents, who love me too. I am a sister to Emma, Maddie, and Carly, and a friend to Jonah and Hanna and others. I am a basketball player and a high jumper. I am a girl who is trying to gain back her testimony, who knows how to pray, and who is learning to listen.

CHAPTER 39

June

The shed where they stored the track equipment was unlocked. I waded through a forest of tangled hurdles and tripped on an old starting block before I found what I wanted: the high-jump bar.

Even when state was over, I didn't stop my practices. But I hadn't used the bar, because I hadn't been ready. Until now.

I cleared height after height after height. Five feet. Five feet two inches. Five feet three inches. Five feet four inches. Five feet five inches. Five feet six inches.

Five feet, six and a half inches.

I missed, badly. The bar came clanging down and I winced as I slid off the mats. That hadn't even been close.

No worries, I told myself. *No one else is jumping. You can try as many times as you want.* I flopped back onto the mats for a minute. Looking up at the sky, which waited for the stars, I told myself that I had all the time in the world, and I believed it.

I missed my second attempt.

Run. Jump.

I missed the third time.

The fourth time, though, I sailed right over, clean, without even brushing the bar. Lying there on the mat, I closed my eyes for a moment.

I did it. I opened my eyes and looked at the bar to make sure it was still there. It was. I closed my eyes again.

I did it. Not in front of the crowd, not when it had counted at state, but here by myself. Not entirely by myself, I remembered. Heavenly Father knew.

"Juliet!" Someone called my name. I sat up.

Carly cut across the infield toward the high-jump pit. "We saw your car in the parking lot on our way home from therapy, so I asked Mom to drop me off. Is it okay if I hang out here with you for a while?"

"Sure. I'm about to go home anyway." I started to slide off the mats, but Carly climbed up next to me and flopped onto her back. I lay back down next to her.

"I saw you clear that," Carly said quietly.

"You did?"

"I'm sorry I wasn't there to watch you at state," she said. "I really wanted to be. But . . . you know."

"I'm glad you were the one who saw me now," I said.

"Is that the highest you've ever jumped?"

"Yeah."

"Way to go."

We didn't say much as we watched the stars come out. I was soaking in the evening, looking at the colors of the sky, smelling the freshly cut grass and listening to people's lawn mowers in the neighborhood around the high school.

Carly sighed. "It's so good to be out here in the world again. A little scary, but good."

"It's good to have you out here in the world again."

"So is high jumping the new basketball?"

"No," I said. "In fact, I think I might try out for the team again next year. Coach Slater probably hates me. There's almost no chance I'd make it. But I think I'd like to try."

"I don't know what I'm going to do next year," Carly said. "Maybe basketball. Maybe wait and try out for cheer in the spring. I might start taking piano lessons again."

"Really?" I said, surprised.

"They have a piano in the center and I kept playing it, trying to remember the old songs I used to know. That helped me."

"It did?"

"Discovering something new is important. They told us that at the center. I know I'd played before, but I felt like I was discovering music again. You know what I mean?"

"Yeah, I do." In the silence that followed, I tried to find the words for what I wanted to ask. I wanted to talk to my sister about Heavenly Father and about her testimony and how she made it strong again.

Just as I was about to speak, Carly sat up and started to climb off the mat. "I guess we should go home now. I don't want Mom and Dad to worry."

"Okay."

We walked across the parking lot and climbed into Old Blue together. Carly rolled down her window. "Remember last summer?" she asked me, taking a deep breath as the summer night flooded into our car and streetlights shone above us.

"Of course."

"Things are different now."

"That's true."

"Would you go back if you could?" Carly's voice was soft.

I didn't answer her for a moment. For me, that summer had been a golden time, an almost-perfect time, a time of innocence. But it had also been a time of ignorance. I didn't know then how much Carly and I would struggle or how strong either of us could be. "I guess I'm not sure."

"Me either."

We pulled into the driveway and I finally said what I'd wanted to say since sacrament meeting a few days earlier. "Your testimony on Sunday really helped me, Carly."

"It did?"

"A lot. You know that scripture about believing?"

"Which one?"

"The one about how to some it is given to believe on the words of others?"

"Yeah."

"I kept thinking of that when you bore your testimony. Maybe you know this, maybe you don't, but I've been having kind of a hard time with the gospel this year. But when you spoke I felt the Spirit and I knew you meant what you were saying. I guess right now it is given to me to believe on your words."

Carly turned and looked at me. "On *mine?*"

"Yeah, on yours. When you spoke, I felt like you *knew.*"

"I do." She laughed a little. "It took a while to get here, but I know."

We were both quiet for a moment. Through the open windows of the car, I heard the neighbor kids calling to each other across the street. I could almost imagine that they were the younger selves of my sisters and me, calling to us now.

"Do you mind if I lean on your words for a little while?" Then I realized that the last thing I should do was give her something else to weigh her down right as she started to come up for air. "I mean, not lean on you like you're responsible for my testimony or something. I mean—"

Carly interrupted me. "Of course you can. Of course I don't mind. How long have I been leaning on you?" She put her arm around me and I rested my head on her shoulder and started to cry.

We had seen each other fall, and we had seen each other fly. We both had battles to fight that were not over yet, and there would be struggles in our futures that we couldn't imagine. And we would see each other fly, and fall, and reach out a hand to catch or offer a shoulder to cry on, all through the years of being sisters. Because that is what it means to have a sister, to be a sister.

EPILOGUE

On my seventeenth birthday, I didn't make a wish. Instead, I closed my eyes and prayed with everything inside of me. I prayed for strength, I prayed for Carly, I prayed for all of us. For everyone standing in that room with me: my family, Jonah, my friends. For people who were not there: Emma and Jonah's sister, Claire.

And here's the thing about prayer: When you open your eyes, things might not have changed. But *you* have changed, a little. You are a person who remembers that she is not alone. You are a person with a little bit of faith that flies up to heaven along with the smoke from the candles.

ACKNOWLEDGMENTS

I am indebted to many people for their assistance in writing this book.

Several girls and women with eating disorders, who prefer to remain anonymous, have my gratitude, respect, and admiration for sharing their stories with me. I appreciate their willingness to tell their stories, and for helping me to give Carly an authentic voice.

Many thanks to Shawna L. Schutz, RN, who worked for ten years at an inpatient treatment facility for people with eating disorders, and who was willing to lend her expertise to the project by reading the manuscript and answering questions.

Jennifer E. Brown, RN, also helped me with medical questions, and Amy Sonntag (EdS, School Psychology) assisted me with information about the psychology of eating disorders.

I also appreciate the personnel at the Center for Change in Orem, Utah, for their assistance, particularly Nicole Hawkins, PhD, who granted permission to cite her excellent pamphlet on the subject. (Please see the author notes for more information regarding pamphlets, books, and Web sites about eating disorders.)

Special thanks to Brandi Koch, who read several versions of the manuscript and was extremely patient and helpful throughout the project.

I am also indebted to Heather Smith, Abby Parcell, Nora Harrison, Libby Parr, Sarah McCoy, Joan Fairbank, Brook Andreoli, Joree Hansen, Becky Bingham, and Jana Hay for their insights. Thanks also to my family: Bob, Arlene, Nic, Hope, and Scott.

This book is dedicated to my sister, Elaine Braithwaite Vickers. It would not exist without her. Because we are close in age, we have gone through many things together, from early dance lessons to high school to parenthood. While our story is different from that of Carly and Juliet, I hope to have captured some of the importance of sisterhood and standing together, because those things have been some of the greatest blessings of my life. Thank you to Elaine, and to Hope, for being my sisters.

AUTHOR NOTES

The following books, pamphlets, and Web sites contain information and resources about eating disorders:

The Alliance for Eating Disorders Awareness, Eating Disorders Statistics, www.eatingdisorderinfo.org/Resources/EatingDisorders Statistics/ tabid/964/Default.aspx.

Anorexia and Bulimia: How Family & Friends Can Help. Center for Change, Incorporated, 2002.

Hawkins, Nicole, PhD. *Battling our Bodies: Understanding and Over-coming Negative Body Images.* Center for Change, Incorporated, October 2006.

National Eating Disorder Association, www.nationaleatingdisorders .org/.

National Institute of Mental Health, www.nimh.nih.gov.

Pipher, Mary, PhD. *Hunger Pains.* New York: Random House, 1996.

Seigel, Michelle, PhD., et al. *Surviving an Eating Disorder: Strategies for Families and Friends.* Revised and updated. New York: Harper-Perennial, 1997.

ABOUT THE AUTHOR

ALLYSON BRAITHWAITE CONDIE received a degree in English teaching from Brigham Young University. She went on to teach high school English in Utah and in upstate New York for several years, and plans to return to the classroom some day. She loved teaching because it combined two of her favorite things—working with students and reading great books. She is also the author of the Yearbook trilogy and *Freshman for President*.

Currently, however, she is employed by her three little boys, who keep her busy playing trucks and building blocks. They also like to help her type and are very good at drawing on manuscripts with red crayon. She enjoys running with her husband, reading, traveling, and eating. Ally and her husband, Scott, live in Provo, Utah.